A Woman's Role
A 1950s Romance

Carol Moessinger

Liselle!

Best Wishes and

Good Reading

Carol Moessinger

ISBN: 1628279176
ISBN-13: 978-1-62827-917-7

Published by Breathless Books, an imprint of
Assent Publishing

DEDICATION

To my grandparents

Jan and Antonia Swincicki
Mike and Mary Moskolik

CHAPTER 1

The days lagged but the years hurried by. It was the summer of 1955.

Outside, the back porch was cooler than the airless kitchen. The early evening sun hung suspended above the trees, and barn swallows darted after invisible insects. The two women sat on the edge of the porch.

Stretching her legs over the steps, Celina curled her painted toenails into the grass. It wasn't that she didn't love her family; she did, but she wanted more than the sweat and struggle that defined their lives. As hard as she tried, she'd never succeeded in convincing her mother, Marian, that there was a world filled with art, music, and literature that lay beyond their small plot of land and the town of Kenville.

"You're alone," Marian said. "Maybe that's what's bothering you. If Bobby had come home from Korea, you'd be busy taking care of your man and your children. It's tough to lose somebody you love before you even start your life together."

Celina leaned against the railing and ran her fingers through her damp hair. She tried to remember Bobby's features, his broad shoulders and somber brown eyes. It seemed so long ago since he was killed in Korea. They started dating on graduation night and were engaged by Christmastime that year. After many long months of anguish and in spite of her grief, she carefully wrapped his picture in white tissue paper. Tears flowed as she stroked each gift he had given her before storing everything in the bottom of the trunk in her bedroom.

"Mom, I don't want to talk about Bobby anymore. He's gone, and it's done. When I see his mother and Kimie now, they don't even mention him."

She twisted her ponytail into a knot and pinned it back up. "It's hard to believe that it's been three years." She breathed a ragged sigh. "I'm done with mourning."

Before Marian could speak, Celina added, "I know you think I'd be content if only Bobby had come home. Maybe I would, but he didn't come home. And I'm not."

She rubbed her eyes with her long fingers. "I think about Bobby, but I think about Martyn, too. Sometimes when Johnny talks or laughs in a certain way, it reminds me of him."

Her mother's voice was a sad whisper. "I light candles for Martyn at church every Sunday, and pray for him every day." They watched a prematurely dry leaf fall. "He was our first son, a good son."

"Remember how he looked out for me? He never allowed Andy or Johnny to pick on me. And I did torment them sometimes." Thinking about her long ago brother, Celina was wistful. "Remember how everybody used to say we looked alike?"

"I remember."

Celina shook her head. "I still can't believe he was killed

the day before his twentieth birthday. And Bobby was only nineteen when he was killed. Just teenagers."

Minutes of silence followed. "They were years younger than I am now when they died. God, they never had a chance at life." Her shoulders slumped. "I hate war."

"I guess everybody hates it." The fingers of Marian's hands laced together. "My heart hurts when I think of Martyn. Losing a child is the worst thing that can happen to a mother, but we have to take what life gives us or go crazy."

Celina hurt for her mother, and patted her hand. "I know."

"Like you said, it's been three years since Bobby was killed. You have got to think about your future.

"You're getting older, and Mike would be good to you. He's a good worker and the same religion. If you married him you'd live right down the road from us. You'd be close by. We'd help each other out."

"Mike and I are like brother and sister. I don't want to be his girlfriend. And I can't picture myself married to a coal miner, even if he worked above ground. And Mike works underground. Besides, he never talks about anything but coal mines and cars. Well, he talks about baseball too, but that hardly counts.

"No, I don't want to get involved with a coal miner. It's bad enough worrying about Dad and the boys down there in those narrow, dark tunnels with the rats and everything. I don't want to be worrying about a husband, too. I couldn't bear to lose someone else I love."

"But you have to move on."

"I am Mom, I am."

"If Mike's not the one, there are a lot of other young men out there."

"Like who? Who's out there for me?"

"There are lots of nice men around. But if you don't hurry, they'll all be taken."

"I don't care." Celina hated the periodic marry anybody who isn't old enough to be your grandfather talks.

"You don't seem to realize that you could end up being a spinster and alone for the rest of your life."

Spinster was a funny word. A dried-up old auntie spinning away the days of her life into the yarn of old-age, sitting back and watching other people's lives being loomed into something beautiful, or at least something useful."I wish you wouldn't say stuff like that. I don't want to be a spinster."

"Well, what are you going to do? You don't want to be an old maid like your friend Harriet Grayhill. You might end up wearing shiny gabardine suits and lace-up pumps, carting books back and forth to the library year in and year out. You have to find a man."

Celina faced her mother. "Where? Where am I supposed to find somebody?"

"You need to get out more. Almost all the girls from your graduating class are married and have kids. You must meet nice fellows when you go out."

"But I want somebody special, a man I can talk to. A man who doesn't work underground."

"Couldn't Pattie or one of your other friends fix you up with somebody?"

In spite of herself, Celina laughed. "Remember the last guy? The one Stella fixed me up with? Jeez, he had a chew the size of a jack ball stuffed in his lip, and he spit tobacco juice out the car window all the way to the movies. When he smiled, bits of tobacco stuck to his teeth and his breath smelled like a sewer."

4

"Was he nice?"

Celina threw her hands up. "Mom! The guy couldn't even brush his teeth or give up his chew for a couple of hours. I'm not that desperate."

"You might have to settle."

"You make it sound like I'm forty or something."

"You will be forty one of these days, and I'm afraid you're going to end up like Harriet."

Anger flared. "Harriet went to college and she runs her own life. She doesn't have to put up with some guy whose breath is bad enough to knock out a mule."

"She doesn't have anybody in her bed at night either," Marian shot back. "Look, I don't want to sleep with Snuffy Smith, and that's that."

Marian stared at the porch ceiling.

Celina's jaw clenched. "Harriet went on vacation all the way to Hawaii and no man demanding his supper at five o'clock told her she couldn't go. What's wrong with that?"

Marian fiddled with the edge of her apron. "Harriet taught school, but teachers don't get paid anything. She lives on her father's money. Her inheritance took her to Hawaii."

"Maybe so, but she had a profession. She got to learn things."

Marian wrung her hands. "I know you wanted to go to college, but Martyn would have been the one to go. Only rich girls go to college. They go to find a man. You're pretty enough to get a husband right here, without wasting all that money."

"But I wanted to go. I bet Martyn would have helped me."

"That's something we'll never know. You've got to care about your future now, today."

"I might not have a man, but I care about my future. I

think about it a lot. I want to be somebody."

"A lonely old lady like Harriet?"

Celina wiped the sweat from her face and neck and looked down at her painted toe nails. She refused to become angry. "I don't want to be alone all my life, but I don't want to live the way I am either."

Marian threw her hands up. "Lost, no direction."

"Will you quit saying stuff like that? I want to do things with my life."

"Like what?"

Celina placed her hands on her knees and rolled her head from side to side. "I want to see some of the world, make my own decisions, get some education."

"Yeah? So?"

"I'm tired of living like I'm not supposed to think for myself, or decide what I want to do and when I want to do it."

"Where's marriage in all this?"

Celina wanted to scream. Instead she closed her eyes and thought for a few moments. "I want to get married, okay. But not if it's the only option available. I'm not getting married just to get married."

She tilted her head back and brushed a few wisps of hair from her face. "If and when I get married, it will have to be to someone special not someone with tobacco in his teeth."

Marian sighed. "You're twenty-three. When people get older, they settle in and tolerate each other, and something like tobacco in a man's teeth might not seem so bad."

"You're doing a swell job of talking me into longing for the joys of marriage." Celina rested her elbows on her knees.

"You know what I mean."

"I'm not going to think about tolerating somebody, or I'll

never get married. Anyway, I tolerate more than I want to already."

Marian flipped the dish towel she was holding at a stray fly. She flashed a smile. "You know what Father Schmidt says, 'Either death or old age solves all marital problems.'"

Celina dragged her hands down over her face. "I can't stand it."

Marian chuckled and changed the subject. "So how do you expect to make your mark, to be somebody?"

"I don't plan to be a clerk at Duxbury's forever. I've been thinking about jobs women can do, like being a female correspondent, a journalist." She screwed up her face. "I'm not cut out to be a nurse or secretary. I'd rather get hired at a newspaper and work my way up. Move from a local to a big city paper. I'll write interesting columns, take night classes, and maybe even get to travel."

Marian stared at her daughter. "Where did you get an idea like that?" Her eyes widened. "You want to go to some city and be a newspaper woman? You don't even know what they do at newspapers."

"But I do. I've been reading about women writers, and some of them are journalists. I've always been a good writer; I won all the awards in high school."

"Marcelina! For God's sake, you can't go to a big city by yourself. What if you got robbed or...or...worse? You listen to me, a husband and family and being near her parents...that's all a woman needs."

"Mom, didn't you ever wish you had done something besides live on this farm and take care of a husband and kids?"

"Maybe, but I don't remember."

"Well, I want something more."

Her voice pensive, Marian said,. "I'm better off than my mother was. When Pap came over from Poland, the only work he could find was in the mines. He worked like a slave ten hours a day, six days a week, digging coal just to pay for Baba's steamship ticket so she could come over, too. After she got here and they were married, she took in boarders to make extra money. She worked as hard as he did so they could buy own land and get out of the coal patch, the shanty town owned by the coal company, and away from the company store."

Marian pointed toward the trees. "They bought their place over the hill there and kept our family going. They worked hard, and us kids worked right alongside them. They were among the few who were prepared when the owners cut the miners' pay and kept so many of them in debt to the company store. If we hadn't had the garden, chickens, and cows, who knows what would have happened? There wasn't any government relief back then."

"But what about when you and Dad were first married?"

Marian grumbled. "In the twenties everybody was supposed to be dancing the Charleston and having a good time, but they weren't good years for coal miners. We weren't married too long when the companies managed to all but break the United Mine Workers, and things got worse."

Her face was that of a woman who had battled her way through a difficult past. "It was bad. People like us struggled to keep body and soul together. But the rich ones? Believe me, they had it easy till the stock market crashed. And a lot of them still had it easy after the crash. The rich never have to suffer much."

Marian ran her fingers around the edges of the dish towel. "After the boys were born, the Depression hit, then you were born, and nothing mattered except staying alive and keeping our place here. Sometimes I wonder how we managed." She sighed. "After that, the war came, and we worried about raising you kids, the Nazis, and the war effort. The government representatives didn't have to tell us how to plant a Victory Garden."

"But things are different now," Celina said.

"Life isn't much different now. Life is never easy."

"But Baba couldn't speak or read English when she came to this country."

With a small chuckle, Marian interrupted. "She's still not very good."

"But you went to school and went as far as eighth grade."

"Yeah, and the teacher locked me in the cloak closet every day till Christmas when I was in the first grade, because I couldn't speak English as well as the others in the class. A lot of the English kids called us hunkies or dumb Polacks, and chased us home and threw stones at us. If I live to be a hundred, I'll never forget that."

"People were ignorant back then."

"People haven't changed much," her mother insisted.

Celina was determined to continue her argument. "You went further than Baba did. I should go further than you."

"You did go further. You graduated from high school and are working in a nice store in town."

Celina rubbed her tired legs. *Some store. I can't even get a promotion.* "Women built tanks and flew planes during the war. But it's been ten years, and we're being told that we can't think or be doctors, professors, or accountants, or anything that takes a brain." She pushed her fingers into her hair. "I want to do things, make a difference."

"You're gonna be disappointed. After the war, the women

were sent home to work in their kitchens, whether they liked it or not."

"That wasn't right."

"Listen Celina, a lot of things aren't right, and God knows life isn't fair. Look at what our family has gone through. At least staying at home taking care of a husband and children gives a woman a reason to get up in the morning."

"Why? Why can't she make a difference in the world and have a family too?"

Marian threw her hands up. "How should I know? You think you're some career woman like Katharine Hepburn in some movie or something. Movies are pretend, Celina." She jabbed her finger at the porch floor. "This is real. Life right here is real."

"But Mom, when we talk about Libby Mezovsky, and how her husband drinks up his pay before he gets home on Fridays, you always say that her life is miserable because of him.

"Yeah. That man would sooner hold down a bar stool than put food on the table."

"If she could get a decent job, then she and the kids wouldn't have to live hand to mouth like they do. She could kick Bill out and take care of herself."

Marian bobbed her head. "Maybe she could."

"Then, if she felt like it, she could let a decent man in her life."

"You better not be talking about divorce. Libby's married and there's no way out of it. Can you imagine how people would talk if she was a divorcee?"

"Mom, her life is hell."

"She's the one who married Bill."

"It's no use." Why can't I say the right thing to make her

understand? Trying to convince her of anything is impossible.

Marian pulled a blue cotton handkerchief from her apron pocket and mopped her sodden face. "This heat is bad enough, but going through the change at the same time, I feel like I'm burning up. I need some water." She got up and went to the kitchen.

"I hope I don't have hot flashes when I go through the change."

"You will." Marian called through the screen door.

Women sure have a lot to look forward to: cramps, the change, and never-ending housework.

A cold, wet nose sniffed Celina's ankle. The nose was followed by the rest of Frankie as he inched out from under the porch. "Okay, boy, I guess you're ready for your supper, too."

The dog sniffed his food dish and snapped at a lazy fly or two. She scratched behind his ears.

Marian stood at the screen door and smiled. "If you married Mike, you could take Frankie with you."

"Mom, you are getting desperate." She held Frankie's loveable face between her hands. "What do you think of that, old boy?"

Marian crossed her arms. "Well, it would be nice to get the family together for a big wedding and then hear the pitter-patter of little feet before too long."

"Oh, Mother."

At that moment, Frankie bounded off around the house, barking with joy.

"That's who Frankie should go with…that is, if my big brother ever gets married."

Her arms still crossed, Marian shook her head. "I don't know about you two. I don't think I'll ever get you married off." She re-tied her pink checked babushka at the nape of her neck. "Thank God Andy is settled and has his family started. And they live close to both Ellen's parents and us."

Frankie bounded toward the house. He dashed back and forth between an advancing dust-and-grime-covered apparition and Celina. She waved to her brother. Johnny's white-toothed smile split his sooty face. "Dad home?"

"Yeah, he's on the couch taking his after dinner nap." Her brother could be an exasperating tease and they often argued, but Celina knew she could always count on him.

Johnny dropped his aluminum dinner bucket, cap, and shirt on the porch floor. "The water gets to be a couple of inches deep in some parts of our section. They can't keep it pumped out. I was in and out of the mud all day and these work clothes are ready to stand up by themselves. The other set's clean, isn't it?"

Marian called from the kitchen, "Yes. But you can't have it till Monday."

"Come on Mom," he muttered. "I can hardly bend over now."

"Tomorrow's Friday, and I'm not dragging the washer out till wash day. I'll throw your pants and shirt over the clothes line and knock the mud off them in the morning."

"I've got to wear these things tomorrow?"

"That's right."

He plopped down on the porch, pulled at the laces in his boots, and pushed the boots off. He peeled away his soaking wet gray socks, revealing wrinkled toes that felt like prunes. "Hey Mom, you got any baking soda for these boots? They're drenched."

He got up and ambled around the side of the house with Frankie close behind. "My supper ready?" he called over his shoulder.

Celina answered, "Yeah. You want coffee?"

"No. Milk."

Marian tossed the box of baking soda to Celina. "Make sure you put half a cup in each one. Sprinkle some on the socks too. I bet they stink."

Light flashed above the trees, and Celina hoped it wasn't just heat lightning tearing across the sky. Many seconds later, thunder rumbled. With each thunder clap, darkness inched closer, pushing itself in front of the evening sun.

"Celina, get in here. You'll get struck by lightning," Marian yelled from the kitchen.

A slight smile lifted the corners of Celina's mouth. Her mother worried too much, but when the first droplets splattered her legs, she jumped up and scurried inside.

"Did anything come from the book club?"

Her mother shook her head. "No. But the rest of the mail's right there on the hall table."

"Never mind then. Maybe the latest selection will come tomorrow."

His broad back shirtless, Johnny sat at the kitchen table, wolfing down pork chops, potatoes, and peas. When finished, he sat back and grinned with satisfaction. "Nobody can say the Pasniewski women can't cook."

The storm rumbled outside. Celina watched her brother, trying to see him through her best friend Pattie's eyes. She had to admit that he was a nice looking guy. Not tall, but broad shouldered with arms strong and muscled from hard work. The crew-cut he finally decided to let grow out gave no inkling that his brown hair was thick and wavy. *No wonder Pattie's crazy about him.*

"Hey Missy, get me some water, will ya?"

At least he doesn't demand like Dad does. She got up and filled a glass. With her father it was always, Celina get this and Celina fetch that. She cringed when she thought about how Tomas Pasniewski would slide his empty coffee cup across the tabletop toward her and remind her not to forget the cream.

Johnny tilted in his chair back and lit a cigarette. He tried to produce smoke rings, but only ragged puffs of gray haze floated from his mouth. "This has been a hell of a week, and I'm glad it's almost over. I'm ready to get out and have some fun."

"And you'll have half the girls in the county chasing you," Celina teased.

"Yeah, and I love it. Ahhh, women. It's great when they follow you around and ask you to dance. Do you think I should let one of 'em buy me a beer?"

Marian slid the last of the dishes onto the cupboard shelf, and spoke up. "Johnny, show respect. And you remember to treat the girls right. I taught you and your brother to be good boys."

"Okay Mom. I'm just talking."

Johnny turned to Celina. "Are you going to the dance at the Polish Hall Saturday night?

"I don't know." She hadn't had much luck at the local dances. She didn't want to waste another evening trying to avoid dancing with guys who'd had too much to drink, but she was sick of sitting home on Saturday nights.

Marian chimed in. "Why don't you go, Celina? There'll be a lot of young people there."

"Yeah," Johnny said. "You've got to get out more, or we'll have to send you to a convent."

"Don't give Mom any ideas." She chuckled.

"Then get yourself gussied up, and we'll go out for some fun. What do you say?"

"Maybe I should. Yeah, I'll probably go."

CHAPTER 2

The thunderstorm ended, sending lumpy clouds rushing to the northeast. Celina set about opening windows. She wrestled the wire mesh screens into place and left the shades up part way to beg in a cool breeze, but the house was still hot and stuffy at bedtime. She tossed and turned all night and woke with her top sheet, blanket, and pillow on the floor.

The storm failed to push the humidity away and dampness weighed down the hazy morning air, causing her wavy hair to spring into unruly curls. She entered the kitchen, trying to tame it. "I hate this hair. I must have twenty bobby pins in it, and it still won't lie down."

"You look fine," her mother said with a snort. "A lot of girls would give their right arm to have a mane of hair like yours."

Celina was not mollified and she set off for Duxbury's. Sweat clung to her forehead before she reached the store. She hoped Grover C. Duxbury III would stay away today, like he often did. She hated the compliments he gave her, and the way he watched her from his office made her skin crawl. He was always polite, but she felt he was evaluating her like he did the mannequins in the store windows.

He was the youngest of five, and the only Duxbury son. Celina remembered stories about how his mother dressed him up like a little girl, and the other children teased him unmercifully for being a momma's boy. Rumor had it he wanted to become a dentist, but followed his father into the business instead. Over his sisters' objections, Grover C. Duxbury II designated him heir and proprietor of Duxbury's Department Store, established 1896.

Celina parked the Hudson in the alley behind the store. She frowned and sighed when she saw Duxbury's black Cadillac parked in its usual spot. *I hope I don't run into him.* She pushed back her hair and tip toed over the puddles from the previous night's storm. The door to the employees' entrance at the back of the red brick building stood ajar.

She heard footsteps inside and her shoulders slumped. It was Duxbury. His chunky body, held up by undersized feet in well-shined wing tips, filled the doorway. It was only eight o'clock, but large half-moons of perspiration discolored his starched white shirt. He approached and Celina noticed the odor of stale whiskey. She recoiled and wanted to hurry past.

He stepped close. "Nice morning. But last night's rain didn't cool things off much, did it?"

"Oh, good morning, Mr. Duxbury. No, I guess it didn't. But it helped a little." She backed away.

He ran a hand over his slicked-back gray hair. "A little is better than nothing, but a little is never enough." His small eyes darted in the direction of the alley.

Celina nodded, agreed, and scurried past him up the stairs and out of the poorly lit basement. In the cloakroom where the employees kept their personal belongings, Pattie Harchak was stowing her purse and gloves in a pigeonhole with her name printed above it.

Pattie dyed her hair. Sometimes it was bright red, sometimes it was orangish red, and at other times it was reddish orange. Today it was strawberry blond.

Celina tossed her purse into her own spot. "Your color's nice."

Pattie nodded and glanced at her face in a tortoise-shell compact mirror. "Yeah, it looks pretty good. But my mom keeps telling me people are talking and saying I'm loose because I dye my hair. I don't see anything wrong with coloring it once in a while."

"I don't either, but you know how people are. They pounce on any little piece of gossip they can get."

Pattie dabbed a finger at the corner of her mouth, removing a stray smudge of lipstick, and then patted her tight waves. "Well I'm not going to let them bother me. Besides it makes me look sophisticated, like Piper Laurie."

She smoothed her dress and turned around to check the seams in her stockings. "We might as well get out there."

"Duxbury's here already," Celina spoke in an undertone. "I hoped he wouldn't come at all this week. I hate running into him first thing in the morning."

"Yeah, he reeks of booze today. But he does own the place and has to come in sometime. And Earl's been yammering all month about getting the winter merchandise orders out. Duxbury'd be working on that," Pattie whispered back.

"Yeah, the order for the Woolrich hunting jackets and pants has been waiting for his approval. I gave Earl the paperwork a week ago and he's checked the forms umpteen times."

Pattie, who missed nothing, often commented on how

Duxbury singled Celina out for compliments and watched her through the half-open office door. She waved a hankie to fan her face and spoke from behind her hand. "So, Duxbury waited for you at the door. You're his favorite, you know." She cocked an eyebrow.

Celina cringed. "I hate when you talk like that, so quit it already. Jeez, he's old and married. And I don't like being around him."

"Yeah, but on the days he comes in, he always runs into you." She tilted her head to one side. "So?"

"So, he gives me the creeps." Celina spat the words out and hurried toward her work station. She wasn't in the mood for Pattie's teasing, and all she needed was gossip starting about her and the store owner. Her mother would be horrified and her father, enraged.

Pattie caught up with her. "I'm sorry. I was just kidding around. You aren't mad, are you?"

"Yes, I'm mad," Celina whispered. "Don't you see how embarrassing it could be?" She loved Pattie and they'd been friends since grade school, but when she started the teasing about Duxbury, it was too much.

Chastised, Pattie sighed. "I guess you're right. If people are talking about my hair, I can imagine what they'd say about something like that."

"I won't listen to that kind of talk anymore," Celina said, not completely convinced by Pattie's apology.

"I won't bring it up again. I'll even give my word. A Harchak never breaks her word."

"Swear to God?"

"Swear to God."

The silence between them was still thick as they entered the main floor near Hardware. The sun glinted through the front windows and dust particles glowed, minute sparkles that drifted around the galvanized watering cans, milk pails, and trays of door knobs.

"I swear to God," Pattie repeated.

"Okay. And I'm holding you to it," she added. "Look at those filthy windows. I bet we'll get stuck washing them."

"I don't know why Harold and Sam aren't keeping this place clean."

"Ever since Memorial Day, they've been up there," Celina pointed to the ceiling, "tarring the roof. And they still have to do their regular work, plus deliveries."

Celina went to her place behind the counter in Women's and Children's Wear. She waited on a few customers, refolded the lingerie, rearranged the racks of women's blouses, and hung up little girls' sun suits. Time moved at a snail's pace. When she checked her watch it was only 10:50. *My God, this day is never going to end.*

Pattie came up behind her. "If I see one more pair of Converse All Stars or PF Flyers, I'm going to scream. I must have unpacked a hundred pairs this morning. That rubbery smell they have is enough to make you gag. You finished here?"

"Just about." Celina hung up the last five sun bonnets. "That's it."

"Good. Let's go up to the meeting."

Once a month the store was closed from eleven to noon, and all the employees were rounded up and ordered to the second-floor meeting room. They would be exhorted to improve their work habits and informed about the world of retail sales.

Years of foot traffic had worn through the varnish on the oak floors and an irregular path meandered through the store to the stairs. The risers creaked as Duxbury's employees ascended the dusty steps to the second story. The store employees had been meeting there since the first Mr. Duxbury bought the place in the 1890s.

"I wish they'd have the meetings in the stock room downstairs. It's cooler." Celina commented.

"Us getting heat stroke isn't going to change the routine in this place."

"Can't anybody change anything?" Beads of sweat formed on Celina's brow.

Grover C. Duxbury was portly and full faced. His second in command, Earl Hartisty, was lean as a beanpole with pointed nose and chin. They sat at the marred and worn wooden table that had stood in the exact center of the room since the store opened over fifty years earlier.

Celina, Pattie, and three fellow employees entered together. Earl swiped a hand across his balding head and leaned close to Duxbury. "How many Polacks does it take to…"

I hate those stupid jokes. They aren't funny at all.

He looked up, saw them enter and cleared his throat. "Let's get the meeting started."

Earl slid a sheaf of papers to his boss and Duxbury called the meeting to order. The employees sat around the table and listened while he rattled off sales statistics, the importance of staying on the right footing for a successful fiscal year, and attention to customer satisfaction.

Celina averted her eyes whenever he looked her way and hoped she didn't look as uncomfortable as she felt. She watched a housefly crawl round and round on a smudged windowpane. Occasionally it buzzed into the room, turned then flew headlong at breakneck speed toward the glass. It crashed into the dingy window, disorienting itself.

Once it got its bearings, it resumed its endless rush round and round the dirty window. Celina marveled at its determination. She wondered if the near-brainless creature willingly entered the hot second-story room devoid of any life-giving sustenance, or was it as unwilling to be there as the sweating humans around the table? She volunteered to open the window to allow some fresh air in. Before wrestling the screen into place, she shooed the fly out into the open air.

An hour later, the silent group filed out after the meeting. Hankies were busy wiping sweat from faces and necks as the little group trotted down to the cooler first floor. It was noon.

"I'm going to end up at the funny farm if I have to listen to that again next month."

Celina chuckled at Pattie's melodrama. "Do you want to go over to The Dairy Bar and get something cold to drink? Then have lunch in the park?"

"Yeah, at least there's a breeze outside."

They claimed the sturdiest bench beneath a red oak tree, sipped icy root beer and opened their brown bags. "I've got warm sardines with mustard and a piece of nut roll." Pattie leaned toward Celina's lunch bag. "You?"

"A piece of *puguch* and a couple of plums."

"Share the *puguch* with me. My mom hardly ever makes it any more. She buys store stuff now. I love the way your mom gets the dough browned just right." Pattie rolled the top of her lunch bag shut and waited. "Besides, I'll probably die of food poisoning if I eat those sardines. They've been sitting in the heat all day."

Celina broke the square of potato-and-cheese-filled flatbread in half and shared her lunch.

"Did you know there are some DPs, displaced persons,

living over at the Halosz's place? I guess they got out of Hungary. My dad said, with the communists in charge, things are so bad in Central Europe that people are better off living in Germany now that the Marshall Plan is working."

"I heard. But when I talked to Harriet the other day, she said that it's only one guy. He's staying at Terez's house. I guess they're related. She's one of the sponsors he needed to get through immigration."

Pattie finished her root beer and stifled a burp. "Do you think he talks with an accent?"

"Of course, he was born and raised in Europe, wasn't he?"

"I wonder if he's cute."

"All us Poles, Slovaks, and Ukrainians and whoever else is from that end of the world look pretty much the same," Celina said. "So I suppose he is ordinary like the rest of us."

Pattie heaved an exasperated sigh and rolled her eyes. "Can't you dream a little, Celina? Maybe he's tall, dark, and handsome."

"Maybe, but I doubt it." She tossed the last few crumbs of her *puguch* to the birds and reached in her lunch bag for the plums. "He's probably bald, skinny, and toothless."

Pattie raised her arms and let them fall on her lap. "Oh, for Pete's sake! You're just being thickheaded. I'll bet he is cute. Handsome like a Latin lover."

"You're the optimist. Me, I'll have to see it to believe it." Celina had been disappointed too many times, especially when her friends set her up with blind dates, to assume the best about an unknown commodity.

Pattie took a bite of the purple plum Celina offered. "You have to be an optimist, especially where men are concerned. One of these days, I know the man of my dreams is going to come up to me and sweep me off my feet. What do you think?"

The sun stood above them as they sat in a circle of shade under the red oak. "My guess is that he already has," Celina said.

Pattie gave her a long look. "Remember when we were in high school? You used to be easygoing. You were more fun in the old days." She scrunched up her mouth, looked down at the dandelions in the grass. "You don't smile anymore."

"What do you mean? I smile. I get along with people. I just don't like being happy all the time, that's all."

"That's not what I mean. I don't want to hurt your feelings Celina, but you act like an old spinster, not like a young person looking for a good time once in a while. Life is too short to be so serious."

Celina leaned back on the bench. She stretched her legs and looked down at her brown flats. "You're beginning to sound like my mother."

"Ever since Bobby got killed, you've been different."

"Well, what do you expect? First Martyn gets killed in the war; he was the brother I could count on to look out for me. Then Bobby gets killed in Korea." She missed them. She had loved them, then one day they packed a suitcase, went away, and never came back. She tried not to be cheerless, but there were times when she couldn't help being downcast and angry.

She twisted her lunch bag into a tight wad and tossed it into a nearby trash can. "We were supposed to get married when he got back from Korea. But he never came back."

A gentle hand patted Celina's shoulder. "I know, I know. But it's been a couple of years already. I don't think Bobby would want you clamming up and holding onto the past. He'd want you to let go and move on."

Celina turned to her friend. "I've let go. I want to move on but I'm stuck. There's nothing here, nothing." Shaking her head, she continued. "I've been thinking about getting a job at the newspaper then after a while moving on to something better."

"What about finding somebody?"

"You really do sound like my mother." She checked her watch. "We'd better get back."

Galvanized pails filled with water, squeegees, and rags, stood in the open doorway when they returned to the store. The two of them shared a long look.

Earl, in his short-sleeved white shirt and hitched-up brown trousers, stepped up to them and sniffed. "Not much business today. Since Friday is window day and Sam and Harold had to stop what they were doing to deliver a washing machine, I thought I'd get stuff ready for you."

He looked up, shaded his eyes with a bony hand. "The sun's on the other side of the store so it shouldn't be too bad out here." He marched into the building.

Pattie's face settled into a frown. "Here we are in our nice dresses and stockings, and look what we have to do. It's not fair," she whispered.

"Do you want to go to Duxbury about it?"

"No, I do not. You know he'd try and make us out to be lazy."

"Well, I guess we wash windows." Celina tossed Pattie a squeegee and faked a bright smile. "At least we're outside in the fresh air, and only a couple more hours before we're out of this place."

They were almost finished when Celina, standing on the top step of the ladder, stretched to wipe a streak from the glass above the main door.

"Are you going to the dance at the Polish Hall tomorrow?

The Swing Kings are playing," Pattie asked.

She draped the damp rag over the top of the ladder. "I've been thinking about it. Johnny is going, and—"

"He is? Oh, you have to go and all of us can sit together. It'll be fun." She added, "And there'll be lots of cute guys there. Please, please Celina. You've got to go."

Celina couldn't refuse. Pattie had been crazy about Johnny since high school. She feigned resignation. "Okay. I guess I'll have to go now." She raised one eyebrow and her eyes twinkled playfully. "And I'm positive there'll be all kinds of cute guys lined up to dance with us."

The windows sparkled, and they lugged the buckets of dingy water to the gutter in front of the store. They set to wringing out the tattered cleaning rags when Celina noticed Terez Halosz's black Ford stop next to the red brick post office. The car door opened and a tall, attractive, broad-shouldered young man with close cropped dark hair emerged from the driver's side.

Still bent over their task, Celina and Pattie looked at each other then back to the good-looking young man. Terez popped out of the passenger side, slamming the door behind her. Together they walked toward the post office.

Pattie whispered. "That's him. The guy we were talking about."

They stood up and pretended to busy themselves with the squeegees and rags while they eyed the young man disappearing into the post office. "He's not short, he's not bald, but he might be toothless," Celina said in an impish undertone.

Pattie grabbed a squeegee and threw it at her. They shared a giggle while they carried the wooden ladder, bucket, and cleaning supplies into the dim store interior.

"Did you notice that he opened the post office door for Terez?" Celina whispered.

"Yeah. He's polite. We've got to find out more about him."

"I'll bet he doesn't chew tobacco."

The round-faced regulator clock that hung next to the office door struck five. Celina collected her belongings and followed the other employees to the office to pick up the small manila pay envelope that contained her week's salary. Celina decided that retail had to be the most boring work in the world.

A tradition, begun by the first Mr. Duxbury and continued down the generations, dictated that the eldest employee be paid first. Mrs. Pinkerton, the senior employee, entered the office first and when she left, she was followed by Sam, Harold, Pattie, and Celina. The youngest, was always the last to receive her pay and the last to leave. She, like the others, accepted her pay envelope from G. C. Duxbury. But when she was about to leave, he reached out and laid a sweaty hand on her arm. "That blue-and-white dress looks nice on you. Wear it more often."

She could feel the heat radiating from his bull-like body. She backed away.

He cleared his throat. "You have a nice weekend, Celina." When she reached the door, he added, "You've been a big help to Earl since you started handling some of the orders. We'll have to talk about a raise. He tells me that for a woman, you've done an outstanding job."

"Thank you, Mr. Duxbury," she muttered and retreated from the airless office only to bump into Pattie. Their eyes met but her friend said nothing, although her raised eyebrows almost touched her reddish bangs and her head tilted with a knowing look.

They left the store in silence. Celina was angry that Duxbury had touched her, and she hated herself for feeling so anxious in his presence. In addition, she was annoyed at the way he talked to her about her job, as though it were a shock that she, a woman, could add a column.

Neither she nor Pattie said a word until they crossed the gritty gravel parking lot. Pattie's eyebrows still danced with her bangs and she held back the words that were struggling to be spoken. Then she pulled herself up to her full five feet and stated, "I'm not saying a thing."

Celina stood three inches taller than her friend. She leaned against her car and instantly pulled her arm away. "Ouch, that's hot." She flung the driver's side door open, and visible waves of heat escaped and engulfed her.

Pattie waited, standing silent with her eyebrows still in gossip mode.

Celina pushed damp wisps of curls from her own face. "So, we're going to the dance tomorrow night. Do you want to drive over together?" she asked.

Pattie's face fell. "Don't you want to say something about you-know-what that just happened?"

"It was embarrassing. I don't want compliments from him. I just want to do my job and be left alone."

Pattie leaned forward and spoke from the corner of her mouth. "I think he likes that you're nice, and not pushy like his wife. So, I think he was trying to be nice to you. As much as someone with all his charm can, that is. What do you think?"

"I'm not supposed to be pushy. I'm an employee for Pete's sake. He's my boss. All I want is my pay envelope."

"Well, that's what I think," Pattie said.

"I just wish he'd leave me alone." She looked up at the empty blue sky. "Don't I have enough problems?"

"All I want is to make some money at the store till I can get a better job." She tossed her purse onto the mohair car seat.

"It's too bad you didn't get to go to college. You could be teaching school by now."

"Yeah, well, I still might someday." Getting at least a little bit of education was part of her plan. She paused. "I've been at that store too long, and I'm glad I filled out applications at the newspaper and bank last month. Sarah Monahan will be resigning from the paper. She said she'd put in a word for me with Mr. Cherriten, the newspaper owner."

"Hey, what about me? I'll be stuck at Duxbury's and you'll be working at the paper."

"Both of us can move on to better jobs, but I don't know where we could find jobs in the same place." Celina tapped on Pattie's car door. "You'd better open the doors or the heat will be unbearable in there."

Pattie threw open the door of her dad's Chevy and shaded her head with her purse. She stood with the corners of her mouth turned down.

"I need to get out of that place, and so do you," Celina said. "Why don't you apply at the bank and Smith's Ladies Wear? And Dad said the feed mill needs a behind-the-counter clerk."

Pattie's face twisted in thought. "I'd like to work at the bank or Smith's, and the mill would smell like fresh ground grain instead of PF Flyers. It's only two blocks down the hill from the paper. We could still meet for lunch."

"That's right. And if nothing comes through at the bank or Smith's, working at the mill wouldn't be bad. Plus, you wouldn't have to get all dressed up."

"Yeah. I'd like working somewhere that I didn't have to wear stockings in the scorching heat." Pattie cocked her head. "Hey, we can be out of Duxbury's in no time."

"And we'd still be able to have lunch together. Hey, we had better get going or the sun's going to eat all the red from your hair," Celina teased.

"*Boga*, God." Pattie ducked into the car, revved the engine, and waved. "I'll pick you up around seven."

Driving home in the old Hudson, Celina tried to get comfortable on the mohair seat. She imagined that she was dancing with the man of her dreams, spinning round and round in his arms. A smile fluttered across her lips.

CHAPTER 3

Saturday afternoon when the clock struck four, Celina had finished cleaning the house and scrubbing the porch. Later, after the supper dishes had been washed and dried, and the kitchen had a final sweep, she hurried upstairs to ready herself for an evening out.

It struck her that she was looking forward to getting out of the house, being with people and having fun. It had been a long time since she actually wanted to go out and scan the crowd for someone to date. She laughed aloud when she remembered how Pattie insisted that there would be a lot of wonderful guys to dance with. Untaken, wonderful guys were pretty hard to come by in Kenville.

Wrapped in her pink chenille housecoat, she trotted down the steps to the shower in the cellar. She stood in the steaming cubicle letting the water flow over her until Marian yelled from the top of the steps. "Celina, you're using up all the hot water. Get out of the shower."

"Okay, I'm out." She dried off and ran up to her room. Her favorite sundress lay across the bed. Picking it up, she smiled. *Maybe it will bring me luck tonight.*

Opening the screen door and stepping onto the porch, Celina watched Pattie's car roar up the dusty drive and stop in the shade of one of the stately silver maples. Frankie raised a weary head from under the sweet shrub bush and sounded the alarm with a low *woof.*

Pattie jumped out and strolled over to the old dog. Petting him, she said, "Some watch dog you are. Can't even stir yourself to come and greet me."

Johnny stood on the porch, grinning and watching her. "You be nice to my dog. He's a big-shot around here you know."

Pattie turned and beamed. "You going to the dance too?" Her eyes followed the buttons down the front of his shirt to his belt to the neat creases in his khakis.

He hopped off the porch. "Sure, I like the Swing Kings and I'm ready to polka." He jabbed a thumb over his shoulder. "And I'm glad that that sister of mine is getting out of the house. We'll have to see to it that she has a good time."

The dog jumped up and bounded toward his master. Pattie stepped aside just in time. "Are you ready, Celina? I want to get there a little early to find a good table."

"I'm ready." Her brown eyes sparkled, and her fine, wavy hair was brushed back. She wore light makeup and fresh perfume.

"Hey, Missy, you sure look a lot better than you did a couple hours ago," Johnny said.

She rolled her eyes. "Well, I was cleaning the house, you know."

He tossed his car keys in the air and caught them. "Mike's waiting for me, so I'd better get going." After flashing a devil-may-care grin, he turned to Pattie. "Hey Red, don't forget to save me a dance." He sauntered to his car and ground the engine a couple of times before it turned over.

"Grind me a pound," Pattie called. He shook his head, sent her a mock scowl, and roared down the tree-lined lane to the highway.

They watched him leave and Pattie's forehead wrinkled. She kicked at a few wisps of drying grass. "Does he have a girlfriend somewhere?"

"Not that I know of." Sometimes Celina's heart ached for Pattie and Johnny. They were so close but couldn't manage to connect. "Why don't you let him know you're interested?"

"I couldn't do that. He treats me like a kid sister."

"You two are always acting like couple of kids, so he doesn't get to see the other side of you."

"What do you mean?"

"Maybe you should show him that you can be serious. That life is more than a Dean Martin and Jerry Lewis movie."

Pattie slid behind the wheel. "I don't act like Jerry Lewis."

"Sometimes you get pretty close." Celina's eyes twinkled as she got into the car.

"I suppose you want me to be grouchy like you. Well, Miss Celina Pasniewski, you are too serious and I can't be like that." Pattie's face turned scarlet.

"Don't get all in a snit. I'm just telling you what I think. Talk to Johnny any way you want. But if you were serious once in a while, I bet it would make a difference."

"What am I supposed to be serious about? How lousy the jobs around here, and that half the population is moving to Pittsburgh or Cleveland or Detroit? If my dad didn't work for the Highway Department, we'd probably have to leave too." Pattie's head swiveled from eyeing the ignition switch to glaring at her passenger. "It makes life easier if I laugh at it. Besides, it doesn't do any good to be cranky all the time, the way the other person sitting in this car is."

"I didn't mean to hurt your feelings." Celina didn't think she was a cranky person. "I'm not that bad, even if I am kind of grumpy sometimes."

"Sometimes! I know you're not like me, but you act," Pattie waved her hand in the air, "like an old lady." She clutched the steering wheel. "You've got to start enjoying life or else it's going to pass you by. And you're going to end up a lonely old spinster like poor Miss Grayhill."

"Hey, I thought we were talking about you, not me." Celina crossed her arms. "There are worse things than being like Harriet Grayhill. I could be married to some drunk who'd spend his pay envelope in the beer garden every week."

Before Pattie could respond, Frankie jumped on the driver's door and pushed his wet nose through the window. "Get away, Frankie. Get. God, his breath stinks. It's worse than Earl's when he's had a wad of Copenhagen in all day. Jeez, did you ever have to talk to that guy just before closing? It's enough to gag a maggot. She yelled, "Get down, Frankie!" and the dog dropped to the ground. "Yuck, look at that, he slobbered on my arm." She grabbed a rag from under the seat and rubbed it across her wet forearm.

"Now you're the one getting all cranky," Celina said.

Pattie tossed the rag over her shoulder onto the back seat. "Well, how would you like it if your boyfriend's dog slobbered on your arm?"

Their eyes met. "Your boyfriend loves that dog."

"Oh, shut up! You're getting me all confused. I just want to go to the dance and have a good time."

"Okay. Let's go."

Frankie continued to snuffle around the car, so Celina called to her mother. "Mom, come get Frankie. He's going to chase the car."

Marian, fanning herself with a newspaper, came out and the screen door slammed behind her. "Here Frankie, come on boy. Come on." The dog marked a tire as his own then lumbered toward the house.

The Chevy chugged down the bumpy lane then Pattie turned the wheel hard and they swung onto the highway. They had covered their hair with filmy scarves, rolled the windows down, and stopped speaking. The car sped past spent daisies growing around fence posts at the edge of the road. A few sprigs of Queen Anne's Lace waved like frilly hankies catching the breeze, and baby milkweed pods climbed stout stems, little fish struggling to the top to spawn.

Celina eyed the small hay fields that skirted the road. "We sure do need some rain. Everybody's gardens are drying up."

Pattie nodded. "Yeah, my dad's been complaining about how dry it's been this summer. He carries buckets of water out to his tomato plants every day after work."

When they reached Kenville, the sun was an orange ball of light in the sky. Its golden glow baked the streets and the two-story clapboard houses. Little boys in striped shirts and blue jeans ran from yard to yard. Most of them were barefoot, but some wore sneakers or battered leather school shoes. Old women in faded housedresses sat on porches and gossiped, and a few people bent over vegetable patches hoeing, watering, and pulling weeds while the evening shadows lengthened.

The stone walls of St. Stanislaus glowed. The church stood silent watch over the town, its massive doors closed but never locked in case some poor soul should need a place to pray in its cool, quiet interior.

Pattie drove up the low hill and swung into the gravel

parking lot behind a long, low-slung, white clapboard building, The Polish Hall. It had been in use as a community gathering place since their grandfathers had helped establish the Polish-American Brotherhood fifty years earlier. A row of small windows devoid of screens had been flung open. It was dusk and mosquitoes and lightning bugs buzzed right through. A few people milled around the side door waiting for permission to enter.

The two young women shook the wrinkles from their skirts, smoothed their hair, and joined the waiting crowd. Someone rang the buzzer and ancient Mr. Antkiewicz in his white shirt and wrinkled trousers stepped forward. He scrutinized each person's identity before he permitted them to enter the fraternal organization's inner sanctum.

When Celina and Pattie reached him, a shaft of snow-white hair fell across his forehead, and the fresh-rolled cigarette drooped from the corner of his mouth. He nodded them in.

After they passed entered the hall's darkened interior, the heat engulfed them in a muggy cloud. Pattie squinted and eyed the empty tables. She found one with a good view of the dance floor. "Let's get that one."

Six large white globes hung from the ceiling and Celina's eyes adjusted to the dim light. Square tables formed zigzag rows along the buff-colored walls. The waxed floor provided plenty of room to dance. One of the members had already sprinkled dry sawdust on the oak boards to make it as slick as possible. People greeted each other with traditional hugs, kisses, and cries of pleasure, all customs brought from the old country and still practiced.

Someone had snatched a chair from a nearby table and propped an emergency exit door part-way open. Couples shined to perfection, waiting for the band to set up, and a multicolored jukebox stood bright and flashing in the corner, silently screaming for attention. A couple of girls walked over, slipped a quarter into the slot, and selected a Frank Sinatra tune.

Celina and Pattie claimed their table, and Janek and Basia Laskowiec, neighbors from down the road, stopped to chat. It was a rare woman who would step up to the bar and order a drink, so Celina was glad when Janek offered to fetch a highball for each of them. A few minutes later, the Laskowiecs drifted off to join several other older couples across the room.

Nursing their drinks, Celina and Pattie watched the crowd grow. People trickled toward the tables in ones, twos, and small groups. Women wore perky pastel sundresses. The men sported Sunday-best trousers, and white or plaid shirts open at the collar with their sleeves rolled up. Their leather shoes were shined to perfection.

As the garrulous, growing crowd increased, the heat in the building increased and by nine o'clock all the exit doors had been propped wide open. A small breeze stirred the heavy air. It drifted through the building carrying the odors of beer suds, cigarette smoke, and restroom sanitizer.

Johnny and Mike arrived. Mike, a stocky young man, had the muscular build of someone used to hard work. His upper arms bulged against his shirt sleeves. He lit a cigarette, blew the smoke into the air, and watched Stella Zaliski and Cathy Wojciechowski walk by. The young women smiled and waved.

"When are you going to ask Stella out already?" Johnny asked.

Mike laughed. "I'm thinking about it. I'm thinking about

it."

Celina was glad that Mike had an eye for Stella. She liked both of them and thought they would make a nice couple. As an added bonus, her mother would have to stop nagging her about marrying Mike.

When the Swing Kings finished tuning up, the crowd was ready to dance. The minute the music started, couples filled the dance floor, and everyone polkaed with abandon. Men, with one arm around their partners' waists, stomped and hooted. Women's skirts swirled as their partners whirled them around the cavernous room.

Mike and Celina partnered up. He was a fine dancer and Celina enjoyed following his lead. Between dances, she looked over his shoulder and watched Pattie gazing into Johnny's eyes. She hoped her brother would get the hint.

Mike turned and glanced in the same direction. "I wish those two would get together already. They're two of a kind."

Celina smiled. "Yeah." Then she rolled her eyes. "Can you imagine what their kids would be like?" Both laughed at the idea of Pattie and Johnny shepherding around three or four noisy carbon copies of themselves.

After a brief intermission, the Swing Kings, carrying mugs of beer, hopped back on stage. They stashed their half-empty glasses under their chairs, and the music started again. Celina noticed a tall young man walk by. He was the one she'd seen going into the post office the day before. She looked up into large dark eyes lined with thick black lashes. Without warning, a delicious unexpected tingle raced through her body and she shivered. She didn't know where to look and was grateful when Mike whisked her away to the beat of the music.

Back at the table she sat next to Pattie, sipped her drink, and tried to see where the guy with the dark eyes had gone.

She spotted him talking to a group of giggling girls and burly young men.

Johnny stepped out of the crowd and following his sister's gaze, raised his brows and smiled. "Hey, you two, are you ready for another drink?"

"None for me, but I'd like a ginger ale." Celina fanned herself. "The whiskey makes me too hot." His smile broadened as he watched her gaze at the tall young man. He took Pattie's order and wandered off toward the bar.

Celina continued to cast furtive glances across the room. The guy was dressed casually in dark trousers and plaid shirt. He looked her way, and for a moment each smiled slightly then turned away. He was definitely the guy she'd seen with Terez Halosz yesterday. She tapped Pattie's shoulder and mentioned the fact.

"Oh, yeah, I saw him earlier. He's cute but not my type. He looks too intense."

Celina continued to watch him. She liked the way he walked with ease through the crowd. She liked the eyes, the olive skin, the dark hair brushed back, and his strong, angular features. She tilted her head. *He doesn't seem too intense to me.*

Pattie had already turned her full attention to Johnny, who was commiserating with Mike and a few other guys about the coal company's refusal to listen to their safety concerns. "Damn bosses, they think they own us. I treat my dog better than they treat us," Johnny said.

A chorus of agreement rose when someone said, "Kettlemore won't spend a dime to keep the roof from falling in on us."

"Stas Halushka said he's quitting before he ends up getting killed," Mike said.

The band played a jitterbug, and Mike swung Celina onto

the floor. Dancing with him was fun, but the stifling heat propelled them toward the open doors to where the air was cooler. They ambled outside and Celina took a deep breath of the fresh night air.

A million greenies and crickets participated in a deafening summer night's symphony. June bugs and moths threw their bodies at the street light, determined to break through the glass and plunge into the light's glow. A few bats darted past, hunting for their evening meal.

After the heat inside, the air felt chilly and Celina shivered. Mike's arm slid round her shoulder. She listened as he described the '49 Chevy motor he had just taken out of a junked car. "The bolts holding it to the chassis were frozen in place, and I had a devil of a time getting them out." He held out a thumb and showed her a blackened nail. "Got this when the wrench slipped."

The small talk waned and she asked why he hadn't asked Stella to dance. When he stammered excuses, she encouraged him to be more forceful. Mike's arm slid away from her and they returned to discussing mines, cars, and baseball for a few minutes. "Let's go back in. They're playing a good song," she suggested.

The glow from a match lifted to an unlit cigarette revealed the features of the intense young man with the close cropped hair and deep dark eyes. He watched them return to the building.

Celina sat out the next dance. She was pleased when she noticed Mike and Stella gliding across the floor. Then the band leader took a sip of his beer, held the microphone to his lips, and crooned a love song. Dark, smiling eyes approached her; the man put his hand out, and with that familiar Eastern European lilt in his voice asked, "Would you like to dance?"

When Celina put her hand in his she shivered, and butterflies did somersaults in her stomach. The hand was warm and strong as he held on to hers and led her to the dance floor. They stood close, swaying to the rhythm of the music.

While they danced, he told her that his name was Stephen Maszaros, that he was from Hungary, and he had been in the United States little more than a year.

She tilted her face up. "Did you leave because of the communists?"

He looked thoughtful. "Yes. For now they hold all the power in Hungary. I wanted my parents to emigrate with me, but they would not leave. He shook his head. "The Hungarians won't make it easy for the Soviet's puppets to control them. Like the Poles, they instigate for their independence at every turn."

Celina wanted to know more, but the music and jostling from other couples made it difficult to talk.

At the end of the set, he asked her to step outside. The low building spilled an arc of brightness into the summer night. In the trees, a symphony of insects played with abandon. Several couples stood close together in the shadows. Others talked. Some necked.

A cluster of giddy girls positioned themselves near a group of young fellows who loitered nearby. The guys spoke in low tones, eyed the girls, and leaned against an old Ford. They smoked and sipped warm beer. The girls, in their pastel sundresses, bobbed in and out of the light like undecided moths approaching candle flames.

Stephen and Celina moved past the chattering girls. He tapped a pack of cigarettes against the back of his hand, and pulled a cigarette. He offered the pack to her.

She shook her head. "No thanks. I don't smoke." In high school, everybody tried smoking, but she had gotten nauseated and turned a sickly green with the first puff. That ended her desire to light up.

He lit the cigarette behind cupped hands and Celina saw the shadow cast by his thick lashes against his cheeks. His hands were big and his arms tanned. A large scar ran from the wrist to the elbow lay thick and open, as though it had healed without a doctor stitching the wound closed. She wanted to ask about it, but didn't.

"Where in Hungary did you live?" Making small talk was difficult. She felt as if she was choking on the words and worried about saying the wrong thing.

He took a long drag on the cigarette, turned his head, and blew the smoke into the darkness. "I was born in the most beautiful city in Europe, Budapest."

"I've read about the capitals of Europe. What's it like?"

"The Danube River divides the city in two parts, the Buda side and the Pest side. I lived on the Pest side where the land is flat and it's industrialized. But Buda, on the other side of the river, is built on hills and more residential. That's where the well-to-do have villas." He stared into the darkness. "And the view from over there, high above the river with the city spread like a jeweled skirt below, is breathtaking. I miss it."

He inhaled, and smoke curled from his mouth when he spoke. "The city is too beautiful to be controlled by visionless communists."

"Will you go back and live there again someday?"

"I don't think so. I plan to create a life here, but I'd like to go back to visit."

"It must be difficult to be so far from home. I'd be homesick." As onerous as life could be in Kenville, she loved her close-knit, reliable family, Clearfield County's rolling hills, and the deer and wild turkey that traveled through the back yard.

After a thoughtful moment, he spoke. "Don't most people want to return to the place they were born? Your first home tugs at you, but there are times when you have to let go." He flicked the ash from the cigarette. "The world is changing with the war and the Soviets in power now. Who knows? When the communist stranglehold is finally broken, I may not want to return, even for a short time."

The sound of stomping came from the building. They stepped inside and saw a group of young men had claimed the dance floor and dancing the traditional Cossack dance that Celina loved to watch. The band played and the crowd clapped and cheered.

The young men had taken their places in a semi-circle. They crossed their arms and with knees bent, they were in near sitting positions. They kicked one foot into the air while balancing on the opposite one and squat-kicked to the rhythm of the fast-paced music. A film of sweat formed on their faces and dampened the backs of their shirts. She couldn't help but admire their strength and agility.

The music blared. The young men sprang to their feet, jumped, whirled, and finally dropped back into the squat-kick position for the finale. Panting, they vaulted to their feet. Sweat rolled down their faces and the crowd roared its approval.

She noticed Mr. Antkiewicz standing a few feet away. He sighed, wiped his eyes and nose with a great white hankie, and shouted for a round of drinks for the dancers. He slapped the young men on their sweat soaked backs as they filed toward the bar. "It does me good to see you keeping up the traditions of the old country. Too many young people forget about the old dances, the old customs."

The evening wound down with the last call for drinks and the final slow dance. Johnny held Pattie close as they swayed to the music. Celina's eyes searched the room for Stephen, but Mike swept her onto the floor. Her face flushed rosy-pink and she swallowed hard when she caught sight Stephen dancing with Cathy Wojciochowski.

CHAPTER 4

Tomas enjoyed a strong cup of *kawa*, insisting that only his technique could make it strong enough. On Sunday mornings he'd practice his coffee brewing ritual by first grabbing the cast-iron grate shaker and shaking the stove's grate till the kitchen windows rattled and everyone in the house woke up.

As soon as the fire was roaring, he'd slide a pot, blackened and burned from use, across the cooking surface and slip it into the space vacated by one of the cooktop's cast iron disks. When the water reached a boil, he chucked in a cup of fresh grounds, stirred it with a long-handled wooden spoon, and gave it five minutes.

When she was a little girl, Celina liked to watch him dip out the still bubbling liquid and pour it from one ironstone cup to another before taking a drink, wondering how he could swallow the scalding, tar-like coffee.

The heady aroma from this morning's brew drifted up the stairs and into Celina's room. She stretched her full length, yawned and peeked at the Baby Ben ticking contentedly on the nightstand. Enticing breakfast aromas lured her. She rolled to the edge of the bed, happy to be alive. As she thought about Stephen, she relived the moments they had spent together. *When will I see him again? Soon I hope.* She swung her feet over the edge and sat there, rubbing her eyes till the morning world focused.

After brushing her tangled hair, she stepped off Baba's hand-woven rag rug and padded across the linoleum-covered floor to the window. Another sunny day. Somewhere on the other side of the trees, a cow mooed, and a dog yipped. A grass-scented breeze floated through the curtains.

Marian had replaced Tomas at the cook-stove. Johnny sat at the kitchen table, wolfing down a plate of eggs, bacon, and left-over fried *pierogi*. When Celina entered, he looked up. "Jeez, Missy, you'd better do something with that hair. You look like a wild woman."

She poured a cup of coffee and used the tip of her spoon to pick out a half dozen floating grounds. "You don't look so great yourself this morning."

As Celina pulled out a chair to sit down, Marian broke in. "You two had better not start arguing. It's Sunday and we're supposed to be getting ready for church." Poised to crack two eggs into the pan, Marian asked Celina what she wanted for breakfast. Celina eyed her brother, who was famous for his appetite. "Are there any *pierogi* left?"

"Yeah, of course. Dad's done eating, and there's," Marian peered into the cast iron skillet, "let's see, five left." She slid the hot potato-and-cheese-stuffed dumplings onto a plate, spooned melted butter over them and passed the plate across the table.

Celina refilled her cup and sat down to eat. "You'd better hurry up if you're going to Mass with us," her mother said.

"I'll be ready. But I'm not very hungry."

"I'll take the last three if you don't want them," Johnny said, eying her breakfast.

She slid her plate across the table and he downed the *pierogi* in a couple of bites.

His face brightened. "Hey, Mom, Celina met a guy at the dance." He rolled his eyes, and covered his heart with his hand. "I think she's in love."

Celina gave him a stern look. His teasing embarrassed her, and if her mother thought there was a romance brewing, she'd never hear the end of it. "For Pete's sake, Johnny, can't you stop being a pain-in-the-you-know-what for one minute? Shut up."

Marian lifted her eyes and her spatula to the heavens and called upon God in Polish. "*Boga, Boga.*" She spun around. "It's Sunday morning, so stop it." She shook the spatula at them. "And I mean it." She took a step in their direction. "Mary, Mother of Jesus, give me strength."

Celina and Johnny looked at each other. Lifelong experience proved to both that they were pushing their luck when Marian said *Boga* and invoked the Blessed Virgin in the very next breath. Celina decided that it must be the change of life that was making her mother more irritable and demanding than usual.

Marian shook the spatula again. "Johnny, stop tormenting your sister, not one more word out of you. You understand?"

Johnny nodded. "Yeah, Mom."

"And Celina, you act like a young lady and have some manners." Marian turned a stern eye her way. "You hear me?"

"Yes, Mom."

When their mother turned away, Johnny focused on Celina and muttered under his breath. "You're like a bear with a sore ass in the mornings." He opened his mouth and roared silently at his sister.

Celina closed her eyes, raised her brows, and turned away from him.

Calm once again, Marian asked, "So who's the fella you met last night? What's his name?"

"He's staying with Terez. His name is Stephen Maszaros. He's nice. And that's all I know." She eyed her brother. "It's not like we're even friends or anything."

"Did he tell you anything about himself?"

"Just that he's from Hungary…Budapest…and his parents are still there."

"Hmm, a *Magyar*."

"A *Magyar*?" Celina asked.

"A Hungarian. They're a pretty ferocious bunch when somebody messes with them."

"How do you know that?"

"Pap traveled through Hungary before he came over from the old country."

Johnny leaned back. "I talked to Stephen a few times and he's a nice guy. I figured you two would hit it off, if you ever met."

Celina decided that it was best not to respond to his comment. "Mom, are we going to early Mass?"

"If everybody gets moving, we will."

Celina stood up.

"Dad's finished feeding the chickens and doing the other outside chores. We'll clean up the kitchen when we get home," Marian added.

Celina hurried to her room and donned a bright yellow sun dress and white cotton shrug. She brushed her hair, swept it back, and pinned it into place, but tiny wavy tendrils managed to escape here and there.

Tomas yelled up the stairs. "Celina, you ready? You better get down here. I'm leaving right now."

"I'm coming."

#

St. Stanislaus' arched stained-glass windows and massive oak doors made the church appear larger than it was. Tomas pulled into the gravel lot and parked next to Charlie Jankowiak's truck. Celina watched Charlie and his wife Anna help their grandkids, who often spent Sundays with them, hop to the ground.

Charlie, a wiry little man with bowed legs, limped. He had gotten hurt in a mine accident when he was forty-five. A runaway mine car had nailed him and he was laid up for months.

Charlie and Tomas had been friends most of their lives. When they were young, it was common practice for boys to quit school at the age of twelve, go into the mines, and work alongside their fathers underground. Times were hard for the immigrant miners in 1913, and a skinny boy's contribution meant a few more cents in his father's pay envelope.

The two boys started out as their dads' helpers, shoveling low coal. They were so small and thin that they could crawl into foot high gaps blasted out from under thousands of tons of coal and rock. They shoveled coal loosened by dynamite blasts back into the open area where their fathers loaded it into mine cars. The coal was then taken to the tipple, weighed, and sold at a good profit by Kettlemore Mining Company.

Charlie could tell a good story. Everybody who knew him

waited for him to warm up with a beer or two and then tell a few tall tales about the practical jokes the miners played on each other. Celina laughed with the rest of them but didn't think she'd like washing the dinner bucket that had a dead rat in it.

The two men slapped each other's backs, and the families chatted as they strolled toward the thick oak doors. The women pinned small lace handkerchiefs on their heads, and once inside, the group separated and each family moved toward its favorite pew.

The faint scent of incense and melted bees wax candles clung to the church's cool, dimly lit sanctuary. The cavernous, echoing sacredness of the place encouraged the parishioners to speak in hushed whispers. Celina genuflected and slid into the pew beside her parents as dappled beams of colored light streamed through the figures of angels and saints frozen in the stained glass.

The congregation heard Father Schmidt's beat-up Buick roaring up the low hill that led to the church, and as if on cue, everyone fell silent. Through the open window, Celina watched the car belch black smoke and rumble into the priest's reserved space.

When the car door slammed, people picked up their Sunday missals and thumbed through them. Father Schmidt was a balding, round-as-a-watermelon man, and he wheezed as he rushed in. Moments later, his head bobbing and his green robes for Ordinary Time flapping around him, he hurried to the altar. Altar boys scurried in his wake, polished leather shoes, socks, and pant cuffs showing beneath fluttering robes.

Marian whispered to Celina. "He's going to get a heart attack if the diocese doesn't get another priest in here to help.

He shouldn't have this church and St. Hedwig's, too. Besides, his sermons are so long that he's always late." Celina smiled and nodded a silent agreement.

The smile still on her face, she looked up and saw Stephen Maszaros' large dark eyes watching her. The pleasant, appreciative look on his face flustered her. She reacted with pleasure then looked down at her missal. Marian turned to her daughter, eyebrows raised.

Celina smoothed her face into a guarded mask and leafed through the book's thin pages, searching for the opening prayer. If a romance happened, she didn't want her mother becoming a part of it.

She couldn't focus on Mass because her thoughts were on Stephen. She stood, sat, and knelt with the rest of the congregation, but during the lengthy sermon her mind continued wandering.

A copy of the mimeographed bulletin lay on the seat beside her. She picked it up and scanned the entries. Her fingers lingered on the last page, and she read and reread the banns of marriage that included those of Kimberly Stuscovich, Bobby's sister. *I can't believe she's getting married. My God, she's got to be too young.* Celina thought a moment. *It's been three years; Kimmie was sixteen when we got the news that Bobby had been killed. Three years.*

She thought back to that bright Saturday morning when the phone rang. Marian answered it. Celina hurried down the stairs and entered the living room. She heard her mother murmuring comforting words into the receiver. Marian turned around, her face grayish. It was the same gray look her mother had had when they got the telegram informing them that her brother Martyn was killed. His B-17 bomber had been shot down over Dresden, Germany, in the summer of

1944. There were no survivors. She'd never forget that day.

Marian held the phone out. "Lucy's on the phone. There's bad news about Bobby."

Celina rushed and grabbed the receiver with both hands. "What happened?"

Lucy Stuscovich's voice was hoarse, and interrupted by sobs. "There was a battle. It lasted for hours."

Weeping, choking, and trying to speak, Lucy finally blurted out, "Bobby and some others were killed." A long rattling sigh came through the phone. "The officer said he was brave and a credit to the nation." She hesitated. "I…I can't talk anymore; I've got to call my sister. So long."

There was a click, and Celina held the phone. She held it a few inches from her face. She stared at it. The dial tone droned. She stared at the little black holes through which she had heard the news. *A battle. Killed.* She turned and looked at Marian, standing sad-eyed in the doorway. Slowly, carefully she returned the phone to its cradle. Tomas came in, put his arm around her shoulder, and led her to the couch.

"Bobby's not coming home," she heard herself say.

Her mind was numb. The three of them sat together for a long time. At last the burning rage that had been building for hours welled up and burst out. She hurled recriminations at the president, the North Koreans, the U.N. "I hate them. All of them. I wish the people they love would die in their stinking wars."

She shook her fist. "Why God, why?" Her face crumpled, and the tears she had held back as long as she was able, streamed down her cheeks.

A shaft of bright sunlight crept through the open window and flooded Celina's face, nudging her back to the present moment. Father Schmidt's voice ground to a halt. She reread the announcement for Kimmie's wedding and folded the bulletin into a neat rectangle. It had been a long time. Such a long time.

She felt a little bump. Marian motioned with a brisk nod of her head that it was time to file up to the front of the church and receive communion. Returning to her seat, she saw Kimmie wearing a cool summer dress, her light brown hair framing her face. She looked so happy with George, her beau, and the rest of the Stuscovich family in the pew beside her.

They left the church and Celina's eyes watered as she squinted into the bright light and unpinned the lace kerchief from her hair. She stepped up to Kimmie, hugged her, and wished her happiness. They chatted about the wedding.

"I'm having three bridesmaids," Kimmie said. "We ordered the nicest pale yellow dresses from the Montgomery Ward catalog. The reception's at the Polish Hall. You got the invitation, didn't you?"

"The mailman will probably deliver it tomorrow."

"You are coming, aren't you?"

"I wouldn't miss your wedding day," Celina said with a smile.

Kimmie hugged her then strode off with her soon-to-be husband.

John and Lucy Stuscovich stood next to Celina's parents discussing the fine qualities of their future son-in-law, a carpenter at the Zeppo Construction Company in Clearfield. Celina smiled and nodded absently as they talked. The sun still bothered her eyes, and she had to dab at them with her handkerchief.

What would life be like today if Bobby had come home? Would he be a coal miner?

Would we have children? Would we be happy? There were no answers; Korea had aborted all the answers. She felt hollow inside as she turned and shared congratulations and good wishes with Kimmie's parents before the families went their separate ways.

As they drifted back to the car, Marian sighed. "It's hard to believe that Kimmie's all grown up and getting married." She avoided Celina's eyes. "Time does fly."

Tomas pulled off his tie, opened the car door, and slid in behind the wheel. "I'd like to know when our daughter's going to find a man." He turned and eyed Celina over his shoulder. "There's too many old maids around here already."

Celina's brown eyes narrowed and her lips pressed themselves into a thin line. She hoped her father didn't know how deeply his words cut her. She stared out of the car's open window, crossed her arms, leaned back in the seat, and spoke. "I do not want to talk about it, especially not in a church parking lot full of people."

Tomas turned the key in the ignition and the car roared to life then eased the car into line. "Well, Kimmie is four years younger than you, and she's got her man."

"My man's dead, in case you forgot."

"I didn't forget. None of us did."

"Then leave me alone."

"Listen here, Missy, it hain't normal to sit and mope for so many years. It hain't normal. You hear me?"

"I'm not moping. I haven't found anybody yet."

"You're not lookin' very hard."

Marian interrupted. "Tomas, leave her alone."

"Like I said, there's too many old maids around here."

Angry and empty inside, Celina stared out the window. "Will you stop it?"

Johnny ran up to the car and slapped the roof. "Hey Dad, I'm going with Mike to look at an old gas station that's for sale. I'll be home later."

Tomas nodded his approval.

Marian spoke up. "Don't forget that Andy, Ellen, and the kids are coming over, and we're eating at two."

Johnny threw his bulletin and missal onto the back seat beside Celina. "Okay, Mom. Two o'clock. I'll be there. Mike too?"

She smiled over her shoulder at Celina. "You know he's always welcome."

Celina wished Mike would marry Stella so her mother would stop trying to force a romance where none existed.

"See ya later."

"Get going." Tomas said as he tossed a glance at Celina, planted like a statue staring out the window. He edged the Hudson forward along with retreating pickup trucks and family cars. When they reached the middle of town, he stopped at the curb near the Main Street Drugstore and sent Celina in for a copy of the Sunday edition of the *Pittsburgh Press*.

Inside, she spoke briefly with Mrs. Pinkerton, who was on her way home from Episcopal services. The elderly lady and fellow employee at Duxbury's seemed concerned. "I'm worried about Mr. Duxbury. He seems preoccupied and not himself lately."

"I haven't noticed anything, but I don't talk to him much," Celina answered. She didn't want to think about her employer on her days away from the store.

They arrived at the house and entered through the back door. "The mess from breakfast hasn't gone anywhere." Marian picked up her apron and tied it on.

In minutes the two women set to work. Celina kept her mind blank as she went through the motions of cleaning up the remains of breakfast and preparing dinner. She didn't want her hurt and anger to be obvious, so she refused to think about the scene after church.

Marian adjusted the draft over the coal fire and removed the overflowing ash pan from the cinder box. The heat from the handle burned through the potholder. She hurried out the screened door and dumped the hot embers onto the pile near the garage.

When she returned, Celina steered the conversation away from herself and her marriage prospects. "Mom, when do you think we'll get an electric stove?"

Marian slid the ash pan back in place. "I'd rather have a furnace installed before getting a stove."

While preparing the potato salad, Celina said, "It's bad enough to spend half your life cooking, but tending a coal cook stove makes it even worse."

"Well, that's what we have to do."

Have to do, have to do. I'm sick of hearing what I have to do. Why can't I just take off and do whatever I want? Celina took her exasperation out on the celery and onion she was chopping.

They heard Tomas outside. He dropped an armload of corn he had purchased from Ray Denny's produce truck the day before. "Celina," he called through the screen door. "Clean this corn and save the husks and silks. I'll feed them to the pigs later." He poked his head inside. "Ray brought cantaloupes up from down south too, but they were bruised and only half ripe. Not worth buyin.'"

Celina stepped out of the sweltering kitchen. A small breeze lifted her damp hair and the air cooled her body as she sat down to shuck the corn.

Marian stood at the door. "How many ears did Dad buy?"

"I've got two dozen here, and there's another dozen left."

"That ought to be plenty. Andy can take the rest home. The kids will like that."

Celina carried an armload of corn into the kitchen. Marian opened the refrigerator door and peered inside. "The strawberry Jell-o's almost set." She spoke from behind the open door. "How about slicing the bananas and stirring them in?"

Celina answered, "I was going to finish the potato salad."

"Do the Jell-o first."

"It's always, do this or do that. It never ends. Cripes, Mother, I'd like to rest on Sunday too, you know." She loped to the pantry, grabbed a bunch of bananas, and did what her mother ordered. Tears stung her eyes. *This is not what I want to do every day for the rest of my life. This is not it.*

Still seething, she finished the potato salad. Isn't there more to life than cooking, cleaning, and working in a store with dead flies in its office windows? She slammed the bowl on the table.

Marian frowned at her. "What's the matter with you?"

"Nothing." Nobody listened when she told them how she felt, so why tell them again.

"Then quit slamming stuff around. You're gonna break something."

Marian pulled two roasters from the oven. She removed the lids and steam billowed up from the fried chicken and *halupkie*. The cabbage roll aroma rode on a cloud of unseen heat across the room. Celina said, "It's so hot that food doesn't even smell good."

Her mother turned. "Okay, what's bothering you?"

Celina clenched her teeth. "I'm tired of everything, and

I'm sick and tired of all this work."

"*Boga.*" Marian slapped her forehead. "How else are we supposed to get food on the table?"

"I don't know and I don't care. I just don't want to do it day in and day out."

"Well, you'll have to do it as long as you live in this house."

"But I don't have to like it." And she didn't like it.

Tomas walked in. "Celina, what are you griping about?"

"Oh, I'm just hot and tired, that's all." It was no use trying to talk to him. He would assert his authority as head of the house and that would end the discussion anyway.

"Don't stay out so late on Saturday night, and you won't be so tired on Sunday."

"You're the one who wants me to go out and find a man," Celina snapped back.

"Don't get smart with me, Missy."

Her mouth clamped shut and she went to the sink to fill the dish pan with soapy water. Discontent spilled through the emptiness inside her as she went through the motions of ordinary life. She wanted to be like her mother and Ellen, her sister-in-law, accept life for what it was, even the possibility of being a spinster, but she couldn't. She didn't understand it herself, but she just couldn't.

#

An hour later, Celina and Marian dragged the kitchen table through the doorway into the cooler living room and threw printed cotton tablecloths over it. Celina had started counting place settings when they heard a car horn tooting and voices hollering.

It was Andy and his family. After piling out of the car, all four of them trouped into the house. Ellen, Andy's wife, had a flat face, high cheekbones, and Mamie Eisenhower bangs. She carried a silver-colored container filled with her special coconut frosted marble cake.

Ellen hadn't learned to cook until after she married Andy and there were many cooking disasters, like the time she left the pinfeathers on the roasting chicken. She took a lot of teasing. Tomas said she was too touchy about a little ribbing.

Andy was barrel-chested and strong as an ox, an older and larger version of Johnny. A ready smile revealed straight white teeth. He was fair skinned, and he combed his sandy hair straight back. Ellen giggled when she told Celina that he could lift her as easily as if he were lifting a doll.

Celina, along with her mother and father, greeted the new arrivals. The family hugged and kissed each other in the traditional way of greeting. Six-year-old Marty and four-year-old Tommy flung themselves at their grandparents then at their Aunt Celina. They both squealed, "Aunt Celina, Aunt Celina, can I sit by you when we eat?"

Their presence lifted her spirits. She hugged them and assured each that he could sit next to her. She enjoyed each hug. *I hope I have boys just like these little guys someday.* They were still young enough to like sharing warm hugs and planting sloppy little-kid kisses on her cheek.

The boys ran to Frankie's spot under the porch. They squatted down, poked their heads into the darkness, and pleaded with the dog to come out and play. Before long, a wet black nose followed by floppy ears and large brown body slid out of his cool den. The patient old dog endured pats and hugs and ear-scratches from the little tow-headed boys.

Inside the kitchen, Andy leaned against the refrigerator.

"Christ, it's hot in here," he said, wiping sweat from his face. "Hey, where's Johnny? The only time I see him is at work."

Tomas opened the corner cupboard and retrieved a bottle half full of whiskey. He unscrewed the top, poured two shots, and slid one toward his son. Lifting his drink and said, "*Na Zdrowie!*" Andy returned the salute. "*Na Zdrowie!*" Father and son threw their heads back, swallowed the Old Crow, and placed the empty jiggers on the kitchen table. Tomas returned the bottle to the cupboard and told Celina to drop what she was doing and get two beers from the refrigerator.

He uncapped the beer. "Johnny'll be here in time for dinner." He ran a rough hand across his chin. "That kid wouldn't miss his mother's cooking."

Father and son left the stifling kitchen to the women and found a shady spot on the back porch. Celina overheard Tomas complaining about loose rock and muddy water at Shirley Creek mine. "A slab the size of a tabletop came down right beside Guido Rizzo on Wednesday. Another inch and it woulda ripped his shoulder off, or worse, killed the poor bastard."

"I heard about that," Andy responded. "At least it wasn't in our section. Kettlemore doesn't have anybody moving the waste rock to the gob piles in the worked-out sections. It's filling up the tunnels."

"Why the hell do they let things slide like that?"

"They think they're saving money, I guess."

"It's almost two o'clock," Tomas announced

The three women raced back and forth from kitchen to living room, placing loaded platters and bowls on the table. A film of perspiration covered Celina's face as she stood near the stove and fished ears of corn from a boiling kettle.

Before Marian called the family together she marched the

boys to the sink, and amid squirming, gasping, and complaining, she scrubbed and dried their hands and faces.

Celina laughed at the sight of their damp hair standing straight up from their well-scrubbed foreheads. "Mom, you're so rough. You're going to scrub their skin off."

Marian looked up. "You've got to keep kids clean or else they could pick up lice or worms or something."

"Ugh." Celina lifted an eyebrow. "Believe me, I remember those scrubbings."

The family gathered around the table and sat down and Tomas said grace.

Marty yelled, "Dig in."

From across the table, Ellen said, "Marty, that's not nice." He stared back at her with big brown innocent eyes.

Tommy picked up a cob of corn in both hands and took a couple of bites while butter dripped from the corners of his mouth. Celina reached over and wiped his greasy face.

A car roared up to lane. Car doors slammed. Tomas looked up and jabbed his fork in the air. "I told you that boy wouldn't miss his mother's cookin'."

The two young men in Levis and white T-shirts stepped up to the screened front door.

Tommy and Marty squealed with delight. They got up on their knees, turned round in their chairs, and cried, "Uncle Johnny, Uncle Johnny!"

"Do I hear my favorite nephews calling my name?" Johnny ruffled their silky hair and, holding their greasy faces in his big calloused hands, gave each a noisy kiss on the cheek.

"Johnny, you're messing them up worse than they were. Their hair is sticking out all over the place," Ellen said.

"Okay, boys, I gotta do this. Your mom says so." A rough

palm reached out and smoothed their mussed-up hair, patting it into place. "But there's nothing I can do about your faces. Aunt Celina can take care of that."

After the commotion, Tomas said, "Sit down already."

Johnny and Mike eyed the table. "Any food left for us?"

"There's plenty on the stove," Tomas looked at Celina. "Bring out some more *halupki* and chicken." He scanned the table. "It looks like there's plenty of everything else."

Celina's good humor drained away. She wanted to refuse but pushed her chair back noisily and rose. *Your obedient daughter will do as she's told.*

"What's a matter with you? Can't you see these fellas are hungry?" Tomas said.

She opened her mouth to speak but thought better of it. All her dad seemed to care about was the men of the family. She would like to ask him what he thought about the women. But on second thought, she knew what he would say and she didn't want to hear it.

While filling a platter with chicken and a bowl with cabbage rolls, she heard Tomas call out. "Bring the coffee while you're at it."

She slammed the ladle onto the sink's drain board with such force that it bounced around, sent tomato broth in all directions, and clattered to the floor. *Why the hell can't he just leave me alone?*

Mumbling under her breath, she picked the ladle up, tossed it into the sink, and started wiping broth from the floor. Ellen ventured into the kitchen. "I'll get the coffee."

"Thanks, Ellie. The milk's in the pitcher at the back of the fridge."

"Don't let that kind of talk bother you." Ellen looked around the refrigerator door. "All old men are like that. They think it's still the 1920s. My dad's the same way. Maybe even worse. Sometimes I wonder how my mother can stand him. He expects to be waited on, hand and foot."

"Is Andy like that too?"

Ellen tilted her head to one side. "No, not nearly as bad as that, but you know how men are; he's pretty much like the rest of them." She wiped her hands. "You know a woman's job is to look nice, be pleasant, and take care of the house and kids. And never complain."

"Don't you get sick of it?"

"Sometimes. Take my word for it, any man will boss you around if he can get away with it." Ellen winked. "He gets away with it only so long. Then I get very unpleasant till he straightens up."

"I'm surprised. I thought you'd never stand up to him."

"Well, you've got to let them know what you won't put up with."

"So, he's better than Dad then?"

"Oh yeah. He's good to me and the kids. He spends too much time hunting, fishing, and chewing the fat with the guys. But then again, you can't have everything."

Celina crossed her arms. "Being an old maid is starting to look better and better."

"It will till you find the right man, then you'd be surprised how much you'll be willing to put up with." Ellen's eyes twinkled.

"I don't know about that."

"I do." The smile on Ellen's face broadened. "You just need the right man."

"But men have the right to rest on Sunday. Why shouldn't we? Why do we have to stay home all the time, do all the cooking, and cleaning, and they get out in the world and give us orders?"

Ellen shrugged and led the way back to the table. She said over her shoulder "If we didn't cook and clean, nobody would."

"Well, it isn't fair," Celina said, speaking softly.

She crossed the threshold and head Andy say, "Hey, Mike, haven't seen you in a while. What are you doing when you're not at the mine?"

Mike pulled his chair closer to the table. "I'll tell ya, I'm doing some auto body work at Kasper's Garage, so I've been keeping pretty busy."

"Oh, yeah. Isn't Kettlemore working you hard enough at the mines five days a week?"

"Well, sure, but I'm thinking about going into another line of work. Detroit is making a lot of cars, and sooner or later those cars are going to need a mechanic. I'll be ready for 'em."

"You gonna quit the mines to work on cars and trucks?" Tomas leaned back in his chair.

"I'm thinking about it." Mike's scowled and shook his head. "Never did like it underground. And I don't like working for a company that would rather save a buck than save my life."

Andy reached for the platter of chicken. "I'll give you that. The company makes money hand-over-fist, and they'd have us working for nothing, like they did when they broke the union in the twenties, if they could get away with it."

"Did you see the fancy Cadillac old Bill Kettlemore was driving last week? Him in his three-piece suit and shiny shoes, strutting around outside, and us coming out the portal filthy and covered in coal dust from head to foot. By God, you can bet he never stepped foot inside that mine. Scared, that's what he'd be, scared." Mike's face hardened into a frown.

"Yeah," Tomas said. "The big shots don't want to get their lily-whites dirty." He fluttered his fingers in the air. "They wouldn't know what to do if they got dirt under their fingernails." He smirked. "They won't step inside the mine, but don't you worry. They don't have no problems sending us down there. When they see us coming out tired and dirty, they don't see men, all they see is dollar signs."

Johnny set down his fork. "Say Dad, what do you think about getting into another business? Starting one like a car dealership or a repair shop or something like that?"

"Couldn't tell ya, Son. When you worked in the coal mines for thirty-five years, you don't know much else." He laughed. "All I know is back-breakin', dirty, and dangerous work. That's all I know how ta do."

He scratched the stubble on his chin. "I suppose a man could make his living fixing cars, but if you ask me, it's risky sinking your money into some business if you're not sure you're going to make it. Everybody I know fixes their own machinery. Can't see how it would work."

"But Dad," Johnny responded. "We can't be sure about the mines either. Things are slowing down. They're not taking coal out like they did during the war. Prices are going up, wages are going nowhere, and a lot of guys are getting laid off."

Mike spoke up. "The companies aren't making it easy either. They're shutting down and not telling the workers till the last minute."

"A lot of guys aren't waiting around," Andy added. "They're going to Cleveland or Detroit before they're on the unemployment line. Joe Clancey said the factories are hiring everybody who wants to work. He said the steel mills in

Pittsburgh are working round the clock."

"What the hell does Joe Clancey know?" Tomas retorted. "You kids are too young to remember it, but your mom and me were desperate during the Depression. We were afraid it'd get to the point where the bank would foreclose on this place. There were some weeks I didn't even bring home a dollar. And that's the truth." He leaned back in his chair. "People like Clancey started saying there was work out west, and the word came out that the government was hiring anybody who wanted to work on Boulder Dam. The one Truman named Hoover Dam. Why he'd name anything after that worthless son-of-a . . ." he eyed the children, "gun is beyond me.

"Anyway to get back to what I was sayin'. So, me, your uncle Stanley, and about a million other poor slobs scraped the last of our money together and went west. We were like a bunch of hobos, hitchhiking, scrimping on every penny and begging for food. We got there and hung around the work site for a couple of months, it was a stinking hot, dusty, brown desert of a hellhole with no trees, and we waited to get called."

Tomas tapped his index finger on the table. "We waited in that damned desert heat and there wasn't even a patch of grass to sit on. And we got no work. We started to run low on money, so what'd Stanley and me do after a couple more weeks? We turned around and panhandled our way back home. Hundreds and hundreds of disgusted men just like us started back east. It was that or starve, which we almost did. Some people were good and gave us food but some would have as soon kicked us like we was no more than stray dogs. Believe me, when I got back here, I was so damn glad to see these hills and these coal patches that I ran all the way up the lane to the house."

He paused for a moment. "I damn near lost the soles off my shoes. They was that wore out. Like I said, I was so glad to be back here, where the grass is green and it rains in the summer. Here I could eke out a living off my own little piece of ground and work in the mines when there was work. I say hold onto your money and your land, and don't trust nobody but yourself and your family."

"But Dad," Johnny said. "It's different now. Coal isn't what it used to be. Natural gas and oil are taking over. Things aren't good here like they are in other parts of the country."

"Nothing's gonna replace coal. Nothing. It's coal and coke that runs the steel mills, and the mills make the steel for everything." Tomas crossed his arms, sat back and waited, defying anyone to raise an argument.

Marty and Tommy, tired of grown-up talk, clamored for a piece of cake.

Ellen chimed in, "Everybody's having cake, aren't they?"

Tomas drained his coffee cup, pushed his chair back, and was about to rise when Marian's eyes locked onto his. He sat down and pulled his chair up to the table and waited for a slab of Ellen's famous dessert.

Marian cut the coconut-frosted marble cake, slipping thick wedges onto everyone's plate. After swallowing the last bit of coconut icing, Tomas pronounced, "Good cake."

Ellen beamed.

Again Tomas pushed back his chair and glanced at Marian. "You boys, ready to go outside?" he asked.

Full and content, the men and children wandered outside to talk and to play.

Marian called, "Keep an eye on the kids."

The women pushed back the clutter, stretched their legs, and sat back to enjoy a cup of fresh coffee and a little gossip before gathering up the dirty dishes.

"Father Schmidt asked the ladies at St. Hedwig's to bring in clothes for

Libby Mezovsky and her kids. I have a couple of dresses that are too small, and she's so skinny that I'm sure they'll fit her," Ellen said.

"How about if I buy a few things from the store for the kids and put them in with your donation?" Celina asked.

"That would be swell. It would be nice to give them something new."

"Somebody ought to knock some sense into that worthless man of hers. Every cent he makes goes into booze," Marian added.

"She should divorce him." Celina chimed in. Both Marian and Ellen turned and stared at her. "Well, she should."

"She made her bed, and she has to sleep in it." Her mother said with a huff.

"I feel sorry for her, but there's nothing anyone can do, except pray that her kids turn out all right," Ellen added.

"I saw her in the store the other day and she looked so haggard. There ought to be something that poor woman could do."

"Somebody at church told me she's on relief. The government is giving away powdered milk, butter, cheese, and beans. That should help feed the kids," Ellen said.

"I guess that's something."

Marian stood. "We can't solve Libby's problems. And we still have a mess to clean up."

Celina washed and Ellen dried. From behind a large bowl she was holding, Ellen made an announcement. "We're going to have a baby."

Celina wiped her hands and rushed over to her sister-in-law and held her close. "Oh Ellie, that's wonderful." She was happy for her, but a tinge of sadness for herself hovered in her heart. Would she ever be the recipient of such hugs and congratulations?

Marian entered carrying a rolled up tablecloth. "What's going on in here?"

"You tell her, Ell."

"We're having a baby."

Marian eyed her daughter-in-law. "I had a feeling you were expecting." She hugged Ellen and patted her on the back. "Does Andy know?"

A faint smile fluttered across Celina's lips when she heard her mother use the word expecting. Marian was still too embarrassed to say the modern word, pregnant, because then everyone would know what the future parents had been up to.

Ellen nodded. Her face flushed with enjoyment.

"When are you due?"

"Dr. Harvey said the middle of November."

Marian insisted that Ellen sit down when she and Celina dragged the wooden table back to the kitchen.

With the tidying up complete, the three ventured outdoors, chattering about the new baby. Marian and Ellen claimed the porch swing. Celina sat on the steps, kicked off her shoes, and sipped a cup of coffee. She wondered what it would feel like to be pregnant, to carry a newborn in her arms, and nurse him from her own breast. Would a husband and family be more important than the career she had planned for her future? Determination crossed her features. *I can do both.*

CHAPTER 5

A serene hour passed when a battered pickup truck followed by a cloud of dust bounced up the lane and pulled up near the house. It was Charlie and Anna Jankowiak. Recognizing the visitors, Frankie sauntered toward the truck and let out a couple of friendly woofs.

Charlie, his cap cocked to one side, crossed the yard with his usual bandy-rooster strut. Anna walked primly beside him.

The boys ran up to them and asked to play with their grandchildren. Anna shook her head. "Their mommy and daddy wanted them to come home, so we took them to their own house." Satisfied, the boys ran off.

"Hey, Marian, go get the bottle and some glasses." Tomas called.

He filled the shot glasses and passed one to each man. They shared a toast, *Na Zdrowie,* and then placed the glasses on the porch railing. Marian went to the kitchen and reemerged with several bottles of beer. Charlie along with the others removed the cap, took a swallow, and closed his eyes.

Tomas, the good host, nodded his pleasure.

The older men settled into their routine of swapping

stories. Gnarled hands cut through the air for emphasis, as they talked about hair-raising experiences and practical jokes that the miners pulled on each other underground.

Tears of laughter escaped Charlie's water-blue eyes. He prepared to retell the story about somebody stealing the food out of his dinner bucket on the days when Anna packed chocolate cake, which was Mondays, because she always baked a chocolate cake for dessert on Sunday.

He leaned forward and rubbed his hands together. "I knew I'd find out who it was when I slipped a laxative into the icing." He bent over laughing and his beer wobbled when he slapped his knee. The bottle teetered and headed for the floor, but Charlie grabbed it before it hit the ground.

He set it aside and choked out, "After the shift, Bart Wilson went running past me looking right and left like he just robbed a bank and needed a place to hide. Ran straight through the parking lot, past the jagger bushes, and jumped into a patch of weeds. All the guys could hear him back there."

Charlie roared and wiped his eyes. "Everybody was laughin' when he came out. Next day Bart came to work and couldn't sit down. "Had poison ivy all over his ass. He must a used a gallon of Calamine lotion for two ta three weeks."

Tomas guffawed, Mike's face split in a wide grin, and Johnnie almost choked on the mouthful of beer.

Charlie took another swig. "Served the bastard right. A man hain't allowed what's meant for another man's stomach." He chuckled and savored the memory. "Never had a bit of trouble after that."

Anna spoke up. "Charlie loves to tell that story. Trouble is that Bart's still mad about them guys laughing and poking fun at him about the poison ivy. And every time they get together and have a few beers, the story comes up. Bart's a joker but he doesn't like it when the joke's on him."

"Well, Annie girl, he was askin' for it. Nobody says much about it now." He held up his beer and smiled. "Unless they have a couple beers in their belly."

A cacophony of nighttime noises rose up and the red sun slid down behind the maple trees. Shadows lengthened, and swallows darted above the yard. They gorged on any unsuspecting insect that caught their eye. As it grew darker, bats swooped above, replacing the swallows in the deep purple-red sky. "Stay near the house or else the bats might get in your hair," Marian warned the boys.

They covered their heads with their hands and ran to Celina. She hugged them close, "Mom."

"You kids do what your baba said, okay. Stay by the house where we can see you. And if you don't bother the bats, they won't bother you."

Marty brightened and turned to his grandmother. "Baba, can we have a jelly jar to catch lightning bugs?" Bats forgotten, they darted around the dim yard chasing the flickering glow of hundreds of tiny yellow-green lanterns that had risen out of the grass.

"Morning's going to come sooner than later," Anna reminded Charlie. "We'd better think about going home." They said their farewells, got in their truck, and set off down the lane. Celina watched the tail lights dance a jig till the truck bounced out of sight.

Ellen followed Anna's lead. "You have to work too, and the boys will be cranky if they stay up much longer. It's time to go."

Celina watched another vehicle disappear, the tail lights dancing till it bounced out of sight.

Mike and Johnny continued to talk about leaving the mines, starting a business in town, or going to a city to work.

Tomas, not inclined to encourage them, stood up and stretched. "Talkin's one thing, but makin' a living is another. You know how hard it was for Pap when he got to this country, and how I had to start in the mines when I wasn't much bigger than those little boys."

The older man slapped at a mosquito. "You were able to finish high school before you started to work. So you know conditions are better now. What you need to do is work at the mines and get a piece of land. Land is the only thing you can be sure of. You take care of the land, and it'll take care of you."

Celina knew that the uncompromising need to own property was stamped into her father and grandfather's consciousness. In Poland, few peasants owned the land they worked. They farmed in the sunshine and fresh air of the northern plains or near the southern mountains, but they eked out a meager living and subsisted on the foodstuffs they grew. Starvation was common under the greedy thumb of tyrannical, aristocratic landlords.

Tomas stepped through the door into the yellow glow of the kitchen and plodded toward the stairs. A large moth beat its wings against the screen.

"What do you think of my idea?" Johnny's voice cut through the dark.

Celina's brow furrowed. "A business sounds fine, but Dad does make a good argument."

"I know how Dad and Pap feel about owning property.

I've heard it all a hundred times…that even after the serfs were freed in the 1840s, they were never more than sharecroppers. I plan to have my own land, but it has to be after I have a business going."

"We're learning how to run things at Kasper's and have been saving for over a year," Mike chimed in.

"A year?"

"Yeah. And we're serious about this," Johnny added. "I've been going in to Kasper's every Saturday that Dad doesn't need me around here. Mike's been working on the vehicles, but mostly I've been ordering parts, helping with the bookkeeping, and cleaning the place."

"Jeez, Johnny, why didn't you tell me?"

"I didn't want to jinx this by talking about it. And I don't want Dad trying to shoot me down."

"You know Dad, all he worries about is making sure he gets that pay envelope every week, and being sure the bank never has an excuse to take this place away from him."

After a moment of silence she went on. "He hates being in debt to anyone. I can't remember when he hasn't paid for everything in cash. He doesn't trust bankers or anyone who could cheat or trick him into being dependent on their whims."

"But this isn't the old country where Pap had to borrow from tavern keepers and moneylenders who charged 200 percent interest. Cripes, the Depression is over."

"My dad's the same way," Mike said, "always worried that the worst will happen. He doesn't trust the banks. He keeps extra money in a half-gallon jar buried in the fruit-cellar floor."

"Cripes, can't they see times have changed?"

"During the Depression, they must have worried all the

time," Celina said. "And when we were growing up, remember how Baba told stories about kids in Galicia dying because they were sick and half-starved, and there was no one to turn to."

Johnny glanced toward the kitchen. "Trouble is they always think it's going to happen again."

"Well, if you took the chance on this business and it didn't work out, you could fall back on the mines, couldn't you?"

Johnny shook his head. "I'll have to make it, because I'm not going back."

"The mines hain't for me either," Mike added. "I dread going through that portal at the start of every shift. One way or another I'm quitting, even if I have to stand on an assembly line all day."

Celina tried to see her brother in the darkness. "Johnny, where would you go?"

"Probably Pittsburgh. I'd try to get on at one of the steel mills. Kasper likes the way I keep his books. So, I'd try to move up in a company where I could work my way into the business end of things."

"I'd hate to see you leave," she said quietly.

"I don't want to, and we're gonna try and make a go of it here." He turned round. "Right, Mike?"

Mike nodded. "We're going to the bank about a loan in a couple of weeks. Old Mr. Wilcox's been talking about retiring and selling his garage. Young Wilcox doesn't want the business. If the old man retires, we'll be ready to step in and make an offer."

"Even if Dad doesn't like it, he can't say you're not prepared," Celina said.

"We're almost ready to make our move. If two guys can be best friends from second grade, they ought to be able to go into business together. Hain't that right, Johnny?"

"Yeah, and we're doing it all by the book, too, do everything legal and keep it fair and square."

She was happy Johnny had a future planned, but she worried about a future for herself. She wanted a career, a husband, and children. She stood up with a sigh. "The mosquitoes are terrible, I'm going in before I get all bit up."

She stepped into the kitchen, "Good night."

It was past midnight, and Celina still tossed and turned in her stuffy room. The fan on top of the chest of drawers whirred and stirred the day's leftover air.

The next morning the sun was a hot blob on the horizon when Celina woke and stretched. Fuzzy-headed and tired, she stared out the window and fretted about Johnny's new venture.

She padded over to the dresser, looked in the mirror and stared into her own eyes. The reflection stared back. Grimacing, Celina had to admit that she was jealous because Johnny knew what he wanted and was going after it. He had enough money saved to go into his own business. *And what am I doing? Nothing, that's what.*

Slipping into a housecoat, she berated herself for being jealous of her own brother. *I'll probably sell women's underwear, slips, and scarves at Duxbury's for the rest of my life.*

The other family members were preparing for work, and the fragrance of fresh coffee enticed her down the stairs.

Tomas and Johnny, in their clean work clothes, grabbed their aluminum dinner buckets, caps, and carbide lamps and shouted their good-byes. Celina murmured good-bye and poured some coffee while Tomas' jalopy sputtered and bounced down the lane. Johnny followed in his Ford.

"Ready for work?" Marian asked.

"Yeah. I've been up for a while. It was too hot to sleep." She set the half empty cup on the table. "Just need to put on my dress, some lipstick, and find my shoes."

"Want some breakfast?"

"Naw, I'll have something later"

"How about some toast?"

"Oh, okay. Are you going over to see Baba and Pap today?"

"Yeah, after I get the washing done, and pick some of the early green beans. I'll take them some." Marian flipped the half-toasted bread she'd placed on the stovetop to brown. "Pap said he's getting too old to haul water to the garden. With this weather and at least a million beetles, their beans won't amount to anything.

Marian set toast in front of Celina. "There's only about a half bushel in our garden that I'll pick. We'll snap them tonight and I'll can them in the morning. Baba's coming over next week to help make jelly. You won't have to help with that."

"Can't the beans wait till tomorrow?" Celina pushed the toast aside.

"What?" Marian's face darkened.

"I don't want to do beans tonight. I planned to go with Pattie to pick up her dress for Kimmie's wedding."

"Well, you can't go. The beans will be too old and tough if we put the canning off."

Celina stood up. "But Mom, I promised Pattie two weeks ago that I'd go with her. She doesn't want to drive to Philipsburg by herself. Besides, Litzinger's is having a sale on summer dresses. I want to see if I can find something."

"You have plenty of dresses."

"You sound just like Dad." Her coffee cup clattered onto the tabletop. "An hour or two of shopping is not too much to expect since I always do my share around here."

"We've got to get this work done."

"I work. I work a lot. And I want some time to go dress shopping with Pattie tonight. I might find something to wear to an interview at the newspaper."

"Duxbury's is a nice enough place to work. You don't need to be trying to get a job at the paper."

"But I promised Pattie I'd go."

Marian's features softened a bit.

Celina grabbed the opportunity. "The store closes at six. We'll leave straight from work and be back early. When I get home, I'll get the canning stuff out, and I know Pattie'd stick around and help. She's a good sport. What about it?"

"Let me think a minute."

Celina threw her head back and stared at the white paint on the tongue-and-groove ceiling. *Why does every little thing have to be weighed out like the fate of the world depends on it?*

"As long as you don't stop anywhere else, I guess you can go. But I'm not looking forward to listening to your dad complain when I tell him you went shopping instead of coming straight home."

"We won't stop anywhere. I know Pattie will help. We'll be done in no time."

The morning seemed a bit brighter as Celina rushed upstairs to prepare for work.

#

As she maneuvered her dusty car into the gravel lot behind Duxbury's, Celina waved and called out to Pattie, who pulled in beside her. "I'm going tonight."

Pattie hopped out of her car and grabbed her purse from the passenger seat. "*Dobry, dobry*, good, good. I knew you'd be able to get away." She busied herself shaking the wrinkles out of the skirt that exactly matched the red flowers on her blouse.

"There is one little thing, though." Celina frowned.

Pattie looked up. "What?"

Snatching her straw purse and lunch, she hopped out of the car and said, "You know I have to help with the canning."

"So?"

"I told my mom you'd help too." She waited for Pattie's reaction.

Pattie shrugged. "Well, I don't exactly have other plans."

They turned and strolled to the employee's entrance. "I'll have to call my mom. She might want me to do something around the house." She winked. "I know she won't, but I always call her anyway."

Celina felt relieved that she didn't have to do the job alone. *At least with Pattie around we can laugh and joke while we work.*

"You know how my mom is. She wants things done when she's ready. Today's the day, and I can't get out of it," she said, apologizing.

Pattie's mouth split into a smile. "I'll stick around. At least you don't have me digging potatoes."

Celina smiled. "Potatoes won't be ready for over a month. Anyway it won't take too long even if we don't start till after six."

Pattie bit the end of her thumb. "Um, is everybody going to be home?"

They reached the back door to Duxbury's, stepped over the threshold and into the dank basement with its lone light bulb dangling from the ceiling.

"Johnny will be home tonight." Celina winked.

"In that case, I'll definitely do it." She looked down at her hands. "I hope I don't ruin my nails. I polished them right before I left this morning."

Celina rolled her eyes and grinned. "*Boga*. God forbid that such a horrible thing should happen."

They hurried through the dingy basement, the clammy air clinging to their hair as they passed broken wooden pallets and empty crates. "So, Johnny's really going to be around tonight?"

"Yeah, he doesn't go out much on work nights. He helps Dad or Pap do odd jobs in the evenings, especially if Andy can't come over."

"Oh, he is a good son, isn't he?" Pattie's face glowed.

"Jeez, Pattie, he's my brother." They scurried up the creaky steps and entered the main retail floor. "This whole place is stale and musty," Celina complained.

They looked around and caught a glimpse of Earl's lanky figure unlocking the front entrance. He flipped the light switches and the overhead lights illuminated flecks of dust hanging in the dimness. Pattie nodded and gestured toward the large panes of glass. "At least the windows are still clean."

In the cloakroom, they tossed their white gloves and purses in their assigned pigeonholes and strode out to the sales floor.

Earl Hardisty waylaid them near the women's fitting room. He stood straight, brushed a bit of lint from a shirt sleeve and raised himself on tiptoe. "I'm filling in for Mr. Duxbury this week."

Earl, a bachelor, had asked three women to marry him in his lifetime, but after brief engagements the weddings never took place. Celina had heard it was because he was so picky. He let it be known that he expected his house to be cleaned from top to bottom twice a week, and that he could not tolerate dirty dishes stacked atop each other if they weren't rinsed first. Earl's prospects for marriage grew dimmer with each passing year.

He rocked back on his heels. "The boss is on a vacation. Took the wife and went off to New York City," he said. "They'll be staying at a big hotel and going to see the Rockettes. Even going to see the Statue of Liberty."

He brushed another piece of imaginary lint from his sleeve. "I'm the boss until he comes back next week. Any questions?"

Celina watched Pattie from the corner of her eye.

Pattie remained silent. "No, no questions," Celina said.

He rubbed his long, thin hands together, breathed deep, puffed up his narrow chest, and sighed in satisfaction.

"Being in charge is a big responsibility, and I gave Harold, Sam, and Mrs. Pinkerton their work assignments already."

He retrieved a lozenge from his shirt pocket and popped it into his mouth. He reached for a small clipboard that sat atop the women's blouses and scribbled a few notes. "You girls must have noticed that the stairs, hallway, and staff meeting room need a good cleaning.

I cannot tolerate the filth that clings to every corner of this store. Your first assignment is as follows: walls dusted, windows washed, furniture polished, and floors swept."

Celina sucked air between her teeth. "What about our real

jobs? I mean, we're supposed to be clerks. What if customers come in? No one will be here to wait on them."

"Already thought of that. Mrs. Pinkerton will leave her station in house wares and stand in the main aisle. If more than one or two people come in, she'll call one of you to wait on them." Earl tapped his clipboard with a clean fingernail and beamed with satisfaction.

Celina raised her eyebrows and Pattie did her best to confront him. "We don't even have aprons."

"You didn't have aprons when you washed the windows last Friday. You're not going to be on your knees with a scrub brush and bucket of soapy water, you know," he said as he brushed lint from his sleeve. "You are just tidying up the hallway and meeting room that's all." With outstretched arm, he pointed to the stairs. "Now, go on up there and get started. Sam has buckets, rags, ammonia, and furniture polish sitting inside the door."

They plodded toward the stairs. Earl called after them. "I plan to give Mr. Duxbury a full report of how the employees follow my directions."

Celina whispered. "If I had another job to go to, I'd quit this very minute. Being a clerk isn't that wonderful, but this is—"

Pattie interrupted. "We need a union like the miners and steel workers. Then he wouldn't be telling us do a janitor's work." Her eyes narrowed. "Hey, what are Howard and Sam doing, anyway?"

"I took a look at his clipboard when he was unwrapping the peppermint. He has them scheduled to clean the basement and whitewash the walls down there."

"Ew, at least we're not down there with the spiders and mice."

"Yeah, I suppose we should call ourselves lucky."

"But they are janitors, you know," Pattie added. "I wonder if he'll have them clean the furnace flue before they whitewash?"

"Who knows." Celina grimaced till her face hurt. "I really have got to get out of this place."

"Both of us need to get out of here." Pattie held her hands out. "My poor nails will be a mess."

"We'll probably look like a couple of ragamuffins when we go shopping tonight." Celina groaned and set to work.

Morning drew to a close. Celina carried the ammonia and water to a window and brushed a few dead flies from the sill. Buffing the glass, she watched the people moving around below and saw Stephen approaching from the other end of the street. She watched him stride into the newspaper office. *What does he do in there?* She sighed and ran a forearm across her damp forehead. A few minutes later, he came out and disappeared after crossing the street. She pressed her face against the glass trying to follow his movements.

Pattie came up behind her. "Okay, it's noon, and I've had it. Let's get something to eat. We can finish the windows after lunch."

Celina followed her down the stairs, but her mind was still on Stephen. His dark hair, his broad shoulders, the way he walked with such a sense of purpose—wanted to know everything about him.

#

In the park, they sipped their cold drinks and stretched their legs. Pattie pushed damp hair from her face. "Jeez, I'll be glad when this day is over."

"We say that every day, and we never do anything about it." Celina watched a gray squirrel scamper across the grass. "Today, I'm stopping in at the newspaper before we go back after lunch. Sarah told me there was a temporary job available, and she'd put in a word for me."

"I'd better check the bank and Smith's Ladies Wear. But I'll wait till later in the week. Maybe go in Saturday morning," Pattie said.

The regulator clock struck two when they finished cleaning the stairs. The hallway and meeting room sparkled. Celina wrung out the rags and threw them in an empty bucket. She watched Earl stride up the steps, carrying his clipboard. *Oh, no, here he comes again.*

"Where's Pattie?"

"She went to the restroom. She'll be right back."

"Okay. This banister hasn't been waxed in years. Mrs. Pinkerton will show you where to find rags and a can of wax. Do as much as you are able, and finish it tomorrow."

Celina could have sworn he clicked his heels before he strode away. She picked up the cleaning supplies. *Pattie is going to love this.*

Pattie returned, and they polished, buffed, and grumbled their way through the afternoon.

After work, Celina dropped her car off at the house, climbed into the passenger side of Pattie's Chevy, and they were finally on their way to Philipsburg.

"What happened at the newspaper office?" Pattie asked.

"Well, when I walked in, Vera Clark, a reporter for the paper, was there. She had on this nice little powder-blue suit and carried a little black briefcase. She was so efficient and businesslike. I wonder if I'll have to buy a briefcase?" Celina crossed her legs. "Sarah came out from behind that army surplus desk and told me she'll be leaving in about a month, so I should be able to start at least a few days before that. Mr. Cherriten's in Pittsburgh buying parts for the Linotype machine, so I'll have to wait for the interview till he comes back.'"

Celina's face flushed. "I can't wait to quit the store. If I never see Earl's snuff covered teeth again, it will be too soon."

Pattie gripped the wheel and stared at the road. "I expect you'll be glad to get away from Duxbury, too."

"Yeah. He's always been sort of peculiar, not saying much of anything and watching us through the office door. And the way he acts toward me, it's so odd. I was really glad when Earl said he'd be gone this week."

"I don't blame you. It's different if the guy is young and single and your type." Pattie hesitated. "Even then, if somebody passed on some kind of rumor. God, I hate to think about it."

Pattie steered the car around the sharp corner in the middle of Osceola Mills. "You don't think he'd do anything funny, do you?"

"No. He's strange, but he has good manners, and his shoes are always polished." Celina didn't know why, but it seemed easier to trust men who were well dressed and well groomed over those who wore work pants with patches and only shaved a couple times a week. Were the ones with clean fingernails more trustworthy than the ones who had to scrub their hands with Lava soap? Were bankers and businessmen better people than coal miners and farmers? Her dad didn't think so. And she didn't know.

"Mrs. Pinkerton told me he goes to the Christian Alliance Church every week. His wife teaches Sunday school there.

She has teas for the businessmen's wives and everything."

Pattie grimaced. "Yeah, he's strange but normal, I guess."

"I guess. But I'm still leaving as soon as that job at the paper opens up."

Celina didn't think about Duxbury unless someone else brought his name up. He was the person who passed out the pay envelopes, and she had no contact with him or his family outside of the store. He was a minor figure in her life.

"I'll go crazy at the store if you aren't there," said Pattie. "I'm definitely checking on those jobs this week."

They parked in front of Loretta's Dress Shop. The brass bell above the door tinkled when they entered the little store with its pale lavender walls and three-way mirrors. Glass cases filled with neatly folded lingerie, hosiery, and blouses stood against the interior wall.

While they waited, Celina peered into a glass case and pointed out some pink lace panties. "Look at these."

"I'll bet girls get guchies like that to wear on their wedding night."

The clerk entered and after exchanging pleasantries, brought out the mint-green dress Pattie had their seamstress alter. She tried on the dress, and both the clerk and Celina smiled, nodded, and voiced their approval.

Celina browsed through the racks, and Pattie urged her to try on a silky sheath she found. She stood in front of the three-way mirror and the clerk oohed while Pattie aahed. It was perfect Celina said, "I'll take it."

The moment the clerk finished ringing up their purchases, the clock struck six and with efficiency, the smiling woman ushered them out. No sooner had the door closed than they heard the lock click behind them.

"She's even faster at locking up than either Mrs. Pinkerton

or Earl. Jeez, she could have caught my leg in the door," Pattie said with a laugh, though they did sympathize with the poor woman whose goal was to lock up and go home.

When they reached the house, they carried their purchases into the kitchen. Pattie modeled her new dress, and Celina ignored the massive pile of green beans waiting on the table.

After donning aprons, the subject of Kimmie's wedding got full attention. Rumor had it that Kimmie had invited two hundred people, not counting the kids. All the close family members were bringing roasters of halupki, kielbasa, rigatoni, and nut rolls, but the volunteer firemen were making the chicken, and the groom's people were taking care of the liquor. Celina and Pattie agreed that the two of them would be the best-dressed girls there, other than the bride, of course.

Marian put them to work snapping beans, and the mammoth pile of produce shrunk. Both Celina and Pattie were indignant as they described Earl's highhanded tactics. Marian laughed till tears rolled down her face when Celina mimicked his preening and posturing from heel to toe before giving out cleaning assignments.

Snapped beans filled several large kettles when Celina announced that she had been job hunting and expected to be working at the newspaper in a few weeks.

Marian grabbed a handful of beans from the pile and looked at her. "So, you're doing it."

"I've been checking around everywhere in town since spring, even the movie theater." She tossed a handful of snapped pieces into a bowl. "I would never have had a chance at the paper if Sarah Monahan hadn't spoken up for me."

"So, my daughter expects to be a career woman like in a Katharine Hepburn movie, writing news stories and carrying around a pencil and notebook."

Celina eyed her mother. "I hope I make it that far. I'm smart enough." She wished that for once Marian would be happy she was trying to improve her life.

They were almost finished when Pattie caught Celina's attention. At her silent urging with glances and nods toward the door, Celina asked her mother why Johnny hadn't come home yet. Marian replied, "Oh, Dad and Johnny went over to look at Pap's farm truck. It wouldn't start again."

"Is that the one they don't have a license for?" Pattie asked as she reached for another handful of beans.

"Yeah. It's too beat up to take on the road anyway."

"Couldn't Uncle Stanley get it running?" Celina asked.

"No. He wanted your dad to go over and look at it."

The women finished their chore and set their bowls aside. They tidied up and swept the kitchen then Marian poured iced tea. Frankie's happy yapping alerting them to Tomas' and Johnny's return, and Pattie beamed.

Johnny flung open the screen door. Greasy smudges covered his face, and his cap had flattened his hair into damp crinkly wavelets. "Hey, we're back. Pap's truck is running like a top."

He strode up to the table, reached for the pitcher, and filled a glass.

Marian groaned. "Your new T-shirt is covered with grease. I'll never get that out." She stood up for a closer look. "Where's Dad?"

"He's coming. He stopped to make sure the chicken

coop's locked."

The screen door opened and Tomas marched in. His cap tipped far back past his broad forehead, and a three-cornered piece of torn fabric flapped around on the front of his work shirt. He announced, "I told Pap to get rid of that damn truck. Christ, its twenty-five years old. Can't even find parts at the junkyard anymore."

He scrubbed and dried his hands, strode to the living room, turned on the television, and plopped down in his favorite chair.

A quizzical look settled on Johnny's face. He put his hands up as if to say, *don't ask me, I didn't do anything.*

Pattie asked to use the phone to call her mother. She tiptoed past Tomas, made her phone call, and came back to the kitchen where she gathered up her purchases and said her good-byes. Johnny rose from his chair and said, "Wait a minute Red, I'll walk out with you."

Pattie looked back at Celina and flashed a delighted grin. Wistful, Celina wondered when she'd have the opportunity to feel that elated when a special someone walked her to her car.

CHAPTER 6

Celina and Pattie wore old clothes to work the next day. If Earl expected them to scrub and polish the whole store, they didn't plan on wearing their best outfits while doing it. He grimaced but said nothing before ordering them to clean the cupboards in the cloak room, wash the windows, dust the ceiling and walls, and carry the trash to the barrels out back. The fountain pen he pulled from his pocket hovered over the ever-present clipboard. "After that, you can clean out the janitor's closet."

Frowns creased their foreheads as they set off for the cloakroom. "I hate that clipboard already, and it's only Tuesday," Pattie snarled. "And can you believe that we have to get rid of old paint cans and floor rags from that closet? My dad and brother do that kind of work at home. I'll bet that closet hasn't been cleaned since the Depression."

"I know, but unless a lot of customers come in, there's no way we can get out of it."

"It's not fair." Tears came to Pattie's eyes, her chin quivered and she sniffed. "We'll look like a couple of tired, old *stara babas.*"

A picture of Pattie and herself as a couple of white-haired old ladies wearing cotton stockings rolled down to their knees popped into Celina's mind. She tried, really tried, but couldn't hold back the side-splitting laughter that erupted as the picture became clearer and clearer.

Pattie's peaches-and-cream complexion turned a blotchy red. "What are you laughing about?"

Doubled over, Celina choked out, "Your face…it's the same color as your hair…s*tara baba.*"

Aghast, Pattie ran to the nearest mirror. Her hands clasped both sides of her face and in a whispered shriek, said, "Oh, my God."

Peals of choking laughter bounced around the empty store. The idea of Pattie sporting red hair with white roots was too much.

"Celina, you stop it. It's not funny."

Celina couldn't stop. She squeezed her legs together so she wouldn't pee herself. "We thought we would be career women. We polish our toe nails and get all dressed up for work, but look at us, a couple of cleaning ladies."

It was so ridiculous that Celina couldn't stop laughing, and soon Pattie chuckled. They looked at each other, dressed in faded skirts and blouses, carrying rags and buckets, and both burst into uproarious cackling, until Earl's piercing voice broke in.

He carried the clipboard in one hand and a galvanized bucket in the other. He demanded to know what was going on.

Harold, Sam, and Mrs. Pinkerton gathered in a semicircle a few feet away, not sure if they should smile or run. They chose to wait and see if there'd be fireworks.

Earl's authoritarian demeanor slipped a tad. "Well, what's

all the commotion about?"

Pattie pressed her fingers against her mouth. Celina wiped her eyes and pulled herself together. She wasn't planning to tell Earl about feeling like a *stara baba*. "Oh, ah, um, we just got to laughing about our drive to Philipsburg yesterday. That's all."

Earl pulled himself up onto tiptoe and rocked back on his heels. "Well, it looks like your chitchat is sidetracking you from your work." He handed them more cleaning supplies and, in his loftiest way, pointed to the cloak room.

"That Earl is such a wet blanket," Pattie whispered, suppressing a stray giggle.

Celina pulled down a box of dusty crumbling invoices and ledgers perched on the shelf above the coat hooks. She noted that one ledger had dates as far back as September 1900. She wiped off the leather-bound books, carried them to Mr. Duxbury's office, and set them on an overstuffed red velvet chair inside the door.

When she returned, she saw Pattie clutching a handful of magazines she had picked up from a pile in back of a narrow, unused closet. With a silencing finger over her mouth she motioned for Celina to take a look.

Flipping through them, Celina saw that they were full of pictures of nude women. "Where'd these come from?"

Gesturing with her index finger, Pattie pointed. "Back there in the closet under some newspapers and empty bottles."

"They're not too old. Who do you think put them there?"

"They were under all that junk, so it had to be somebody

who didn't want anybody to know about them."

"It must have been Duxbury, or maybe one of his sons," Celina suggested.

They flipped through the pages and Pattie pointed. "Look at the size of the titties on this one. Those things can't be real."

Celina looked at the picture of a young woman with breasts so large they looked like they would explode. Wearing only stiletto heels and a fur boa slung over her shoulder, the platinum blond had her legs crossed, and she reclined on a velvet settee. "Jeez."

Pattie looked down at herself. "These can't compete."

Celina looked down at her own small breasts. "Neither can these." She flipped through a few more pages. "Nope, can't compete."

Pattie puffed her chest out and pushed her breasts up with her hands. "Now?"

Celina laughed. "If we had to make our living that way, we'd starve to death."

"Yeah, I hate to admit it, but…" She looked around. "Oh, Jeez, what if Earl comes waltzing in?"

"He told us to clean out the closet, didn't he?" Celina tossed magazines and liquor bottles in a wastebasket and picked it up. "We'll get rid of these. Let's toss this stuff into the trash barrel before any of the men around here see it, or they'll be carting it off."

Pattie loaded her arms. "Mrs. Pinkerton would have a heart attack if she saw magazines like this."

"She'd probably go into spasms."

"I'll bet she's never even seen herself naked."

"For Pete's sake, Pattie, let's just dump this stuff."

"Well, I bet she hasn't."

As they headed back into the building, Pattie caught Celina's arm and whispered. "Do you ever think of being naked with a man?"

"Yeah."

"Well?"

"Well what?"

"What do you think it will be like?"

"What do *you* think it would be like?"

"I asked first."

It was too late. They reached the door and entered the cavernous basement where Harold and Sam had dragged dank packing crates and musty boards to the door. "How's it coming down here?" Celina asked.

Sam, short and stout, straightened up and spat a glob of brown tobacco juice out the door. "I'll be glad when we get this mess outta here." He rubbed his shoulder with a grimy hand. "It'll take another day, and my back's killin' me. The old woman and me want to go to the ball game tomorrow night." The beak of his cap caught a cobweb. "Probably need ta take half a dozen aspirin ta sit through it."

Harold, the younger of the two, removed his frayed cap, beat it against a dusty leg, pushed his thick hair back, and replaced the cap at a jaunty angle. "You girls going to the game?"

Celina eyed the two men and wondered how their wives liked being naked with them. She almost shuddered. *I hope it's dark whenever it happens.*

"Is Shirley Creek playing?" she asked.

Since the early days of baseball, the coal companies encouraged and supported the miners when they formed teams. Many of the miners were excellent ball players, and the owners encouraged rivalries between mines. Ringers, and the winning teams they played for, were often given preferential treatment in work assignments.

"Yep, Shirley Creek against Deer Hollow. Should be a good game. Both teams had a couple of guys who play as good as any ringer." He nodded. "Yep, them guys are good. 'Course, we're rootin' for Shirley Creek."

Pattie chimed in. "Shirley Creek's playing. We're going, aren't we Celina?"

Sam spat again. "Well, we wouldn't miss it. Too bad they're not playin' as much as they used to. Years ago, when the competition was fierce, the wife'd pack a picnic lunch on Sundays and we'd make a day of it."

Harold leaned against a stack of pallets and lit a cigarette. "Too many cars and television sets are takin' people's minds off the game." He blew smoke into the rafters. "I played third base in my younger days. Was pretty good, too." He coughed and cleared his throat. "Yeah, it's too bad they don't play like they used to. Some of them games was as good as watching the Yankees and Dodgers." He scratched his head. "Players good enough for the majors came out of local teams. Ones like Billy Hunter, the infielder from Punxsutawney, who was an all-star in '53. Remember him?" Harold asked Sam.

"Yeah, yeah, sure do. Played for the St. Louis Browns."

"And this very summer Mumbles Tremel, the guy from Lilly in Cambria County, is pitching for the Cubs." Harold lifted his cap then jammed it back on his head. "That's somethin' to be proud of. Comin' from middle-of-nowhere places like this and ending up in the majors."

Earl's voice bounced down the steps. "What's going on down there? You working like you're supposed to? It hain't lunchtime yet."

In one voice, Harold and Sam shouted. "Yeah, we're

workin'." They turned to the pile of lumber they were dragging out.

#

"Why didn't you tell me about the baseball game tomorrow night?" Celina asked her brother that evening at the supper table.

He pushed the plate away after eating the last piece of blueberry pie. "Sorry, Missy, I've been real busy lately."

She waited for him to continue, but he said nothing. She cleared the table, but didn't let the subject drop. "I thought the companies weren't sponsoring games anymore."

"They're not. They tell us there's no money for uniforms or equipment." He tipped his chair back on its rear legs and rocked back and forth. "A bunch of us guys were talking Saturday night and we decided to get together for the fun of it."

She pulled out a chair and sat down across from him. "At least you're still playing."

"Yeah, you know how it is with the mines, baseball isn't important anymore. But we're gonna play as long as the guys want to get together." He stretched and rolled his neck. "Let's go outside where it's cooler."

They sat on the edge of the porch and watched a humming bird race from flower to flower. Frankie wandered over and rested his head on Johnny's knee. The insect chorus had started and the sun, an orange fireball, took its time sinking into the shadowy west.

"It's hard to believe that summer is almost half over," Celina said with a sigh.

"Half over." Johnny leaned back and cupped his hands

behind his head.

"Are you worried about something?" she asked.

"Nah." His arms dropped and he shook his head. "But I wish Dad could see that the mines aren't going to last forever. Stubborn. Won't listen to anything."

He rested one foot up on the edge of the porch. The dog moved a few inches and curled up on the floor nearby. "Everybody knows at least one mine that's shut down in the last year. Coal's not selling like it did even a few years ago."

"Do you think Shirley Creek will shut down?"

"They laid off some guys and are talking about a four-day week, but I haven't heard anything about a shut down." He curled one calloused hand into a fist and smacked it into the other palm.

He lowered his voice. "Mom in the kitchen?"

Celina peered through the screen door. "No, she's watching the television with Dad."

"I don't want her to hear this, 'cause she'll start worrying. But I'm thinking the company's up to something. They're cutting corners everywhere and won't put one more penny into that place than they have to."

"But that's how they always do things," she pointed out.

The muscles in his neck tightened. "But it's not safe in there. Roof supports aren't holding and the dust levels are too high. I don't think we have enough prop timbers or cross bars to keep the roof from falling on us. Christ, we can hardly find a few lousy wooden wedges to tighten up what's there. The bosses are pushing to get more and more coal out, so the roof stress is only gonna get worse."

"Can't you do anything?"

"I've gone to the boss. Mike's on the verge of getting fired because he won't stop bitching about safety issues. Neither of us wants to get fired. We don't have enough money saved yet."

"What does Dad say?"

"He said that's how mining works, but admitted it's been riskier than usual. Those old-timers have been underground so long that they've seen a lot of roof falls and men dodging rock and slate."

He paused a moment. "Charlie keeps harping about listening for changes in the underground noises. I spend half my time watching which way the mine rats are running and the other half listening for changes in the rock sounds. I guess for now that's all I can do."

"Dad was complaining about the roof a couple of weeks ago, that it's weak and there aren't enough supports." Celina added. "He said that one of these days there could be a roof fall and somebody could get killed."

"Yeah we all complain, but he thinks somehow we'll squeak through this, that the mines will keep on working, and everything will be hunky dory."

Celina turned to watch the lowering sun. "I wish all of you would get out." What would she do, and what would her mother do, if Dad or Johnny were hurt or killed? Celina couldn't let herself think about it.

"The company's not going to tell us anything till they're sending in a rescue team or pushing us out the door in a layoff." He ran a hand over his close-cropped hair. "I don't know what men like Dad and Andy get from closing." He spat again. "It's not like the company owners care about any of us. As long as they're making money, they don't give a damn about the miners."

"Dad's been doing it an awfully long time. He'll never quit. Especially, not after he told that story about Boulder Dam.

But what about Andy?" She worried for her other brother.

"I don't know." He cleared his throat and spit into the dry grass. "But I'm ready to get out."

"Can't the union do something?"

"They can't stop a company from closing. I already told you that it's a constant battle just trying to keep the roof from falling in. Like Dad says, 'haul off and run like hell when it starts coming down.' Nah, they can't do a damned thing."

Celina watched the sun disappear behind the low hills. "I'm scared. It's like life is splitting apart or something, like we're wandering around, not sure what to do next."

"Trying to make believe that the mines will always be working and these little pieces of land will always support us doesn't help." He stood up. "It's getting late. I need to get some sleep."

She slapped at a mosquito nearby. "Yeah, I'm tired too. Earl has us cleaning the store from top to bottom. I guess he wants the place gleaming when Mr. Duxbury comes back from New York."

Dark clouds raced in from the southwest as Celina drove to work the next morning. They threatened rain and scuttled across the sky until late afternoon when they disappeared. At the end of another day of cleaning, Celina and Pattie rushed to their cars and opened the doors to let the heat out before climbing in for the drive home.

Pattie tossed her belongings inside the Chevy and groaned. "I'm tired, tired, tired. And I'm sick of Earl and his stupid clipboard." She wiped her sweaty brow. "I think I'll throw it in the trash tomorrow. I'd like to throw him in, too." She used both hands to push her red locks away from her face. "He hasn't put his lily-whites in soapy water all week." Her eyes narrowed. "I hate him."

Celina's damp blouse stuck to her back, tendrils of damp hair stuck to her forehead and neck, and she wiped her face with a limp hankie. "Pattie, will you stop complaining. I want to go home, get something cold to drink, change my clothes, and go to the ballgame. When I get there, I want to watch my brother and his friends play, and I want to forget this place exists."

"Aren't you mad about this horrible week?"

"What do you think?" Celina covered her eyes with her damp hands, slid her fingers to her chin, and down her neck.

"Well, then act mad."

"If I act mad, I'll start screaming, but I'm not going to. I'm going home, and I'm going to cool off."

She climbed into her car and pulled the door shut. "Once I cool off I'll be in a better mood. I'll see you at the game, okay?"

Pattie's mouth turned down at the corners. "Okay, see ya there, around six."

"Don't forget about your hair."

"Oh, Jeez, I'll fade." Pattie rushed to her car and jumped into its stifling shade.

Celina drove and thought, and thought and drove. Her life had come to a near standstill, caught in a slow-moving vortex going round and round in circles, yet going nowhere. She feared that every month and every year that passed, dragged her further and further away from a career, a husband, a life. *I want out. I want to find a straight road and follow it. But what if there aren't any straight roads?*

She stepped on the gas and wished she were braver, at

least as brave as her grandmother had been when she packed up her few belongings and emigrated from Eastern Europe sixty years earlier. *Baba got on that steam ship all by herself and left her family and home forever. And me? I can't even get out of Duxbury's.*

#

She arrived at the ball field twenty minutes before the game, and a dozen cars and a few pickup trucks were parked under the scattered apple trees that lined its grassy edge. She spotted Bart and Shirley Wilson, two of the early arrivals, who perched atop the sagging bleachers. Three of their grandchildren climbed the bleachers and perched on Bart's lap.

Men in faded pants and shirts and women in housedresses chatted and milled around looking for a good spot to view the game. Girls in summer dresses and their pigtails flying, took turns jumping rope at the edge of the dusty field. Boys in striped shirts and well-patched jeans ran around the bases, yelled, and spit in the dust as though they were big leaguers.

Celina stood under the low-growing branch of an apple tree and kicked off her shoes. She had changed into green shorts and a sleeveless striped blouse which flattered her slim figure and long legs. A blue thermos bottle of lemonade stood next to the tree trunk. She spotted Pattie, waved, and called over the din. "Hey, over here."

Pattie, dressed in matching pink cotton shorts and a blouse, hastened toward her tapping the crystal of her watch. "Six o'clock, right on time." She tossed a thick flannel blanket on the ground. "They haven't started yet, have they?"

Pattie craned her neck in the direction of the field where a knot of young men stood near a backstop made of chicken wire. They talked, scuffed at the dusty home plate, and knocked dirt off their shoes. "Johnny here?"

"Yeah. He brought me."

"I don't see him." She shaded her eyes and stood on tiptoes. "Wait. There he is. And there's Mike. My mom said she saw him with Stella Zaliski. If you want him, you better get out there and give Stella some competition."

"Nah, she's nice, and I hope it works out for them."

Pattie scanned the group of young men and giggled. "How did you end up with such a cute brother? Oh, I mean he's just so, you know, handsome."

Celina shaded her eyes and looked over the group. "Hmm. I wouldn't say he's handsome, cute maybe, but not handsome.'"

"You quit that. You're just making fun of me." Pattie waved her off and returned to watching the young men warming up for the game.

The first inning started and they sat down, opened the thermos, and shared lemonade. The players kicked up clouds of yellowish dust with every play, and the score mounted. Whenever there was a run or an out, the crowd cheered or yelled out unsolicited advice.

A couple of old timers spat tobacco juice, pushed their caps far back on their heads, and grumbled that the kids nowadays didn't know how to play the game, not like they used to in the old days.

At the bottom of the fourth inning, Mike demonstrated some of those old-time skills by creating a cloud of choking dust when he flopped on his belly and slid into second. He avoided the tag for a double play.

Johnny was next up to bat. He stepped up to the plate. Strike one. Celina held her breath, and Pattie screamed,

"Come on, Johnny."

Strike two. *Come on, Johnny, hit it.* The last pitch whizzed toward home plate. The bat hit the ball with a loud crack. The ball sailed over the spectators and into the trees. A homerun and three men scored. Celina and Pattie jumped to their feet and cheered for Shirley Creek at the top of their voices. Flushed, Pattie turned to Celina. "I love baseball, don't you?"

Pleased, Celina agreed. "Ummhum." *Pattie you are so love struck I can't believe it.*

She was caught by surprise when she heard an accented male voice. "Your brother's a good baseball player." Celina's stomach flip-flopped, and she turned to the person who had crouched down beside her.

She blinked, smiled, and stammered. "Oh, Stephen, hi, I didn't know you were here." *Jeez, I sound so stupid.*

Pattie turned. "Hi Steve. Isn't it a great game? Aren't they doing swell?" Before he could answer she asked, "Do you play baseball?"

"I've played in a few baseball games, but I know a lot more about soccer. What's the score?"

"Nine to six, Shirley Creek." Pattie grinned. "I know they're going to win."

She jumped up. "Hey, I think I'll go over and congratulate Johnny on his homerun." Her small body, topped with its red hair, bobbed into the crowd as she made her way to the dugout.

Stephen sat next to Celina. She could feel the heat from his body and it made her sweat. She hoped he didn't notice how flustered and anxious she had become. After a long pause, she cleared her throat. "This is only the second game they've played this summer. I guess people can watch baseball on television, though."

He radiated confidence, and when he spoke he was so close that she could smell cigarettes and the scent of aftershave. She wanted to lean closer still.

"It's too bad the companies have stopped sponsoring games." He gestured at the noisy crowd. "It looks like the whole community is out cheering for their favorites."

"Yeah, but how did you know about the companies not sponsoring the games?"

He wrapped his long arms around his knees. "I've been talking to Johnny and some of the other guys off and on, and the subject came up."

"Oh." *Johnny hadn't said anything.* "Um, how'd all you guys get to know each other?"

"I met them at Kasper's Garage. Johnny was in the office and Mike was working on my aunt's car." He tilted his head and nodded. "While I waited, we talked about cars and sports. And a lot of things."

"Oh." *That brother of mine, he should have told me.*

Without realizing it, she found herself staring at the long, wide scar on his forearm.

His eyes followed her gaze then moved to her face. She looked up at him and reddened. She turned away quickly and wished Pattie would come back. "You're wondering about the scar?" he asked.

She searched her mind for a way to be evasive and could find nothing. "Well, yes, I was. But it's none of my business, really."

His eyes were tender and his voice low. "If you look at me, I'll tell you."

Feeling inept and silly, she turned to him. Their eyes met. He smiled a brief little smile and Celina returned it.

He shifted his weight, held the arm with the wide flat gash

out in front of him, and rubbed his fingers over the scar. "Hmm. Where do I start?

"Like most Hungarians, my family opposes the Soviets and the communist puppet government. Of course, we always watched what we said, since if you were overheard by the wrong people your whole family could be in trouble. In the privacy of our home, we talked of emigrating. But in the end, my parents could not bring themselves to leave the place where they had spent their entire lives." He moved closer. "I decided I had to leave, but everyone else stayed behind. And a small group of us banded together to make our way west.

"Three of us…Wasyl, Theo, and I…had been friends since childhood and stuck together like brothers. When it came time to leave, we gathered only what we could carry in our rucksacks and traveled at night, since the communists would not hesitate to make it very difficult for us if we were caught.

"At dusk, on the second day of the journey, we came across a rundown tavern on a side road. The place was a ramshackle building with a low ceiling lit by kerosene lamps. We should have known better, but we stopped there.

"We realized we'd made a mistake when we took our drinks to a table and a foul-smelling man with uncombed hair staggered up to us. He slammed his glass on the tabletop. Spittle flew when he barked, 'You three, what are you up to?'

"I spoke up, using the story we concocted in case we were challenged. 'We're students on our way to check on our great-aunts. Our parents have not received a letter in weeks, and they are worried.' Wasyl and Theo played along. Casually, we reached for our drinks. The drunken man stood over us, sucking in heavy breaths and the last of his beer.

"Wasyl pointed to me and said, 'Here, our brother will

have your glass filled.' The drunkard stared at me. I stood up and motioned to the barkeep to fill his stein and walked to the bar to pay. Before he put the beer to his mouth, the drunkard clasped my shoulder to steady himself. The other patrons were now more curious and edged closer.

"I wanted to get out of there. I caught Theo's eye and nodded to my friends. They stood up and stretched saying it was time to move on and find a place to sleep, but the drunkard lurched toward Theo and grabbed his arm. Theo shoved him away, and the three of us ran toward the door followed by the drunkard and his cronies.

"I saw the glint of a knife blade. One of them had turned on Theo. Wasyl and I stepped in. I tried to talk our way out of the situation, but there is no reasoning with a drunk who wants to fight. The knife was turned on me. I put my arm out to stop the blow, and it cut through my jacket and shirt, right through to the flesh. Wasyl pushed me and we ran into the darkness. They were so drunk that they couldn't make a good chase.

"We stopped somewhere out in the country near an empty road. I heard a cow bell ring. We rested at the edge of an orchard. Theo tore a shirt into strips and wrapped the wound as tight as possible. Wasyl gave me a jacket he had rolled up in his rucksack."

Stephen glanced at Celina and ran a finger down the length of the scar. "It looks bad because the flesh was laid open, but it wasn't a deep wound."

"What happened next?"

"We traveled at night, avoided main highways, and crossed the border into Austria and left Hungary behind. It was such a relief when we got there. We stopped at the first town we came to. I speak German and communicated with the officials. They helped us reach the American Embassy in Vienna, and I was put in contact with my sponsor, my Aunt Terez. She vouched for me and said she would help me any way she could."

"What happened to your friends?"

He watched a flock of birds scatter above the trees. "Wasyl went to France where he has family, and Theo settled in Canada."

"Do you ever hear from them?"

"Yes, we correspond regularly, and Wasyl wants to come to the United States once he gets his financial affairs in order. Theo says he is happy in Canada."

"I can't imagine what it must be like to be uprooted from your home, and get caught in a bar fight, plus having to travel in secret to avoid the authorities. Were you ever afraid?"

"Yes." He paused and looked up. "Once, we heard border guards' voices nearby, and were afraid they'd start shooting if we made the least little noise. We were absolutely silent for what seemed like hours before we moved on."

"Are you glad you came here?"

"Of course. You can't imagine how much less complicated it is to travel here. No one has to show papers or a passport when they move from one state to the next. And we don't have to watch every word we say."

He sighed. "The war almost destroyed Central and Eastern Europe. And now that the communists are in power, people feel like aliens in their own countries. They don't know who they can trust; it's a sad place."

"You've been through a lot."

He shook his head. "Not compared with many other people."

They sat in silence for a few moments. "We need a lighter

conversation." He tilted his head and spoke softly, close to her ear. "Coming here has been the best thing I ever did. I met you."

Celina tried to appear composed. But her heart thumped. She turned to him, and their noses almost touched. She couldn't restrain a little smile when their eyes met. They exchanged a long and tender look. Stephen leaned back, one arm behind Celina. They sat quietly for a few minutes and then Pattie came bounding toward them.

She stopped in her tracks, stared first at Stephen and then at Celina, and stammered, "Uh, uh, the game's almost over, and we're going to the dairy bar, are you coming?"

The two of them grinned. "Sure, we'll meet you near the backstop when they finish up," Stephen said.

Pattie turned and walked to the dugout, tripping several times when she looked back over her shoulder at the couple, so close on the blanket on the grass. Surprised contentment settled over Celina, sitting there beside a man she hardly knew. She had never felt so close to anyone before.

From her vantage point on the grassy slope, she watched Pattie dash up to Johnny, her arms flailing and jaw moving. He cast his eyes in their direction. Celina's eyes sparkled. "I think we're getting some attention."

His lips almost touching her ear as he spoke. "Hmm, I suppose we'll be the object of interest for at least a little while."

She tried hard to act casual. "I suppose so."

Pattie, standing next to the split log the baseball players used for a bench, continued to wave her arms and tap a foot at Johnny. Celina smiled. "She wants him to look this way but not be obvious about it." She could tell that her brother had commenced his usual teasing, and soon the two figures near the backstop were laughing and Pattie plopped down beside Johnny.

Amused, Celina said, "You know, I'll be in for the third degree as soon as Pattie catches me alone."

Stephen smiled. "What are you going to tell her?"

"Hmm, what will I tell her?" She shifted her position and shared a thoughtful look with him. "What will I tell her?"

She could feel his breath on the side of her face. "You could tell curious friends that it is love at first sight."

Happiness rushed over her. "Should they believe me?"

"Yes. When I danced with you the other night, I felt it. Didn't you?" He waited for an answer.

Butterflies tumbled through her stomach and started a wild dance that set her heart thumping. "Yes, but I…I don't know what to say."

"You don't have to say anything."

"I mean…." Her fingers rested on the wide flat scar. "I guess you caught me off guard."

Stephen's hand covered hers. "You are right; I shouldn't rush you. But once you get to know me, you'll see that I tend to make quick decisions about the important things in life." An impish look crossed his face. "And I'm always right."

She recovered her equilibrium and teased. "Always right, huh?" She jumped up, and smoothed her shorts. "The game's over. Shouldn't we go?"

He shook and folded the blanket, and as they strolled to the backstop, they shared knowing glances each time someone craned a neck to observe them.

CHAPTER 7

Celina avoided Pattie's questions as long as possible, enjoying the wonderful new emotions that enveloped her. Pattie fussed, fumed, and sputtered, but Celina needed to hold the new feelings close to her own heart for a while.

Friday afternoon finally arrived, and all five employees looked at each other in relief when at last, Earl declared the store shipshape and ready for the boss' return on Monday.

His clipboard with its dog-eared sheets and scratched out lists rested on the corner of Mr. Duxbury's desk. A few specks of snuff clung to his teeth when he spoke. "All right people, here are your pay envelopes." He inspected the name and contents of each envelope before passing it on to the employee.

Pattie waited at the back of the store and fell into step with Celina. They trooped down the stairs, through the newly whitewashed basement, and out the back door.

"If you don't tell me what's going on with you and Steve, I'm going to burst and I'll never speak to you again." Pattie could contain her pent-up frustration no longer.

Celina tried not to laugh as she tucked the pay envelope

into her purse. "Okay, but there isn't much to tell."

"I don't care. Tell me anyway." When Celina hesitated, Pattie stopped walking. "Why are you refusing to talk about the most exciting thing that's happened to you in your whole life?"

"I'm not refusing to talk." *I'm having delightful daydreams about Stephen.*

"Yes, you are. You haven't said a word since the ball game, and friends don't hold out on each other like that." Her eyebrows touched her red bangs. "You act weird sometimes."

"I'm not acting weird."

"Yes, you are. Or else you would have told me all the details."

"Well, Stephen and I like each other…a lot. And we're seeing each other. We haven't had much time to talk about anything. And you already know that Johnny drove me home after we stopped at the dairy bar."

"Yeah, I wish I hadn't driven myself so Johnny could have taken me home, too. Are you going steady?" Pattie opened her car door.

Surprised, Celina, answered. "I'm not sure. Maybe this is all going too fast. We hardly know each other."

"You two looked pretty lovey-dovey the other night."

"We did?"

"Well, he was making eyes at you, and you were making them right back at him. And you talked so quiet nobody else could hear you. Don't tell me you weren't because I was watching you. You're in love and you won't even tell me, your best friend. I should be the first to know."

"Even before I'd tell him?"

"Yes, everybody tells their best friend first."

"You haven't told me that you love Johnny."

"Well, we never got around to talking about it. Besides, you know. I mean, you do know how I feel about him, don't you?"

"Yeah. I know."

"Do you love Steve?"

"I can't stop thinking about him, and I wish I could be with him every minute of the day."

"Well, then? Aren't you going to say it? That you love him."

"I'm not sure that I should."

"Why?"

"He's not going to stay around here. What if he just leaves or something terrible happens?"

"Shame on you. That's being superstitious. Anyway, you haven't sinned enough for God to point His finger at you and give you special punishment. That's for people like Hitler and Stalin."

Celina's face burned. "You're making me feel stupid."

"Well, that's no way to think. Did he kiss you?"

"Jeez, how would he have had a chance to kiss me with the whole crowd around gawking at us?"

"Hmm, that's true. When are you going to see him again?"

"He's driving me home from the dance tomorrow night."

Pattie clasped her hands and grinned from ear to ear. "Oh, it's so exciting. I just love love, don't you?"

Celina grinned. "Sometimes you are such a goof."

"I'm just romantic, that's all."

"After losing Bobby, I don't know—"

"Celina, you stop that. That's a stupid thing to say. Korean War widows lost their husbands and are marrying every day. Betty Cakanac got married and has a year-old baby already."

Pattie narrowed her eyes and crossed her arms. "I don't want to be mean, but you're not thinking right, or maybe you're in a rut. Is hanging onto Bobby's memory better than going out and taking a chance on loving someone else?"

"I don't want to think of it that way."

"Listen, I love you like a sister and I don't want to hurt you, but there has to be a reason why you won't let go."

"Well, what if he leaves in a few weeks and I never see him again?"

"What if he does? You'll at least have taken the chance."

"Pattie, you don't know how much it hurts to love somebody and they say they'll see you soon, but they disappear forever. I was just a kid when Marty died, but I remember feeling so weary and everything around me looked drab for such a long time. It was two years before my mother packed away his things." Celina's apprehension about losing another person she loved had become a burden weighing her down.

Pattie was silent.

"When Bobbie was killed, I was full of hate. I'd been cheated by life, and I couldn't even make the people responsible pay for what they'd done. I don't know if I can take the chance of going through something like that again."

"But what if he doesn't leave and you wouldn't take the chance? Then how would you feel?"

An uneasy sensation clawed at Celina's stomach. "I.... I.... Jeez, Pattie I want to do this right. I want to so bad."

Pattie pressed on. "Anyone can see that Steve's crazy about you. And in case you didn't know it, Cathy Wojciechowski has been chasing after him since before you even met him. So don't fool around too long."

"Cathy? How do you know that?"

Pattie's voice dropped. "Mrs. Pinkerton told me."

"How would she know?"

Pattie nodded somberly. "She's friends with Harriet, and Harriet is friends with Terez, and Terez told her. I guess Cathy's even called him at home. Can you believe that?"

"She called him first?" Celina marveled. Only loose girls called young men at home. Nice girls were required to wait till they were asked out by the guy they liked.

"You know Cathy. She doesn't care what people think. And anyway, that's what Mrs. Pinkerton said."

The heat of jealousy crept up Celina's neck and onto her cheeks. "I thought she was interested in Ed Hagarty."

"She's interested in Steve too." Pattie brightened. "Hey, you're jealous."

"You are getting a kick out of this, aren't you?"

"You're my best friend, and I will do whatever it takes to wake you up. You need to come out of that fog you've been in and fight for your man."

"For Pete's sake, that sounds like something from the movies."

"Maybe so." Pattie squared her shoulders. "Movies can be like real life. And, I can tell you one thing, if Cathy ever sets her sights on Johnny, I'll scratch her eyes out." She brushed her hands together. "I'll do it, too."

"Okay, okay, I believe you." Celina responded, taken aback by her friend's intensity.

Driving home, she passed Shirley Creek mine with its low, gray buildings dusty and hunkered against the hillside, and thought about their conversation. Surprised at how jealous she became when Pattie told her Cathy had called Stephen, she couldn't clear her head and needed a few minutes to think.

A few miles further on, she pulled over and parked along the overgrown side road that led to an abandoned tipple. No coal had been taken out of that mine since twenty-five men were killed in a methane gas and coal dust explosion at the beginning of the Great Depression. The emissions were so bad that the Kettlemore Company rushed the men on the rescue team out of the mine and sealed the entrance. The charred and mutilated bodies of her great-uncle, Jurek, and twenty-four others were left where they had fallen.

Once upon a time, the massive, blackened, skeletal remains had been a productive place. The tipple was shaped like a ski slope, taller at one end than the other, with railroad tracks going right through it. Now, the wind sighed through the collapsing structure and Celina could almost hear long-dead miners grunting to push mine cars to the top of the track, then tipping and emptying their loads into waiting transport vehicles. The company sent the fruit of their labor out on railroad cars to stoke industry and heat the homes of the northeast.

She walked up the steep bank to the jagged hulk of a building that had once been the busy focal point of a thriving mine. The roof was gone in places, exposing slumped rafters. Windows had been knocked out and shards of glass lay scattered on the stony ground. The walls dipped and swayed drunkenly against the sky. A warped piece of rusty pipe, buffeted by the light breeze, sounded a death knell as it swayed clinging to the side of the ruin.

Scavengers had pulled up sections of the railroad track leading to the tipple. Only wooden ties were left. They lay rotting amid weeds that grew through the coarse black-and-red residue left by generations of coal laden mine cars.

A few gnarled sumac trees grew out of the small mountain

of shale and red-dog mine refuse on which the tipple perched. Dandelions and quack grass grew in scraggly tufts between the scattered railroad ties.

A few gray, splintered mine cars, some with small, round, numbered, brass tokens, the miners' chits, still attached, were like twisted corpses that lay scattered, helter-skelter, around the property. Pieces of rusting, misshapen steel wheels and bent gears grew out of the sickly grass in lopsided disarray.

Celina's clothes stuck to her, and she shaded her eyes with her hand. She stopped to rest on a railroad tie that someone had pulled up but neglected to haul away. She looked back at the building where a long flight of rickety stairs leaned precariously against a wall like a crippled miner no longer able to stand on his own.

The site was so quiet and devoid of human disruption that the swallows flew through holes in the roof and perched on the broken windows. A sparrow landed on a mine car a few feet away and watched her curiously.

With her chin in her hands and her elbows on her knees, she examined the desolation and thought about what Pattie said. *She was right. I am afraid Stephen will leave and I'll be all alone again.* "I don't think I could stand that," she said aloud.

A robin lit on a piece of debris. She straightened up, and the startled bird flew several feet and settled on a rusting wheel. The bird stayed there for a moment, just out of reach, and then it flew further on. *What if I don't take the chance?* She didn't want to think about that, but images of spinsterhood and living a fruitless life, one like Harriet's, edged in.

She surveyed the barrenness. *This deserted place belongs to the past.* It was there where her grandfather, fresh off the boat from Poland, started his life in the United States, working ten hours a day and living in a shack that he was forced to rent from the coal company. It was there where her dad and Charlie, a couple of twelve-year-olds, learned their trade. *Now nobody wants it. Not even the junk man comes here to collect scrap.*

Walking to the edge of the rise, she studied the winding road that led away from the old mine. A few cars sped by on the highway that passed through Kenville to the world beyond.

She was sure no one remembered the miners entombed under her feet, or noticed that the tipple had fallen into ruin. Would Shirley Creek and Deer Hollow end up the same way? She heard a car approach. It was Terez Halosz's black Ford. She watched it pass her by.

She checked her watch and hurried back to her car. *Boga, Mom will be going through the ceiling and Dad will be complaining about his supper.*

When she got home, Tomas' jalopy was parked in its usual spot. She jumped out of the car and ran into the house.

Marian, wearing a plaid housedress and her graying hair covered with a babushka, pulled the iron skillet over the open fire.

Celina rushed to the stove. "I'm sorry I'm late. I'll fry the ham."

"So where were you?"

"I stopped by the old tipple and walked around a bit."

"Why? You're supposed to be helping with supper." Marian handed Celina a long-handled fork. "Besides, there's got to be snakes under all that junk piled around out there."

"I needed some time to think." Celina watched her mother from the corner of her eye and hoped she'd understand. And she hoped they'd have dinner ready before Tomas came up from his shower. "I did get some of the cobwebs out of my head."

"If you need time to think, you have to do it after supper is over and the dishes are done. There's too much to do around here to take the time to go up to that godforsaken place."

"Yeah. Okay." Making her mother understand that she needed some time and space was hopeless. Marian Pasniewski's priorities were family, home, and work. Nothing more, nothing less.

Celina placed the silverware on the table, retrieved the cream from the refrigerator, and set it next to Tomas' place. The percolator gurgled on the stove and sent the aroma of coffee through the house.

Tomas raised the latch, pushed open the cellar door, and lumbered into the kitchen. He had taken his shower, but the wrinkles around his eyes held traces of coal dust, and his lashes were lined in black, as though someone had painted them with a mascara brush.

He drew a heavy wooden chair away from the table, plopped down, and pulled well-darned gray cotton socks onto his knobby feet. The right foot was twisted and missing its big toe. "I'm glad to be home. Cripes. My back is killing me."

Marian served his dinner and Celina poured his coffee. Before he could grumble, she refilled his cup.

After supper, while he snored on the couch, Marian said, "Oh, I almost forgot to tell you. Stephen, Johnny's friend, the one you danced with, called asking for you. His number is on a slip of paper next to the phone."

Celina rushed to the living room, slowed down to tiptoe past Tomas, then dragged the phone as far into the hallway as the cord would reach. She lifted the receiver carefully and put it to her ear. *Thank God, no one's on the party line.* She dialed the number and Terez answered. After the usual small talk,

Celina took a deep breath. "I'm returning Stephen's call. Is he there?"

It seemed like hours while she waited for him to pick up the receiver. *Oh please God, don't let the Kolariks or Johnsons pick up the phone, please.*

In less than a minute, the deep rhythm of his voice reached her from the other end of the line. He came right to the point, telling her that he had agreed to deliver a packet of invoices for Johnny that evening. He wanted to know if she would like to ride with him to Philipsburg to drop it off.

"Wait. I'll check with my mom." She knew her parents' rules, and checking with her mother was at the top of the list.

Marian sat at the table with a cup of coffee in her hand. To Celina's surprise her mother approved. "Johnny told me Stephen is a nice and respectable young man." Celina could have hugged her brother as she danced back down the hall to give Stephen her answer.

After hanging up, she quietly slipped through the living room, set the phone back on its little stand, and quietly climbed up the stairs to her room. Once there, she readied herself in record time.

Her heart pounded when she saw the black Ford stop under the maple trees. Stephen crossed the yard with long strides and Celina met him at the door. Marian waved them off, then called from the porch. "Watch for deer crossing the highway since it'll be dusk when you're driving back."

The car windows were rolled down, and Celina adjusted the glass side window vent to keep the wind from pulling at her hair. The large brown envelope propped between them on the seat slipped to the floor; and she picked it up. "I'm curious. What's in this?"

"Just some invoices and tax records Johnny organized for

Doc Kasper."

"I haven't talked to Johnny much in the last couple of days. I guess he still wants to learn about the bookkeeping end of the auto business."

Stephen glanced at her. "He's determined to learn as much as he can." He sped up on a straight stretch of road just past the lane. "Johnny and Mike are planning for the future. They want some kind of stability to offer a wife and family."

Studying his profile, Celina considered what he just said. "In spite of some of the crazy things he does and his sense of humor, my brother is a sensible person."

"And you?"

She smiled. "Let's see. Pattie spends half her life telling me I'm too serious. But I don't think I am. I think I'm realistic...levelheaded."

"But are you happy, Celina?"

His question caught her off guard. "That's difficult to say." She flipped the envelope over a couple of times. "Happiness isn't a word that goes with everyday life."

"Why not?"

"Well, you work hard and make the best of things. Maybe you'd like to be happy, but that doesn't mean you will be. You just do what you have to do. That's all."

"Don't you want to be happy?"

"Of course, doesn't everybody?"

"Some people don't," he replied. "I think some people enjoy being miserable and making everybody around them miserable."

"Well, I think everybody wants happiness. Maybe they don't know how to find it, but they want it." *Even Dad, Earl, and Mr. Duxbury must want to be happy, but they don't know how to do it.*

"But there are people who don't know how to be happy."

"I suppose so," she said.

"I think there are."

"What about you? Is your life happy?" Celina asked.

"No, not every day. But I agree with what you said about working hard and making the best of things."

"How did we get onto such a difficult subject?"

"It was Johnny and the envelope you're holding."

"Well, let's change the subject."

He reached across the seat and pulled her closer. "You were too far away. "He grinned, then added, "But if you'd rather not—"

"Oh no, I like being close to you." She blurted out.

"I like being close to you too." He pulled her a wee bit closer. "I saw you today up there near the abandoned tipple. Do you walk there very often?"

"Hardly ever. I don't get much privacy at home and wanted some time to think."

"What were you thinking up there alone on the hilltop?"

"About taking chances on things, and about where my life is going. I got a lot sorted out."

"Were you thinking about Bobby?"

Surprised that he knew about Bobby, she shook her head. "No, I was…oh, I hate small towns where everyone's life is on display."

"Johnny mentioned him. And I know only what my aunt told me, that's all. They said he was killed in Korea."

"Yes, he was." She wondered what Johnny had said.

"Tell me about him."

"Well, he was a quiet person and loved it here. He never wanted to leave Kenville. We didn't start dating till after high school. Eventually, we fell in love and planned to be married." She sighed. "But he was drafted and sent to Korea. He cried the day he left for basic training." She stared straight ahead, through the windshield. "He was killed two months before his tour of duty was up."

"Do you still love him?"

"He was a part of my life. When he was killed, I was bitter for a long time. I felt cheated. I hated everybody and everything, especially the army. It took me too long to move on. I think I'm beginning to understand why."

"Then you're over him?"

"Yes. He's a warm memory now, but I do know I'll always regret that he didn't have a chance at life. I feel the same way about my brother, Martyn, who was killed in 1944. Both of them were still in their teens when they died." Her voice dripped with sarcasm. "They died in wars some 'great leader' started."

The two of them were silent for a while. "That abandoned mine, it's a melancholy place," Stephen said.

She nodded. "The ruins are distracting all by themselves."

"Why do people want to stay in Kenville? Has this part of the state ever been prosperous?"

Celina thought for a second. "It's not prosperous by a lot of people's standards, I suppose. But people here are used to it. Some people, the old timers who lived through the Depression, or their parents who were immigrants, believe they're prosperous. They have their little pieces of land and live as independently as anyone, I guess."

"How do people survive?"

"They work in the coal mines, the brickyard, or the cigar factory, other than that, there isn't much here."

She told him that her grandfather and father had worked in the abandoned mine before it was shut down. "As usual, the coal company fought unionization and skirted safety regulations, and there was a methane explosion. It killed a lot of men. After that, they sealed the mine and opened Shirley Creek."

She continued. "My dad started mining when he was a kid. He still tells stories about how Pap allowed him to keep no more than twenty-five cents a week from his pay as spending money."

"It must have been a hard life for a boy, a hard life for the whole family."

"But Dad's proud of how hard he worked, and he likes to brag about how much tougher miners were in the old days. So things really are better now."

After a moment of silence, Stephen spoke softly. "You looked beautiful, standing up there with the wind swirling around you."

Their eyes met and she wanted to kiss him.

They pulled in to the freight depot and he delivered the brown envelope to the man behind the counter. A minute later he returned waving a receipt.

As they drove back, Celina wanted to continue their earlier conversation. "Tell me about you. I know you're from Hungary and your parents are still there, but what about your future?" She wanted to know, and dreaded what he might say.

"I want a normal life again in a country where I'm not being spied on. As soon as I can, I'll become a citizen. And I want a stable future…a secure job." He reached for her hand. "I want a wife and family."

A small, "Oh," escaped her. She caught her breath. "That's a lot. What kind of work do you want?"

"I'm fortunate. I have had a university education. I know several languages, and speak English well. Those skills give me more opportunity than most immigrants would have." He glanced at her. "I know I can take good care of a family. I've been in touch with several colleges here in Pennsylvania. I've given them my credentials for teaching Russian and European History."

Celina's brow furrowed. "Why in the world are you here, in middle of nowhere, if you can do all that?" She turned his hand over and ran her fingers over the calloused palm and fingers. "And your hands are a working man's hands, not a teacher's."

"I'm here because my Aunt Terez sponsored me and has allowed me to stay with her until I find a position. It's only a couple hours' drive to the schools I am interested in. That makes the interview process much easier."

"Oh."

"And I'm pretty good with my hands. So far I have repaired her chicken coop, replaced the rotting shelves in her fruit cellar, and mended what seemed like one hundred miles of fence. Does that answer your question?"

Heat rose in Celina's face. "I'm sorry, but it seems so strange that someone with your background would come here." Her breath caught in her throat. "You'll have to leave soon."

"Not until the school year starts in late August, that is, if I'm accepted by one of the schools."

She feigned moderate interest. "Where do you expect to go?"

"There is a good college near the Ohio border called Westminster, and I believe I would fit in well there. In Pittsburgh, Duquesne University is an excellent school. I would be happy with either one."

I knew it. I knew I shouldn't let myself get interested in him. She bit the inside of her lip and had the childish urge to hit him because it had been so easy for him to break through every boundary she had erected.

"What's wrong? You're so quiet."

Celina looked at her watch and said, "It's getting late. I have to get home."

"Wait a minute, what's the matter?"

"It's just that, well, it's just that," the words rushed out, "I don't want you to leave."

"I've been trying to tell you that I want you to come with me."

"What?"

"Come with me when I leave."

"I can't do that."

He pulled the car onto a side road and turned off the engine. "Why not?"

"I wouldn't leave unless I was married. It wouldn't be right."

He slid closer and whispered, "Isn't loving someone right?" They were so close. He brushed her cheek with his lips then Celina tasted his first kiss.

Headlights lit up the highway, and a car filled with yelling teenagers, careened down the nearby road. They pulled apart. In a throaty whisper, she said, "I really do have to go home."

He turned the key in the ignition and pulled the car onto the highway. "I'll pick you up for the dance Saturday night?"

Her eyes sparkled. "Yes."

CHAPTER 8

Celina daydreamed about Stephen, sighed, and polished the glass case surrounding Duxbury's Ladies' Intimate Apparel. She paused to stare at the silky nightgowns and lacy negligees and thought about what it would be like to wear something like that on her wedding night.

Her reverie was disturbed by a commotion. At the front entrance, Harold in his khaki work clothes marched inside. He veered away from Earl, who had motioned him indoors by jabbing a thumb over his skinny shoulder.

Harold tramped, one boot lace dragging, from Hardware past her toward Men's Attire. He tied the lace, stood up, and crossed his arms. A frown pulled the corners of his mouth down to his jutting chin where specks of tobacco juice rested amid the stubble.

"Harold, what's the matter?" She whispered loudly.

He pointed to the entrance where a stout woman in a gabardine skirt and starched white blouse stood speaking to Earl. "That old bitc..." he back peddled, "excuse me, excuse my language. But that old biddy's tellin' Earl she don't like the way I sweep the sidewalk in the morning."

He poked the air with a crooked finger. "She's a bossy old bat and I hain't taking no orders from her." He crossed his arms. "I take orders from the boss and Earl. Not from some bossy old woman."

Minutes passed, and they watched Earl nod, scratch his head, and rub the back of his neck while talking to Harriet Grayhill, who stood framed in the doorway clutching her pocketbook to her chest.

Pattie strode up to Celina. "What's the matter?"

Harold explained that he was sweeping the sidewalk and pushing the dirt into the gutter as usual, when that Miss Grayhill came right up to him and pointed to some candy wrappers. She told him to pick them up and put them in the trash.

He stared into Pattie's eyes. "I don't pay no attention to the cigarette butts, they'll wash down the sewer with the next rain, but I always wad up the paper and throw it in the can on the corner." He glared in Harriet's direction. "I don't want her comin' round acting like I don't know how to do my job."

They watched Earl smooth his thin hair with both hands and call out. "Harold, come on over here."

Celina couldn't imagine Harriet being a troublemaker. When the woman was in charge of the high school library, she patiently explained arcane verses of poetry and praised the virtues of world literature to any student who would take the time to listen. Celina listened and learned to love literature because Harriet Grayhill shared her knowledge so willingly.

Harold brushed off his shirt sleeves, crossed his arms, frowned deeper, and strode across the store. A few minutes later he uncrossed his arms, said a few words, and rearranged his cap. The three separated. Harold walked past Celina, winked, smiled, and headed to the basement.

"I'll ask him what happened later," Pattie said before heading back to boys and men's clothes then turned around. "Is your mom still doing summer apples tonight?"

"Of course."

"I'll come and help. I like doing all that stuff that we don't do at our house anymore."

"Thanks." Work always went faster with more help, and Pattie made it fun.

"Good morning, Celina." Harriet approached, placed her pocketbook on the glass case and retrieved a book, still in its new, crisp paper-jacket. "This one, *Steamboat Gothic* by Francis Parkinson Keys, came in the mail yesterday and I thought you would like to take a look at it."

Celina examined the book and thanked the elderly woman for her thoughtfulness. "I've just finished *My Cousin Rachel* by Daphne du Maurier. I'm glad I read it, but can't say I'd want to read it a second time."

The two discussed the book briefly before Harriet offered an explanation. "You probably noticed that I had a little misunderstanding with Harold, just there. Sometimes he can be so touchy."

Celina nodded and Harriet proceeded to purchase six pairs of very large pink panties, cotton.

Taking the paper bag from Celina, she rolled the top tight. "I hear that you and that nice Stephen Meszaros are courting."

Celina's eyes widened. She didn't know what to say. "Oh. Um."

Harriet's lips curled upward and fine lines creased her plump face. "I see him with his Aunt Terez at the post office. I like him." Her small blue eyes twinkled. "Very handsome if

I do say so myself."

Celina felt her cheeks heat. "Um, yes, he is very nice. Did Terez say we were courting?" *It was such a nice old-fashioned term.*

"Of course, and she said it to Ethel Pinkerton on the party line." She patted Celina's hand. "Now everybody we know is buzzing about the new romance."

"We're just dating. I hope people don't think too much of it." Celina knew she should have expected people to be going on and on about her and Stephen as soon as word got around.

"You know how people are. It makes life more interesting if there's something to gossip about. It breaks up the monotony."

"I guess you're right." She liked Harriet, so solid and sensible.

#

Storm clouds gathered as Celina and Pattie strolled to the dairy bar to pick up their cold drinks for lunch. They returned to the store, trudged up the stairs to the meeting room and sat down at the recently polished table. Pattie peered into Celina's lunch bag.

"Jeez, all you have is two summer apples and peanut butter and jelly. Not too fancy." Pattie examined the waxed-paper wrapped sandwich. "At least it's homemade bread. How come that's all you got?"

Celina unwrapped the sandwich. "Mom's been running over to get Baba every day this week. They've been making blackberry jelly and she wants to get the applesauce done too." She passed an apple to Pattie.

"Is that blackberry jelly on there?"

"Yeah."

"Want to share?"

Celina gave Pattie half her sandwich. "What'd you bring?"

"Let's see." She reached inside her own lunch bag and found a Hershey Bar. She squeezed, and melted chocolate squished out the ends of the wrapper. Dropping it in the wastebasket she said, "I don't think we want that."

"Harold was in a real snit this morning, wasn't he?" Pattie noted.

"Yeah. But when he talked to Harriet, things got straightened out."

"We had a nice night for the midsummer dance, didn't we? A lot of couples paired off before it was over," Pattie bit into the peanut butter sandwich.

Tenderness spread over Celina's face as she remembered how close Stephen held her during the slow songs and how much she loved the scent of him.

"Um-hum, it was a swell evening."

"Did you notice Mike and Stella?"

"Yeah. They look good together. I'm glad they're dating."

"You never were interested in him."

"No. And now I won't have to worry that my mom will keep bringing his name up all the time as a marriage prospect."

A few moments passed, and Pattie slid her chair closer to Celina. "Did you and Steve do, you know, anything after you left the dance?" she whispered.

Celina thought about the tender caresses, the long kisses, and the hesitant touching. "Jeez, Pattie. That's kind of private."

"Well, did you?"

"We kissed a lot and stuff."

Pattie's voice dropped even further, and she tore at the corners of the wax paper lying on the table. "You know how I feel about Johnny. I love him so much I can hardly stand it." She avoided Celina's eyes. "We almost went all-the-way. And God, you wouldn't believe how hard it was to stop."

"You shouldn't be telling me this."

"But I need somebody to talk to and you're my best friend."

"But he's my brother, and it makes me feel sort of weird. Did you talk to him about what could happen?"

"We talked. He says he wants to do it, but he can wait till we're married."

"Waiting till you're married is the best. Jeez, you two are talking about getting married?"

"Yeah. He wants to get out of the mines and start his own business. Then we'll get engaged and set a date."

"You haven't said a word to me. When did all this happen?"

"When we saw you and Steve together at the ball game, you looked so in love. And you hardly knew each other. That's when we realized we wanted to be together too. And it sort of just happened."

"I'm really happy for you, but you caught me off guard."

"You know I've been waiting for Johnny for such a long time, ever since we were in high school. And I want him, all of him, right now."

"But you've got to think. What if something happens? You know what I mean. It could ruin all your plans."

Pattie covered her face with her hands and looked at Celina from between her fingers. "Do you think I'm a horrible person?"

"Oh, God, no. If you're in love, you want to do it. But

you've got to be careful."

"I know. I will." Pattie lowered her hands. "What about you and Steve? Do you want to do it with him?"

Celina took a long breath. "Yeah."

"Are you going to?"

"For Pete's sake, Pattie, we're talking about being careful and waiting till our wedding night, remember?"

"What about using rubbers? They're supposed to work."

"That's what they say, but what if one leaked or something? Then you'd be counting the days till your period and worrying yourself sick. Remember, this is my brother we're talking about. And I don't want you two having a shotgun wedding."

"I don't either."

"Okay, so remember that you have to be careful."

"Yeah, be careful. I know it's important…be careful."

They stood up, brushed a few crumbs off the table, and went to the door. "I'm serious, Pattie. If something happens, it could mess up your whole life."

"Yeah, I know."

Rain began beating on the roof. It slid over the gutters in sheets and splashed onto the street below. Thunder rolled loud and long. Celina chuckled.

"What's funny?"

"When we were kids, I used to be afraid of thunder, and my dad always told me not to worry. He'd get down on one knee, point up, and say, 'You hear all that noise up there, first it's far away then it gets closer and closer?' I'd nod and he'd say 'Well, that's because the angels are getting ready for a party up there, and it takes them a while to roll the beer barrels across heaven.'"

Patty laughed. "And you believed him?"

"Of course, he's my dad. He'd tell me that the angels were setting up the kegs where the sun was shining above the clouds." Celina stopped on the stairs. "Then Daddy would muss up my hair and tell me to go play, but to stay inside."

"I never thought your dad would, you know, be nice to you if you were scared. He must not be as cranky as I thought."

"Don't get your hopes up. He's mean and bossy most of the time."

Mr. Duxbury and his wife, Marge, entered the store. He shook the rain drops off a large black umbrella. She yelped. "Grover, please! You're getting water on my dress."

"You sure can tell that hair color came out of a bottle. And it clashes with her purple lipstick." Pattie whispered.

"But that dress must have cost a fortune. And her shoes and purse match."

Duxbury looked up at Celina and Pattie, nodded, and a tight-lipped smile crossed his face. He followed his wife to the office. Marge's voice drifted through the open door. "You aren't keeping close enough tabs on those girls. I saw the two of them standing on the stairs gawking at us when we came in. You'd think these foreigners would appreciate what you do for them but they're insolent, that's what they are. Grover, you must tell them that they are here to work, not gawk. They'll be stealing merchandise from under your nose if you don't watch out. You know how those...." Her voice became muffled when the door closed.

Marge Duxbury came into the store no more than once a month. Celina shook her head in disgust. "She's a witch. She thinks she's better than us."

Pattie nodded. "Must be that hoity-toity Newark, New Jersey, family she comes from. He's no prize, but I don't know how he can stand her."

They scurried to the main door to watch the rain for a few minutes before they had to get back to work. They found Stephen smoking a cigarette under the awning. He stood near Harriet and Terez who stopped talking long enough to glance from him to Celina and trade smug, knowing looks.

As the little group exchanged pleasantries, Pattie called out. "Hey, Steve, what are you doing here?"

His eyes met Celina's as though they shared a secret. "I'm expecting a telegram. I'm going to run over to the newspaper office when the rain slows down."

Flicking the half-smoked cigarette into the water rushing into the culvert a few feet away, he stepped into the store with Celina and Pattie. They waved to the two elderly women who were becoming engrossed in a discussion about Kimmie Stuscovich's wedding.

He glanced back at them. "Those two ladies do love to talk. A lot more must happen in this small town than I thought."

"So Steve, what's the telegram all about?" asked Pattie.

"A position. I'm expecting to hear from one of the schools I've contacted."

Celina noticed Earl peering around the now half-open office door. He came out, and pulled the door shut with a little click. Rocking from his toes to his heels, he watched the three of them. Then with his head erect and his thin lips pulled into a tight line, he approached. He looked at his watch and cleared his throat. "Ladies, this is a place of business. Don't you have customers to attend to?"

Stephen answered for them. "Yes, sir, they do. I have been taking too much time questioning your clerks about the proper shirt and tie for the upcoming wedding."

"Ah. Well, in that case," Earl said, "Miss Harchak, please take this gentleman to Men's Attire and show him our merchandise."

Celina was so annoyed that she wanted to stomp on Earl's big feet. Stephen winked, and she strode back to women's wear. He followed Pattie to the men's department. From the corner of her eye, she watched Pattie hold ties against several different shirts. At last, Pattie rang up the purchase and gave Stephen the shopping bag.

He stopped at her counter. "Miss Pasniewski."

"Yes, may I help you?"

"I would like to purchase something beautiful for someone beautiful. I'm sure you know who I mean. What would you recommend?"

Celina played coy. "A nice box of handkerchiefs, maybe?" The pure white squares of embroidered cotton always served as an appropriate, innocuous, gift.

"No. No," He teased as he walked along the glass case and paused in front of the lingerie. Their eyes met and they kept moving. He pointed to several bright silk scarves. "I'd like to see those."

Celina removed several scarves from the case and placed each one in front of him. He pulled an emerald-green rectangle through his hands and asked for her opinion. She pointed to one she liked best.

"I'll take it."

The rain ended, and he left with his purchases. The sunny afternoon brought a steady trickle of customers through the store. Wedding gifts were big sellers, and mothers wearing housedresses stopped and looked at school clothes and pencil boxes.

That afternoon, on the way to their cars, Pattie said,

"After Queen Marge," Patty poked her nose in the air, "left, Duxbury stood at that office door and watched every move we made. And can you believe that Earl coming up to us like that?"

Celina raised an eyebrow. "Stephen's a quick thinker. He caught Earl totally off guard. I wish I could think that fast."

"I want to ask you something." Patty opened the door and they both stepped outside.

"Okay."

"Why do you call him Stephen instead of Steve?"

"It's what he's always been called. Besides I like saying his full name. It sounds strong." Celina paused. "And I'm showing respect for his parents, who I'll never meet. That's the name they gave him when he was baptized."

Pattie cocked her head. "That sort of makes sense."

They climbed into their cars, and Celina called out through the open window. "Hey, are you still coming over tonight?"

"Yeah, I know Johnny won't be home." Pattie's red head glistened in the sun. "And I must have told you five times, I don't mind peeling apples. I like doing kitchen work with you and your mom, and your baba is going to be there. It makes me feel like I'm doing my share."

"Okay. See you later."

After supper, Celina wanted to flop into a chair and watch the John Cameron Swayze *Camel News Caravan* show on the television with her dad, but instead, she eyed the baskets on the back porch. Three bushels heaped with apples awaited. She slammed the screen door, and hoped to relay a message to her mother through her grandmother. "Baba, tell Mom we can't do all these tonight."

Baba Dombrowski in her tattered maroon brocade slippers, faded house dress, and plaid apron tied around her ample hips, poured coffee into a mug and looked over her spectacles at Celina. "Ellen's coming. She will help."

Marian warmed up her own coffee, and said, "Andy's dropping her off. The kids can play outside. And maybe Dad'll take them for ice cream. The apples won't take that long, and when we're done he can take the kids along when he drives baba home."

She peered into the cook stove's firebox and adjusted the damper to save a few embers for morning. "Pattie's coming too, isn't she?"

"Yeah. She'll be over after supper."

Baba, using the table for support, lowered her creaky body onto a chair. She took a long, slow swallow of coffee. "See, we have plenty of help. You got jars washed, kettles ready?"

"Yeah, Baba, everything's ready."

"Then get knives."

Marian called. "Tomas, we need a basket brought in."

Grumbling, he plodded through the kitchen in his stocking feet. "I'm gonna miss the news about Eisenhower sending some kind of military advisors to Indochina."

"Well, hurry up, and you won't miss it."

"Okay, woman, okay."

Pattie arrived first then Ellen and the boys trooped in. Three generations of women peeled and sliced apples and tossed them into the large kettles of water spiked with vinegar.

Baba nodded silently while the others nattered on about everyone they knew. With Pattie's help, Celina told the others about Harriet's encounter with Harold.

Tomas carted in the second bushel, and when it crashed to the floor, Pattie jumped and cut her finger. She ran to the sink to rinse it off while Marian looked for a bandage. Celina noticed Baba Dombrowski roll her eyes at the ceiling while Marian fussed over Pattie's injury. The old woman muttered something about today's girls being weak babies who would not have survived in the old country.

"Harriet told me that everybody knows Stephen and I are seeing each other, because Terez told her over the party line." Celina said, reaching for another apple.

Baba nodded. "You get all the news on party line. Who needs television?" Baba didn't watch television, but she liked the telephone and the gossip it provided.

While the women worked, Tomas and the kids, with Frankie at their heels, carried buckets of apple peels and cores to the pig sty, and tossed them into the trough where the porkers' pink snouts snuffled and rooted to find the tender morsels first.

After the pigs had their fill, the boys followed Tomas to the wire-fenced chicken coop, and the Rhode Island Reds got a treat. The hens scratched, pecked, and chased each other in circles until peels, cores, and seeds flew in all directions. Tomas warned the boys about putting their fingers through the wire. "Gonna get your fingers pecked off if you stick 'em in there."

The sun dipped low in the sky when Celina reached into the last basket to retrieve the last apple. She tossed it in the air. "I thought we'd never get done."

Pattie sat back, turned her hands over, and examined the fingers. "My hands are like prunes, and my fingerprints are gone." She blew on her wrinkled finger tips and lifted the edge of the bandage to examine the small wound. "But the nails are bleached nice and white."

When Baba stood, Celina noticed that she pursed up her face above Pattie's head. At seventeen, the tough old woman left Poland on a steamship to America to take part in an arranged marriage. It always amazed her how brave her grandmother must have been.

Baba started cleaning off the table and Celina retrieved the mop and pail from the pantry. "Don't bother," Marian said. "I'll get the floor tomorrow when we're done with the applesauce."

"I think the morning sickness is over now," Ellen announced when Celina offered her a cup of fresh-brewed coffee. She stirred a spoonful of cream and some sugar into the cup, lifted it to her mouth—and gagged. Clasping a hand across her face, she ran to the bathroom. Marian followed. Celina rose from her chair, but Baba motioned her to sit down and leave them alone. "She'll be all right in minute."

"Shouldn't the morning sickness be over already?" Pattie threw a tentative look at Celina. "She's five months along already."

The old woman sighed. Baba, pragmatic as usual, said, "She could have it till baby comes."

"Jeez, I didn't know it could last that long," Celina marveled. The thought of being nauseated and vomiting for nine months was not an appealing one.

"Sometimes it does." Baba shrugged.

Eyes wide with concern for Ellen, and their own future dealings with morning sickness, Celina and Pattie needed each other for moral support. "You okay, Ell?" they asked when the women returned.

"Yeah. I was hoping it would pass, but it didn't." She pushed the cup away without looking at it. "Is there any ginger ale?"

The screen door slammed when Tomas and the boys burst into the house. Marty and Tommy held melting ice cream cones that dripped down their arms. Tommy ran up to his mother and thrust the cone in her direction. "Want some strawberry ice cream, Mommy?"

Ellen smiled and averted her eyes. "Not right now, honey. Mommy's full."

"Okay you boys, come over here and I'll wipe your hands."

"For Christ's sake Marian, let 'em eat their ice cream. You said to get 'em ice cream. Now you won't let 'em eat it." Tomas grumbled.

Ignoring him, Marian wrapped the cones in paper napkins, scrubbed their faces and hands with a wet cloth, and gave the treats back to the boys. "There."

"Jesus Christ." Tomas grunted and turned on his heel. He went into the living room and flopped down on the couch.

"I wanna go with Pap-Pap."

"No, Tommy," Ellen said. "You know you aren't allowed to sit on Baba's couch when you eat."

He sent a pleading look to his grandmother.

"You listen to your mother."

The boys found a spot in front of the Hoosier cabinet and slid down onto the kitchen floor. They licked the strawberry ice cream as it melted into soggy napkins. When finished, Marty wiped his hands down the front of his shirt. Baba Dombrowski laughed, Marian shook her head, and Ellen threw the leftovers into the trash.

Pattie's head flew up and she stretched her neck to look out the door when she heard Frankie scrambling to his feet and jumping from his usual spot on the porch. Andy, in greasy work pants and stained tee shirt, followed by his younger and slimmer look-alike, entered the cluttered kitchen.

Frankie, sad eyed, stood at the door and yipped for

attention. Johnny said, "Settle down, you," and the dog, panting, sat staring through the screen.

Tomas yelled from the living room. "Did ya get Pap's truck running?"

Johnny stood behind Pattie's chair and kneaded her shoulders with strong fingers. "It's running," he called out. "But who knows for how long."

Baba shook her head. "He swears at it and kicks fenders when it breaks down. Someday he's gonta shoot it." The men grinned.

Celina visualized her pap, feet apart and cap askew over his bald head, squinting through the sights of his shotgun at the truck's rear end. She chuckled.

"Ahh, Pap loves that truck. Besides, he wouldn't waste a shotgun shell on it." Johnny guffawed.

Tomas stood in the doorway. "That damned thing belongs in a junkyard."

"Well, Dad, the way I see it, he's bound and determined to hold onto that thing, even if he has to get poor old *Kwiat* from the pasture to pull it."

"He's right, Dad." Andy added, "One of these days we'll be hitching that old horse to the front bumper."

"Christ. I'm sure as hell glad I wasn't over there. That truck hain't worth workin' on."

Marian nodded in the direction of the little boys. "Tomas, watch it, will you?"

He shifted his weight against the door frame. "What? I'm just sayin' I'm sick of workin' on that junker, that's all."

"Hey, Dad," Johnny said, "Uncle Stanley found a good windshield at the junkyard. He wants you to go over and help him put it in next week."

"Oh, hell."

Everybody, even Tomas, laughed.

He pointed to the boys. "I'll tell you one thing, I'm glad I was busy watchin' them two little boys over there tonight. Tell your daddy and Uncle Johnny what you did while they were gone."

The boys ran over to their father and told him about how they tipped the buckets of apple peels into the wooden troughs and watched the pigs squeal. Tommy scuffed his feet across the floor demonstrating how the hens scratched and scattered apple peels all over the chicken yard.

"See. You're hard workers like your dad, hain't you, boys?"

"Yep, we sure are."

Ellen stood up. "It's getting late. We had better be going." She turned to the boys. "Say good-night to everybody, kids."

While she gathered their things, Andy instructed the boys to give everyone a good-bye hug. "Get your things, Baba, and I'll drop you off at the house." Three adults and two children were packed into his pick up when they set off down the lane.

The dog whined at the door and Pattie looked up at Johnny's smudged face. "Want to take Frankie for a walk?"

"I'm too tired...let's sit on the porch for a while."

Once they were out of earshot, Marian whispered to Celina. "Those two are getting pretty serious, aren't they?"

"It looks like it. I guess he's going over to her house for Sunday dinner sometime soon."

"Oh, it is serious."

Celina rinsed the dishcloth and wiped spots of apple juice from the sink drain board. "I'm glad they've finally gotten together."

"It's time he settled down, and Pattie is a good girl...a little bit scatter-brained, but a good girl." Marian covered the kettles of apples with clean dish towels. "Is he talking about getting her a ring?"

"From what she says, he wants to get that business started first."

"But he's making a decent living right now, and Pattie can work until the kids start coming along."

"Mom, you know he hates going underground. He's not like Dad." She shook her head. "He really wants out. And so does Mike. And Johnny says a lot of the mines are shutting down."

"Does he think Shirley Creek will shut down?"

"He doesn't know. Don't worry, if they start layoffs, Dad will be one of the last to go."

"What about Andy?"

"A lot of men have more seniority. I guess he'd have to find something else."

Marian wrung her hands. "There's not much besides the mines around here."

"He could drive to State College and still live here. Or he might have to go somewhere else to work."

"He can't leave. I couldn't stand it. We'd never see him. We wouldn't get to see the boys grow up." Marian folded a dish towel and sat down. "I remember how empty and lonely it was when Dad went out west during the Depression." She blinked back tears. "I cried like a baby when I saw him coming up that lane. I was that glad to have him home, money or no money."

"I don't know what to tell you, Mom."

"You know Celina, it tore my heart out when Martyn left for the war. He was only nineteen," she lowered her eyes, "a nineteen-year-old who flew more than twenty bombing missions and never came home." Her lip quivered.

"Sometimes I think about his body falling out of the sky over Dresden." Tears spilled over onto her cheeks. "I hope he was already gone by then and didn't know what was happening."

She slapped the towel onto the table. "It's best for you kids to stay close to home. Even if you do end up working for the newspaper, at least we'll be together."

Celina patted her mother's thin shoulder. "I don't know, Mom, there's so little here."

"Well, families should stay together."

"Yes, they should, but people have to work."

The two mused in silence for a while, the sun had set, the night was warm, and the greenies were singing. "Mom, I'm so tired, and I have that interview tomorrow. I need to get some rest. Good night."

Burdened with a sense of responsibility, Celina climbed the stairs to her room.

CHAPTER 9

The next day at noon, Celina crossed the street and stepped up to the screened doors of the *Weekly Messenger* newspaper office. She pulled the door open and entered. The penetrating odor of fresh ink and damp newsprint hit her in the face.

A four-foot-high wooden partition ran the width of the room and served as a barrier, as well as work space. It partially obscured several cluttered army-surplus desks, bulging file cabinets, and an overburdened bulletin board.

Newspaper clippings, typed sheets, and handwritten notes flowed over the bulletin board and found their way, tacked or taped, halfway across the back wall. A red geranium in a cracked, terracotta pot stood sentry over piles of paper clips, rubber bands, and pencil stubs.

Sarah Monahan, whose job Celina was applying for, looked like a female Bob Cratchit sitting at the corner desk and hunched over her work. The rhythmic sound of a well-oiled printing press hummed in another part of the building.

A plumpish man, with his suit jacket removed, sat at the desk closest to the door. His fingers flew over the keys of a

Smith Corona typewriter. After each line, he slammed the carriage back with such force that Celina thought the machine would fly off the desk or fall apart before her eyes.

The man whipped a packet of paper out of the machine, removed three wrinkled sheets of carbon paper used for making copies, and plopped the finished pages into a wire basket. Without looking up, he asked, "Who are you?"

Celina informed the reporter that she had come to speak to Mr. Cherriten about a job. The man stretched, opened and closed his hands several times. "Harry's in back. Have a seat and I'll get him."

The man stood up and jerked his head in the direction of the humming printing press.

"I'm Edgar Cherriten. I'm the business end of this paper."

"Nice to meet you." She waved to Sarah and sat down on one of the heavy wooden chairs that stood against the wall. She tried to see over the partition but it was too high. Only the large clock and the upper portion of the bulletin board, with its river of flowing paper, were visible.

Several editions of the newspaper littered the waiting area. She scanned a back issue. It was much smaller than Sunday's *Pittsburgh Press*. The floppy, half-sized pages contained pictures of family reunions and community events, and news about a local serviceman. She counted two weddings, three births, and a funeral. The police report announced that Bill Mezovsky had been picked up for drunken driving.

She examined the classifieds and noticed that employment opportunities for women filled less than half a column. There were open positions for a secretary, a day girl, and a cleaning lady. Jobs were scarce in Kenville.

She craned her neck and watched the clock's second hand drag itself round the large round face. At last, a middle-aged man with thinning sandy hair and bushy eyebrows burst into the office. The pocket of his green and yellow plaid shirt bulged with a thick-barreled fountain pen and many scraps of paper. He thrust out an ink stained-hand. "Miss Pasniewski, I'm Harry Cherriten."

Standing up, Celina stretched to reach his hand and the outer edge of the divider dug into her upper arm.

He pointed to a saloon-like door at the end of the partition. "Come on around. Call me Harry," he said, after motioning for her to sit down at one of the cluttered desks. He strode back and forth, his skinny arms flailing while he spoke in short, quick bursts. He rambled on about the newspaper business, the fickleness of the reading public, the menace of television news to the print media, and the communist threat. But he asked her very little about her qualifications.

He stopped for breath. "Have you ever seen a printing press in operation?"

"Um, no, I haven't."

The ceiling fan whirred in slow circles above them, the metallic odor of ink on newsprint stifled her breathing, the hum of the printing press filled her ears, and Sarah Monahan sat unmoving at her desk.

"One of these days you'll have to stop by and I'll show you," he jabbed his thumb over his shoulder, "how we operate our press."

Harry Cherriten smiled broadly, shook her hand, and ushered her to the door.

On her way out, Celina ran into Vera Clark, prim and neat in her crisp summer suit, carrying her small briefcase in one gloved hand.

"Celina, did you talk to Mr. Cherriten?"

"Yes, yes I did."

"Well, what do you think?"

"It was very interesting...very informative." She thought about the speed of Harry Cherriten's chatter and how rapidly he moved from subject to subject. She wasn't sure if she had had an interview or not.

Vera smiled. "Harry's one of a kind."

"Yes, yes, he is." Celina's mind was still whirling.

She shook the little briefcase. "Edgar is waiting for these notes." Vera smiled and went inside.

The bright sunlight blinded Celina for a moment. She rushed to the park.

Pattie waved. "How did it go?"

She sat down and sipped tepid root beer. "It was a strange interview. The place was so disorganized, it had a strange smell, and machines rattled and clattered the whole time I was there. And Mr. Cherriten talked a hundred miles an hour. I hardly understood what he said."

"But did you get the job?"

Celina shrugged and shook her head. "I don't know. He didn't say."

"Did he say when he'd let you know?"

"No. He talked about everything else though...the governor, the president, the pope, Linotype machines. And he said he's sick of people complaining about school consolidations. They write letters to him instead of the school board. He told me people have been complaining about the dry weather for weeks." She smiled. "He got real huffy when he said 'they act like I can do something about it.' But he didn't say a word about calling me or giving me the job."

Pattie bit into an apple. "That's weird." She scuffed the dirt with her foot. "I wonder if he has more than one job open."

"I should have asked, but he was talking faster than Uncle Vicktor does when he's all riled up about politics."

"He must be some talker."

Squirrels chased each other around the trees, and a breeze tugged at the waxed-paper-wrapped sandwich on Celina's lap.

"I hope we won't be working at Duxbury's for the rest of our lives," Pattie said.

"There's still the bank, Smith's Ladies Wear, and Woolworth's."

"Yeah. The bank's the best choice."

Pattie eyed her wristwatch. "It's time to go back to the dungeon."

Celina returned her belongings to the cloakroom and took her place behind the counter. She watched mothers carrying squirming babies or shepherding older children into the store. Rambunctious little boys ran their sticky fingers over the clean glass cases. Little girls wandered between the racks, touching the crisp cotton dresses and examining the contents of each pencil box filled with rainbow-colored notepads, erasers, and pencils.

Mrs. Pinkerton folded her arms across her ample, white-bloused bosom and shot stern looks at any child who crossed the line of civility. She walked up to the offenders and stared down her nose and over her bosom at them until they slunk back to their mothers' sides.

"Mrs. Pinkerton can scare the wits out of the worst kid," Celina whispered.

Pattie laughed softly. "She used to follow my brother around every time we came in here. He was such a brat."

Somewhere nearby, someone cleared his throat. Celina located the source of the cough. Earl stood near the Woolrich coat rack, mouth puckered, rocking from heel to toe and cradling the clipboard in one arm. She rolled her eyes and Pattie marched back to Men's Attire.

At the end of a long day, Harold pushed the accumulation of dust bunnies around with his broom, Celina and Pattie used ammonia to clean finger marks from the glass cases, and Mrs. Pinkerton, back at her position in house wares, finished ringing up the day's last purchase of two galvanized watering cans and a cast iron skillet.

When the last customer stepped out onto the sidewalk, the older woman followed him to the door, pulled it closed, and turned the heavy key in the lock. In a synchronized motion, Harold at the other end of the building closed the door, locked it, and pulled the shade over the glass. With the customers gone, the little group congratulated each other on how well they had managed the day.

Harold addressed Mrs. Pinkerton. "For a minute there, I thought you'd have to grab that Miller kid by the scruff of the neck and toss him out in the street."

"Harold, I was a school teacher before I married Mr. Pinkerton. And I can still do the teacher's glare with the best of them."

"Sure looks that way. That kid shriveled up three sizes before he went running back to his mama. You musta been a good teacher."

She accepted his compliment. "Thank you, Harold."

Pattie and Celina made their way to the cloak room. "Did you know Mrs. Pinkerton was a school teacher in the old days?"

"No. Did you?" Celina reached for her purse.

"No. And I'm glad she didn't work at our school. Can you imagine her looking over that chest at you all day long?"

Sam called out that it was time for everybody to get their pay envelopes. He marched to the office.

"I sold sixteen pair of boys' shoes, and I can't tell you how many socks this week," Pattie commented.

Celina shrugged. "With school starting and hunting season coming up, we'll be busy for a while."

"Hey Sam," Harold said, "you get your huntin' license yet?"

"Yeah, picked it up last Saturday." Sam raised his hands, holding an invisible shotgun, aimed, and pulled an invisible trigger. "Pow. Can't wait to get them dogs out. I'm ready for some fried rabbit. The old woman makes it so tender it falls off the bones."

"Squirrel's better. Got a better taste."

"I say rabbit's better."

Harold looked at the three women. "We need ta take a vote. Okay ladies, what do you say, rabbit or squirrel? So far we got one rabbit and one squirrel."

"Mrs. Pinkerton?"

"I like rabbit."

"Pattie?"

"Rabbit."

"Celina?"

"Squirrel."

Sam's smug grin revealed yellow, tobacco stained teeth. "Hah, rabbit wins."

"You don't know what's good. Hain't that right, Celina?"

"I'm with you, Harold. Squirrel tastes better especially when it's fried in butter. It's even better left over and cold after supper."

"Hey, my mouth is waterin' just thinking about it." Sam rubbed his hands together. "And all we're havin' tonight is hot dogs and beans."

"It's Friday and I have to eat fish." Pattie chimed in.

"Not me, I'm Methodist," Harold said.

Earl opened the door and stepped out of the office. "Mr. Duxbury has your pay envelopes. Go on in, Mrs. Pinkerton."

One by one they trooped into the office and back out again. Focused on counting their money, they wandered toward the door. Celina was last as usual. Pattie waved the latest issue of her favorite romance magazine. "I'm going out to the car and get started on this issue. See you in the parking lot."

The well-appointed office smelled of alcohol; it brought back memories of the times when Celina was very young and the Friday nights her father had come home drunk, though he hadn't done that for many years. She recoiled at the odor. The red velvet armchair near the door still held the stack of ledgers she had piled on it during Earl's mandated cleaning spree. The blotter on the large oak desk lay tattered and marked with ink stains. Mr. Duxbury stood behind his desk and held the last small manila pay envelope in one hand and a ten dollar bill in the other. "Do you remember that raise I mentioned a few weeks ago?"

Celina nodded. "Yes."

"Do you want to talk about a raise?" His thick neck reddened and he shifted his weight from one small foot to the other.

"Well sure, all of us would like a raise."

The diamond in his gold ring winked in the afternoon light as he leaned both hands on the desk. "We're talking about you." He straightened up, folded the ten. "I could put one of these in your pay envelope every week."

He wiped his perspiring face, swallowed hard, and his eyes

darted around the room.

Celina glanced toward the half-open door. "Is everyone getting a raise?"

"No, I said we're talking about you."

"It seems like an awful lot of money."

The late afternoon heat took its toll, and a trickle of sweat dripped off his chin. "Not if you earn it." Still clutching the bill, he smiled and held the envelope out to her. "How about it?"

"I asked Earl about a promotion a couple of weeks ago, since I'm helping him with the invoices and records. He said the added responsibility was part of my job as clerk." She waited for his response, and she chastised herself for standing there like a scared child.

He grinned. "You know that only men hold supervisory positions." The grin faded from his face. "And you know that's not what I was talking about."

She knew, and backed up a step. *My God, what's he going to do?* "My family is waiting for me. I'd like to take my pay envelope and go home."

He held the envelope out to her. When she reached for it, he lunged across the desk and grabbed her arm. She tried to pull free, but his fingers dug in.

Still clutching her arm, he came round the desk. "You know what I'm trying to say, don't you? You know, don't you?"

She lied. "No, I don't." Her heart thumped, and she tried to twist free. "Let go."

His grip tightened and he pulled her closer.

He pulled her to within an inch of his flushed face. His chest heaved. His breath spread over her averted face, and she felt like she was going to gag. "If you're nice, you could earn extra money and pretty things, too." He cooed and his grasp tightened. "Wouldn't you like that?"

Fear gripped her. *How am I going to get out of here?* "Let me go." She pushed against him and tried to get away.

His fingers dug deeper into her arm. Celina blinked back tears of pain in a desperate attempt to keep him from knowing how scared she was. Each second was an eternity of dread. He maneuvered past the desk and thrust her against the paneled wall. A painting in a gilded frame clattered to the floor. He snarled. "I thought you were so inexperienced, so naive. But you're no innocent girl, are you?" He shook her. "Are you?"

At first Celina managed to dodge his wet panting mouth and crude attempts to kiss her. He pinned her against the wall as she struggled, and pressed himself against her. She could feel the bulge in his pants against her stomach. "I've been watching you." He pressed harder.

Her arms ached. Between compressed lips she hissed. "Let me go." Her fear was transforming itself into a primal struggle to extricate herself from danger.

With one hand he grabbed her face, grunted and a flaccid wet mouth clamped onto hers. She clenched her teeth, but he pried her mouth open and pushed his slippery tongue inside.

Celina gagged. *God, help me, please, please.* He fumbled with her blouse tearing several buttons off and tugging at her bra. With his full weight against her, he pulled up her skirt and pushed his hand between her legs. She screamed, "No!"

He clamped one hand over her mouth, muffling screams of fear and rage. Celina squirmed, twisted, and kicked. His weight was too much and as he dragged her to the floor; he fumbled with her garters and yanked at her panties. She fought and freed both hands then pushed hard against his chest, and he reeled back for an instant. She jumped up and darted for the door, but he caught her skirt. She kicked and yelled, "Get off!"

The office door creaked and swung open.

White faced and slack jawed, Harold stood there. After a long silent moment, he spoke. "I didn't see nothin', and I don't know nothin'."

Framed by the light behind him, the unwilling witness fell silent. Grover C. Duxbury struggled to his feet. Celina rushed to put the desk between herself and Duxbury.

"I was in the cellar lockin' up and heard a commotion." Harold pointed to the gold framed picture on the floor.

Celina kept her eyes on Duxbury and backed away from the desk. "I'll just wait," Harold said, pointing to the main floor, "out there in the store till everybody's outta the building." He pushed the door wide open, looked back over his shoulder, and stepped a few feet away.

Celina grabbed her pay envelope from the desktop.

Spraying spittle, Duxbury jeered. "Who do you think you are? You damned cheap hunky bitch?"

She scowled and tucked her blouse back into her skirt. "Go to hell."

"Whore."

The word stung; and tears pricked her eyes, but her disgust and anger held them at bay. On her way out, she took a neatly ironed hankie from her skirt pocket and wiped her mouth and tongue. She turned, threw the crumpled piece of cloth onto the desk, and left the room.

Harold held his cap. "Night Celina," he said.

"Night Harold. Thanks."

"Nothin' to thank me for."

"Yeah." *Thank you, God. Thank you, Harold.*

Celina rushed down the steps and out the back entrance. She looked down at her hand clutching the pay envelope and saw the ten-dollar bill protruding above the folded flap. Rage welled up. Outside in the sun, she tore the bill to shreds and hurled it against Duxbury's black Cadillac. "Pig. Rotten, stinking, pervert pig."

A heartbeat later, all the inner energy at her command drained away. She felt weak and wobbly, and her knees almost buckled. When she reached her car, her entire body trembled.

Pattie sat behind the wheel of her dad's Chevy, engrossed in the romance magazine. Folding the corner of a page down she looked up. "You know that I've been waiting here a good ten minutes. Where— Oh my God, Celina. What's the matter? You're white as a ghost. Your blouse." Pattie jumped out of the car. "You're shaking like a leaf."

Trembling, Celina took Pattie's place on the car seat. Her chin quivered. Her eyes filled with tears, and she blinked hard. *I'm stronger than this. I will not let myself cry. I can't.* Pattie touched her shoulder. "You're scaring me. Tell me, what's the matter?"

Celina clutched her midsection, doubled over, and bit her lower lip. "In a minute."

Harold, his head bowed, scurried to his truck. He didn't wave like usual. "What's the matter with Harold?"

In the window above them, Celina saw the sun glint off the diamond in Duxbury's ring as he ran his hands over his sparse gray hair. "Duxbury," she croaked.

Pattie looked up. Her eyes widened and her mouth dropped open. "Oh God, what'd he do?" Pattie grabbed Celina's arm and she winced. "Tell me."

Celina's chin quivered and she blinked harder. Her head

throbbed.

Pattie knelt next to the car, struggling to remain calm. "Now tell me, did he…did he…rape you?"

She shook her head. "No."

"Oh *Boga*, thank God." Pattie's forehead rested on the edge of the seat. "Can you tell me what happened?"

"He grabbed me when I reached for my pay envelope. I fought as hard as I could. But I couldn't get him off me."

She put her hands over her face. "I was so scared. Harold walked in, said he heard a commotion, and…and I got away."

Pattie looked up at the now empty window. "That rotten dirty old pervert bastard."

She patted Celina's shoulder. "It's okay. It's okay. I'm here."

The trembling continued. Celina drew a long shaky breath. "I never thought he'd do something like that." Her body shuddered. "How could he do that?"

"You never know what's going on inside some people's head. You okay?" Pattie squeezed her hand.

"Yeah."

Celina blinked, but that didn't stop two large tears from rolling down her cheeks. "He called me a hunky bitch and a whore."

Pattie's face turned to stone. "Lousy stinking john-bull thinks just because he's rich and wears a suit to work, he can hurt you and call you ugly names." She smoothed Celina's hair. "Are you going to tell your mom and dad?"

Celina's pallid face drained of all color. "Oh, God. No. I can't." She shivered. "My mom would die of shame, and God only knows what my dad would do."

A moment of silence followed. Pattie sighed. "Yeah, it's best not to say anything."

"I've got to go home and act like nothing happened."

"You need some time to calm down first."

Pattie thought for a moment. "I know. We'll go to my house. It's Friday and your mom doesn't have anything for you to do. I'll give you one of my blouses, and you can comb your hair, rest, and have a cup of tea. Mom will be making supper and Dad will have his nose in the paper, so they won't notice anything."

"Yeah. Okay."

"I'll call your mom and tell her where you are. Okay?"

"Sure."

#

Celina sat in the Harchaks' dining room sipping tea from a small porcelain cup.

Pattie tapped her on the hand. "Um, look at your arm," she whispered.

She inspected the purple spots the size of quarters that stood out against her tanned skin. "Aw, Jesus."

Pattie pursed her lips. "Let me think, let me think. Grab your tea and let's go upstairs."

Celina followed her friend and thought about what happened. *I tried, really tried to avoid Duxbury. I was always polite and reserved, never gave him a reason to think I was interested in him. Could he have attacked me because I asked Earl for a better job title, and a raise? No, that doesn't make any sense.* She shook her head and couldn't imagine how that could have caused Duxbury to act the way he did. She asked herself over and over again. Why did he do it? Why?

The two of them tiptoed past Mr. Harchak dozing behind his newspaper, and they ascended the carpeted stairway.

Once in the bedroom with its canopy bed, ruffled curtains, and girlish wallpaper, Pattie went straight to the bottom drawer of the dresser and retrieved a bottle of liquid tan cover up.

"It's a good thing I never throw anything away." She smoothed and feathered the flesh-toned liquid onto Celina's bruises to conceal them. "I knew being a majorette would come in handy for something, someday." Pattie leaned back and asked. "How'd you get the bruises?"

Celina rushed through the story. Duxbury had clamped onto her arm with his meaty hand and held even tighter when she tried to break free. Telling Pattie about the ten dollars, he had offered her, made her shake with indignation.

"Are you going back there?"

"I'll have to. Mom and Dad will start asking questions if I stay home."

"Well, I'll be right there with you. I won't let you out of my sight, not for a minute. We'll even go to the bathroom together."

In spite of her pain and humiliation, Celina laughed and hugged her dearest friend. "You're a good person, Pattie Harchak."

Returning the hug, Pattie patted Celina's back then suddenly sat bolt upright. "Oh, *Boga*, are you going to tell Steve? I mean Stephen."

Fear gnawed at Celina's stomach. "I can't tell him."

"If you're serious about him, you probably should. He's bound to notice something's wrong and ask about it."

"But I can't tell him something like that. What if…"

Pattie raised her hands in a sympathetic gesture. "I know what you're going to say, but I know he's not going to blame you. You've got to trust him."

"I trust him. But it's just that this is such an awful thing to talk about." A wave of dread passed through her. "I can't just say, 'guess what happened today?' and tell him."

Pattie lowered her eyes. "It won't be easy, but you should." She clucked. "I mean, you don't have to say it that way, but you need to tell him."

"I don't want to."

"All right. But I think you should."

"I know you're trying to help, and I do appreciate it." Celina looked at her watch. "He's coming at seven. I need to go home and scrub myself clean before I see him."

"Okay. Johnny and I will meet you at the movies." Pattie peeked in the mirror. "I can't wait to see if Piper Laurie's hair is the same color as mine."

"Pattie, you're crazy."

The little redhead patted her hair and stared into the oval mirror above the bureau. "I like red hair, that's all."

As they walked to Celina's car, Pattie patted her shoulder. "Do you have the liquid tan?"

"Yeah, it's right here."

"Okay, we'll see you later then. Do you think you'll want to stop at that pizza place?

It's the newest thing. It'll be fun."

"Yeah. I won't be able to eat anything, and it'll give me an excuse not to eat at home. If Mom thinks we're stopping someplace, she won't badger me about it."

At seven o'clock, Stephen pulled up to the house and knocked on the back door.

Marian and Tomas sat at the kitchen table sipping coffee.

Celina opened the door and introduced him to her parents. Tomas, in his stocking feet, stood up and reached out to shake his hand. "So this is the fella who my daughter has her eye on, huh?"

"Dad!"

"What?"

Marian chimed in. "We're glad to see you, Stephen. I guess you two are going to watch a Piper Laurie movie with Johnny and Pattie."

"So it seems," Stephen replied. "She's Pattie's favorite actress."

Tomas tapped his scalp with a gnarled finger. "It's the hair. That girl thinks she looks good in red hair. God knows why. She's a little flighty, if you know what I mean." He held out his hand and wobbled it like a shaky bird flying through the air.

With force, Celina cut in. She refused to listen to anyone, even her dad, showing disrespect to the friend who had comforted her. "Pattie's a good person and is always there when someone needs her."

"I said she was flighty, that's all."

"Well, it sounded like you were ridiculing her."

"Cripes. You're touchy tonight."

Impatient, she looked at her watch. "We'd better go or we'll miss the beginning of the movie."

She avoided the questioning look in Stephen's eyes as they left the house.

"Is something bothering you? You are in a bad mood."

"I'm okay."

"Want to talk about anything?"

"No."

"Are you sure?"

"Yes."

During the movie, Celina replayed the incident in Duxbury's office in her mind. *Why did he do it? Why?* Her face flushed red with anger when she thought about the names he had called her. Hunky. Whore. Bitch. Again and again, she examined her own behavior, and although she knew he watched her from behind the office door, she could not recall a single occasion when she might have given him the wrong impression. She wondered if Duxbury was jealous because of her interest in Stephen. *I am absolutely positive that I never even once gave him a reason to think I was interested in him, and the thought of him touching me makes my skin crawl. But what else could it be?* Filing out of the theater, she tried to shake the incident from her mind.

#

They trooped into the Pizza Parlor. The restaurant sported mottled gold walls, small red topped tables, and black wrought-iron chairs. They ordered a plain pizza pie and soft drinks, from the kid at the counter.

A dark-haired young man, wrapped in a flour-covered apron, brought the pizza pie and a handful of paper napkins to their table. Before taking a sip of her coke, Pattie examined the circle of baked dough, tomato sauce, and melted cheese. She lifted the corner of a piece and wrinkled her nose. "How do we eat this? There's no fork."

The kid smiled and wiped his hands on his dusty apron. "Slide a wedge onto a napkin, and hold it so," he pantomimed holding a slice, "and bite into it starting at the point."

Each of them took a piece and bit into the steaming slices.

"It's different. I like it," Celina marveled. Strings of cheese stuck to the napkin, and tomato sauce soaked through it. "Sort of messy, though."

Pattie wrestled with a slice, turning it every which way trying to get a good spot. "Hey, Red, it's going to get away if you don't take a bite," Johnny said.

"I don't want to smear my lipstick."

"You'd be beautiful with no lipstick at all."

"Aw, Johnny." She blushed and took a bite. "Hey, this is good." She swallowed. "It tastes better than it smells."

Stephen sat back and observed Celina "You aren't eating much, and your mom said you didn't have dinner."

"Yeah, Missy, aren't you hungry?" Johnny asked.

Pattie shot Celina a quick look.

"I have to watch my girlish figure, you know. Piper Laurie is real competition."

"Well, you'd better eat something, or else I'll let Mom know you're skipping meals."

"Quit it, Johnny. If she doesn't want to eat, she doesn't have to," Pattie said.

Surprise crossed his face, and Pattie back peddled. "Well, it's just that women don't like to be told what to eat."

"I was just teasing."

"Let it drop, okay? I'm not hungry, that's all," Celina said.

Stephen quietly watched the little exchange.

On their way home, he pulled off the road near the abandoned tipple. He reached over to take her in his arms. She winced.

"Why did you draw back?"

"I didn't."

He ran his hand over her upper arm, and she flinched. "Don't you want me to touch you?"

"Of course, I do. My arm is just a little sore, that's all."

He stroked her arm. "I can't see anything. Did you hurt yourself?"

The liquid tan had done a good job of covering up the bruises. She searched her mind for an answer.

"You've been irritable all evening. Tell me what's going on."

She was silent.

"Are you afraid to tell me?"

She nodded.

"Did you wreck your dad's car?"

She almost choked but managed a wan smile. "No. If I did that, you'd have heard him yelling all the way down to the main road."

"Celina, come on."

He held her close and kissed her forehead. He twirled a lock of her hair around his finger. "You know you can tell me anything, don't you?"

Tears welled up and she nodded. "Um-hum."

"Then what's holding you back?"

Her chin quivered. "It's so hard to talk about."

"You don't have to look at me while you're talking if you don't want to."

She turned her face to the window. "Okay."

"Now tell me."

With Stephen's encouragement, Celina recounted what had happened in Duxbury's office. How she had gone in for her pay envelope. How he grabbed her arm and the struggle that followed. She related everything that happened until Harold, with head bowed, hurried past her and Pattie in the parking area.

When she finished, Stephen's face was chiseled stone. He

drew her close and she curled up against him.

His hand rested on her hair.

"Do you think I'm an awful person?"

"My God, why would you ask that?"

"People always think it's the girl's fault."

"You don't believe that, do you?"

"But it's what people think."

He scowled. "It's not your fault. And we need to report this to the police."

"No! My parents can't find out. My mother would be humiliated, and my dad would end up either killing him or killing me. It would be nothing but trouble."

Anxious, she pulled back and continued. "Everybody would gossip. Besides, who would believe me? I'm only second generation. My grandmother can't read or write English, and my dad's a coal miner with a sixth-grade education. People would side with the businessman who went to college, drives a big Cadillac, and whose family has been here forever." She shook her head. "No. No I don't want the police."

"Wouldn't Harold stand by you?"

"No, he wouldn't. He said he didn't see anything and didn't know anything. Look, Harold has a wife and kids to support. He doesn't want to be dragged into something like that. He'd never get a job anyplace in town if he spoke up for me against somebody like Duxbury."

"I thought America was the country of justice for all."

"There's a lot more justice for people like Duxbury."

"Then I'll take care of it."

"No. I don't want you or my family involved."

CHAPTER 10

Monday morning dawned bright and sunny, but Celina was filled with a dark dread at the prospect of facing Duxbury. In front of the mirror, she pinned her hair back and tried to muster up courage she did not feel. *I'm tougher than this. I have to go in there and act like nothing happened.* She slipped into her shoes and trudged down the stairs to the kitchen where Marian stood at the cook stove. "You want an egg before I shut the damper?"

"Naw, I'm not hungry"

"Coffee?"

"No. Not this morning."

"Your color's off. Is it time for your period?"

"No."

Marian crossed the kitchen, reached out and felt Celina's clammy forehead. "Are you sick? Maybe you should stay home."

"I'm okay. It's just that the stove makes it so stinking hot in here."

"I know. There's some secondhand electric ranges at the furniture store, I should go and look at them."

"Yeah." Celina checked her watch. "It's time to go."

When she reached the traffic light at the corner, she noticed Pattie shifting from one foot to the other while waiting in the parking lot behind Duxbury's. The sun glinted off her red hair, and she shaded her eyes with her pocketbook.

As Celina stepped out of her car, she looked up at the office window. A sick feeling settled in her stomach, and she clenched her teeth until they felt like they were ready to crumble. "Well, I guess it's time to go in."

"It'll be okay, you'll see."

"But I just have to show him I'm not scared." *Even though I my head throbs, and my stomach is sick.* "I feel like I'm going to vomit."

"You'll be okay. I'm right here."

Celina entered through the back door and into Duxbury's territory. The close air in the basement seemed mustier, the distance between the door and the stairs longer, and the steps steeper.

Pattie, her red head bobbing, marched in lockstep. They climbed the stairs and crossed the main floor. After they stowed their purses and lunches in the cloakroom, Celina smoothed the frown from her forehead. "Okay, I'm ready."

"Me too."

Mrs. Pinkerton stared at Celina's tight face. "Morning, Celina. Morning, Pattie."

I wonder if Harold blabbed.

Harold came in after sweeping the sidewalk. Head lowered, he looked up through the frayed edges of his cap. "Mornin', ladies," he said and hastened to the basement door.

Sam, carrying a stack of galvanized milk pails, scampered past them. "Mornin'."

"Morning, Sam."

He dropped the pails behind the counter and several of the milk buckets rolled across the floor. He scurried after them, looked up from his task. "Hey, you two got your dancin' shoes polished for the big wedding?"

Pattie smiled. "You know it."

"Me and the missus got an invite. She got towels for a wedding present, yellow ones with flowers."

A wave of relief washed over Celina. Sam was just being Sam.

People drifted in and out of the store. Shirley Wilson, her hair in pin curls, waved. She ordered canning supplies from Mrs. Pinkerton, and on her way out, stopped to chat. "Morning, Celina."

"Morning, Shirl. How are you doing?"

She patted her bobby-pin covered head. "I didn't have time to take my hair down and comb it this morning. Before Bart went to work, he said I had to order more canning jars because we got so many hot peppers this year. You know how coal miners love eatin' those things."

"Yeah. They are good."

"Well, I had better get going before anybody sees me with my hair up. Bye."

Around ten o'clock, three mothers with eleven children between them entered. They shepherded the youngsters in Celina's direction. She helped the chatty women hold up plaid cotton dresses with eyelet trim in front of the giggling girls.

The boys played cowboys. They ducked between the racks of dresses and skirts. Invisible guns popped and invisible bullets whizzed by.

Mrs. Pinkerton stood sentry. Her frown assured the grown-ups that neither the sheriff nor the posse would get out of hand. She made sure the boys' prying little eyes stayed away from women's intimate apparel.

With their dress buying completed, the girls carried paper bags containing their first- day-of-school purchases. All eleven children congregated around the "School Days" display, and each one chose a pencil box even though classes would not start till after Labor Day. The smiling mothers shooed the children toward Men's and Boys' Attire.

Half an hour later, Pattie, frazzled and tired, ushered the brood to the exit and returned to her station. During a lull, she looked to Celina. "I don't think I want more than three kids," she announced.

At lunchtime, they sat under the oak tree in the park. "Do you think Duxbury will show up today?"

A spasm clutched at Celina's stomach. "I hope so. As much as I dread it, I want to see him and get it over with. Otherwise, I'll be worrying till tomorrow or till whenever he finally comes in."

"I guess I can understand how you feel. If you have to get a tooth pulled, you might as well get it over with."

Tight-lipped, Celina smiled.

Late Tuesday afternoon, Duxbury entered the store and dashed to his office. He looked neither right nor left. His clothes were in disarray, the white shirt was yellowed with perspiration and spotted with stains, and one scuffed shoe was untied. Greasy strands of gray hair stuck to the back of his head. He had a black eye.

A minute later his wife, Marge, marched in. She wore a fresh white skirt and yellow pullover and carried a straw purse. Not a hair out of place. Celina watched her strut to the office, the heels of her wedges clattering like castanets against the oak floor. At the office door, she turned and scanned the employees who stood watching her. She glared when her eyes rested on Celina.

Earl rushed to Marge's side and she squawked. "Every time I come in here, those…those people are standing around. Don't they ever work?"

He followed her into the office and closed the door. The sound of muffled voices rose and fell. Mrs. Pinkerton wandered past the door several times.

In an instant, Pattie was at Celina's side. "Did you see how awful he looked?"

Celina had seen him all right. He was a loathsome sight and she had not a drop of compassion for him. Today, she didn't want to vomit. She wanted to pummel him into oblivion. She wanted to kick, and scratch, and punch, and give him another black eye. She wanted to give Marge a black eye for good measure.

"You all right?"

Her fists clenched. "I'm a little shaky, but today I'm ready for him." She patted her hip. "I have one of my dad's hunting knives in my skirt pocket."

"What are you carrying that thing for? You could stab yourself."

Celina almost laughed. "You sound more like my mother all the time."

"Well, you could. You know I won't let you out of my sight."

"I know, but I want to be ready in case he comes at me again and the knife makes me feel safer."

"Jeez, Celina."

At that moment, Earl slid out of the office and whispered a few words to Mrs. Pinkerton and Harold. He ran a bony hand across his face and reentered the office.

A few seconds later, Mrs. Pinkerton joined Celina and Pattie. She cleared her throat and spoke. "Since Harold and I are the senior employees, in the future neither he nor I will leave the store until the rest of you are off the premises." She crossed her arms. "It's a modern business practice, you know."

Celina held her breath.

Pattie nodded. "Hmm, yes, business."

"Yes, indeed." The most senior employee turned and strode back to house wares, where she busied herself dusting off butter churns and canning supplies.

"She must know more than we thought," Pattie whispered.

Exhausted at the end of the day, Celina wanted nothing more than to go home and feel safe with the people she trusted and loved.

"What do you think was going on in that office all afternoon?" Pattie asked as she rolled open her car window.

"I'm not sure, but I've never seen so many Duxburys in this place before. When you were in the restroom, both of his sons came in and went straight to the office. They have to know what happened."

"Yeah, it's been like a beehive in there all day."

Celina scrutinized the office window. "I wish I were out of that place."

"You'll get a job, you'll see." Pattie reached into the back seat of her car and came out with a small brown bag. "Here's an extra bottle of liquid tan in case you need it."

"Thanks, the marks are getting easier to cover up. They're

starting to turn green and yellow. See you tomorrow."

#

The next morning, when Celina climbed out of her car, Pattie was waiting for her. *Good old Pattie. She's a real friend.*

Pattie bolted up to her. "Celina, I have something to tell you."

"What?"

"The night before Duxbury came into the store looking so bad. That would have been Monday night. He was at an after-hours bar over in Dubois. Stephen found out where he was and went in there looking for him."

Celina's face blanched and her stomach turned over. She put her hand to her mouth. "Oh, *Boga, Boga.*" She did not want either Stephen or her family involved.

"It gets better," Pattie continued. "I guess Stephen followed him outside, grabbed him by the front of his shirt, and pushed him up against that black Caddie of his so hard that Duxbury's feet weren't even on the ground. He roughed him up a little bit and nearly scared him to death. That must be how he got the black eye."

Pattie sighed with satisfaction and brushed her hands together. "That old pig won't bother you anymore. "But don't worry, I'm still going to keep my eye on you all the time."

"I can't believe it." Celina's throat constricted and her stomach cramped.

"Well, it's true. Johnny was with him."

"You told Johnny. Why?"

"I had to tell him. He is your brother and has the right to know when something's wrong."

"Aw, Jesus, Pattie." She didn't want either Stephen or Johnny getting into trouble.

"What's the matter?"

"You don't seem to realize that they could get picked up by the police."

Pattie guffawed. "They won't. If Duxbury says anything, the cops could put him in jail. What he did to you is a crime in this country, you know."

"But I don't want them taking that kind of risk, and I sure don't want my mom and dad to find out."

"You worry too much." Pattie glanced around, lowered her voice, and spoke from the corner of her mouth. "You saw how Duxbury's wife struts around with her nose in the air like she's better than everybody else. Acts like her you-know-what doesn't stink. I bet she'd divorce him if he made her look bad."

Pattie pointed her nose to the heavens and waved an invisible hankie. "Then, of course, she'd take him for all he's got. So, you see, he won't say anything."

Celina was unconvinced. "But Stephen's not a citizen yet. He could be deported." Tears filled her eyes. The strain of forcing herself to stay calm and pretending nothing had happened was taking its toll. Impotent anger swirled inside her. "He should have stayed out of it."

Pattie would have none of it. "You're too upset to think straight. He didn't commit a crime. Nobody else saw. All he did is bump into some fat guy in a parking lot. I'm telling you, don't worry."

"Why didn't he tell me first?"

"Because you'd have tried to talk him out of it."

Her friend was right. But she wanted to deal with what happened in her own way.

"He did it to protect you."

"I understand that," Celina said, annoyed and trembling. "And it means a lot to me that he took that kind of chance. But I don't want him taking risks like that. And I wish I could give him a good talking-to right this minute."

What she wanted to do was scratch Duxbury's eyes out, scream at Pattie, and tell Stephen to butt out. Instead, she sucked in some air, turned and entered the store's back door, marched through the basement and up the stairs to the cloak room. At that moment, she had the most god-awful headache of her life.

Late that morning, Pattie sidled up to her. "You still mad?"

"I was more worried than mad."

Pattie looked toward the door. "Well, here he comes."

Celina's stomach cramped. She glared in Duxbury's direction as he walked past. On this day, except for the black eye, he looked as he always had, carrying his jacket, wearing his starched white shirt and polished wing tips. He lumbered through the store, went to his office, and pushed the door shut.

Earl appeared and snapped. "Get to work. Everyone get to work."

Pattie gave Celina a knowing look then ambled back to the men's department.

Her stomach still churning, Celina grabbed the cleaning rag from the shelf beneath the cash register. She busied herself wiping away the miniature handprints adorning the fronts of all the display cases.

Halfway through the chore, she looked up. Five well-behaved children filed through the Main Street entrance, followed by a very thin woman. Celina recognized Libby

Mezovsky in a too-large dress; it was one that Ellen had donated to St. Hedwig's a few weeks earlier. Thin brown hair streaked with gray fell in limp wisps from the ponytail at the nape of her neck. Like a mother hen, Libby clucked quietly, steering the young ones through the store.

The little brood stopped in Men's Wear. Libby's bony hands held blue jeans and striped polo shirts up for inspection. The three boys shuffled around nearby. Celina watched as Pattie helped them try on many pairs of shoes. Libby did much foot squeezing for size, and the kids admired their feet in front of a mirror. Each child had been fitted with new school shoes.

The girls wandered over to the Women's Attire and fingered the crisp cotton dresses with the eyelet collars. They pointed and pleaded, but Libby purchased socks.

The kids spotted the stack of pencil boxes. The girls oohed and aahed over the rainbow of colored paper. This time all five tugged at their mother; they whispered urgently, pointing to one or another of the cardboard cases. Libby's gaunt face flushed red. She pointed to the door and ordered all five out. Still pleading and with tears in their eyes, they filed out onto the sunny street.

Mrs. Pinkerton stepped up to Celina. "That poor woman, her man is nothing but a no-good drunk." She sniffed. "She has all those children and you can be sure none of them will ever amount to anything. Couldn't even afford thirty-nine cent pencil boxes. It's a shame, that's what it is. That good-for-nothing man of hers should be tarred and feathered."

Celina watched Libby follow her scuffling brood till they were out of sight. *Boga. Why does she have to live like that? The church gives them clothes, and a basket of food at Christmas, but what else can be done? Bill should be taken out and shot.*

"I hope you're wrong about those kids, Mrs. Pinkerton. They deserve a chance at life, too."

For a brief time, Celina forgot all about Duxbury. She purchased five sets of school supplies. *I'll get these wrapped and put them in the mail with no return address. They'll get them in plenty of time for the first day of school.*

#

A dark shadow of anxiety followed her for days. When she wasn't waiting on customers, Celina worried about Stephen. She watched and listened for any odd signs of trouble, terrified that the county sheriff might pay a visit, but all was quiet. And Duxbury either stayed away from the store or spent his time behind closed doors.

A week passed and she decided to return Tomas' hunting knife to its rightful place in the closet under the stairs. She opened the door and the odor of mothballs bounded out.

Inside, it clung to the coats and scarves stored for winter use. Celina climbed over the steamer trunk, the one that sailed across the Atlantic with Baba when she came from Poland. She placed Tomas' knife in the pocket of his Woolrich jacket, backed out of the closet, and closed the door.

That evening Stephen called, and they made plans for the weekend. Celina said nothing about the information Pattie had given her.

#

On Friday Earl made an announcement. "The boss has gone to Philadelphia on a buying trip." Once again, Earl himself would shoulder the responsibility for the wellbeing of the store and its employees.

Celina hoped Duxbury would stay in Philadelphia for about ten years.

Mrs. Pinkerton strode up to her and whispered. "You remember when I mentioned that Mr. Duxbury hasn't been himself for a long time."

"Yes."

"There is a reason for it." The older woman cleared her throat. "Earl told me that he isn't really on a buying trip. He's gone to a place for people who," she glanced around the room and whispered quieter, "have a disease from drinking too much."

"Alcoholism?"

Mr. Pinkerton held her finger to her lips. "Shh," she whispered. "Yes."

Celina whispered back. "Will he be gone a long time?"

"I don't know."

Mrs. Pinkerton continued to whisper. "His wife made the arrangements." She lowered her voice further. "It's a sickness that makes them do things out of character."

Mrs. Pinkerton cast her eyes around the empty store. "A strange sickness."

It struck Celina that it was the same kind of strange sickness that Bill Mezovsky had, but everybody wanted Bill either shot or tarred and feathered.

Driving home, she noticed purple ironweed and feathery goldenrod blooming along the road, the first signs of autumn. *I don't care if Duxbury had a sickness or not. I'm glad he's gone. And I hope he never comes back.*

That night at the drive-in theater, glad to feel safe and protected, she nestled in Stephen's arms. She told him about

Duxbury's sudden decision to go to a hospital for alcoholics. He rested his cheek on the top of her head and said nothing.

Now that Duxbury was gone, she overcame her fears for Stephen and Johnny. She pulled back and looked at him. "Why didn't you tell me about you and Johnny going to Dubois?"

"Um, how did you find out about that?"

"Pattie told me a couple of days ago."

"That woman! I knew Johnny shouldn't have told her. She couldn't keep quiet to save her life."

"I wish you had told me."

"You were still so scared that I didn't want you having more to worry about. Besides I couldn't let him get away with what he did. I had to do something. It was the only way I could look out for you and keep the police out of it." He held both her hands. "You aren't angry, are you?"

"I've been too scared to be angry. I was worried you'd get into some kind of trouble…get deported or something."

Again he held her close. "You aren't supposed to be worrying about me." He kissed the top of her head. "I had to be sure Duxbury knew that he would have me to answer to if he ever approached you again."

"Weren't you at least a little worried that you'd get into trouble?"

"No. I wasn't going to let someone hurt you and get away with it, because I love you and want to protect you."

Tears stung Celina's eyes. It meant so much that he took a risk like that for her. She murmured against his cheek. "I love you. I love you so much."

Stephen's mouth covered hers with deep, lingering kisses.

A loud rat-tat-tat sounded on the roof of the car. They both jumped. Stephen grinned. "Oh no."

Pattie and Johnny stood beside the car smiling like two mischievous kids. They carried popcorn and soda pop. Stephen reached over and rolled the window down. "What do you two want?"

Johnny stuck an arm into the car. "Popcorn? Or do you have more important things going on?"

Pattie batted her eyes. "We're parked right behind you, but we can climb in the back seat and keep you company. We don't mind sharing our popcorn."

Celina chuckled.

"Oh, no you don't." Stephen said.

The popcorn-wielding pair stared at each other in mock disbelief. Johnny placed his hand over his heart. "They don't want us in their car."

Pattie shook her head. "I can't believe it." Giggling like kids, they wandered off.

Stephen turned to Celina. "Now, where were we?" He leaned close to her ear and said softly, "I want to hear those words again."

"I love you, Stephen Meszaros." She looked into his dark eyes. "I do love you."

CHAPTER 11

Stephen's voice and image lived in Celina's thoughts. She was happy. Prickly little tingles rushed through her body when she thought of his kisses, his touch.

On the Saturday morning of Kimmie Stuscovich's wedding she hopped out of bed. *Will I be anxious when I stand in front of the priest wearing a white gown and veil? How will I feel when Stephen takes my hand and slips the ring on my finger as we exchange vows?* The joy of anticipation flooded her.

After grabbing her housecoat, she danced around the room and looked into the mirror. Wavy tendrils stood out in every direction. She continued her dance. Twirling to the window she looked out and raised her arms to heaven. *What a glorious, wonderful, magnificent day.*

She floated down the stairs and into the kitchen. Johnny looked up from his breakfast. "Hey, Missy, you'd better do something with that hair or you'll scare Stephen away."

She went up to him, grabbed his face, squeezed it between her hands, and planted a noisy kiss on his forehead.

"Holy cripes, woman, what's the matter with you? Get away," he said.

"I'll have you know that I have wonderful hair."

He grabbed a piece of toast. "I can guess who told you that. I'm going to have to give him a talking to."

Celina raised her eyebrows, fluttered her lashes, and grinned. Turning away, she stepped up to the cook stove and reached for the coffee.

Smiling, Marian stood with her hands on her hips. "So that's what's been bothering you lately. For a couple of weeks, you looked so awful I thought you were sick, but all this time, you've been lovesick."

Celina and Johnny shared a quick glance. She knew he'd never reveal what had happened in Duxbury's office.

"You caught her, Mom." Johnny winked.

Celina danced over to her brother and tapped her spoon on his head. "Quit it already," he said as she flitted away and sat across from him at the table. Their eyes met; he grinned, and she grinned. "Jeez, Missy, I wish you'd fall in love every day."

She giggled then sighed. "Am I in love?"

"It's either that or you're ready for the nuthouse."

"Brother of mine, I'm glad you dragged me to the dance at the Polish Hall that night, so I refuse to argue with you today."

Their ever-practical mother returned the discussion to breakfast. "You want pierogi?"

"Two."

"Two, that's all? You're going to starve to death. How about an egg?"

"I'm not hungry."

"It's love." Marian's eyes twinkled. "Ah, to be young again."

Tomas tramped in carrying a bucket of coal. *There he*

is...the love of my mother's life.

"What are you three talking about?"

Marian's eyes rested on Celina. "Looks like you got your wish."

"What?"

"Celina is serious about Stephen. The young fellow you met a while back."

Tomas placed the bucket next to the stove. "I like him. Johnny and Andy like him. A good worker, too."

He leaned against the sink. "The Poles and Magyars are tough, and we take care of our own." He turned to Celina. "Did you ask him to Sunday dinner yet?"

"Not yet, but I will." She thought about Stephen roughing up Duxbury. *Dad, you don't know how right you are.*

"Dobry. Dobry. I'll see what he knows about Poland's greatest king, Jan III Sobieski. You remember that he led the Polish army and saved Europe from the Turks when they invaded Vienna." Tomas turned to his wife. "When was that, Marian?"

"1683."

"In 1683."

"Oh, Dad. He might not know Polish history."

"Sure he will. He lived next door to Poland all his life, didn't he?"

There's no use arguing with him. She nibbled at her breakfast. "It's a beautiful day for a wedding."

"You have your gift wrapped and dress ironed?" Marian questioned Celina.

"Yeah, the gift's on the hall table and the dress is hanging on my closet door."

The phone rang and Celina answered. "Johnny, it's Pattie for you."

He picked up the phone and a few minutes later yelled from the living room. "What time's everybody leaving for Kimmie's reception?"

Celina yelled back. "Mom and Dad are leaving around two. They'll pick up Pap and Baba at their house, because Uncle Stanley and Aunt Vera are going to the wedding mass. Stephen's picking me up at three, and we're going straight to the reception."

At two o'clock, Marian, holding a package wrapped in white paper and tied with a white ribbon, waited for Tomas to shine his shoes. She paced the floor. "Be careful you don't get polish on your pants."

She wore her best black dress, the one with the maroon posies splashed across the skirt and bodice, and had pinned her silver-streaked hair into place in the style she had worn as long as Celina could remember. Tomas sported the blue suit and wide tie he wore for every important occasion. She expected that he'd wear it to her wedding, too.

"Don't forget to save seats for Stephen and me," Celina called as they left.

She heard Marian reprimand Tomas as they stepped off the porch. "Quit yanking at your tie." He grumbled an answer Celina didn't catch.

Alone in the house and still starry eyed, she scanned her reflection in the hall mirror. The dark pink sheath clung to her body in all the right places.

She flipped open a book from the book club, tried to read, but couldn't concentrate. Tossing the book aside, she got up and stood at the window and sighed, pretended she was in Stephen's arms.

A cloud of dust signaled his arrival. She grabbed her purse and the wedding gift, strode to the back door, and watched him approach. *Oh, he is so strong and handsome. I'll be so proud to show him off at the reception.* Almost embarrassed, she smiled. *I'm getting as bad as Pattie.*

Frankie, lying on the porch with his face between his paws, watched them lock up the house and stroll to the car.

She peered into the open window. "Where's Aunt Terez?"

"I drove her to the church for the wedding mass. Harriet will take her to the reception." He rolled his eyes. "They couldn't wait to start talking."

Celina laughed and slid close to him.

"You look beautiful, and you smell good too," he said.

Stephen wore a dark suit, snowy white shirt, and the printed tie he purchased at Duxbury's. "Thank you sir, you don't look bad yourself."

Late arrivals were forced to park several blocks from the reception hall. Hand in hand they strolled under a cloudless summer sky, passing St. Stanislaus then weaving their way between vehicles in the overflowing lot, to the Polish Hall.

"It's a perfect day for a wedding."

Stephen smiled. "Um-hum."

It took a minute for her eyes to adjust to the dimness inside the door but soon everything came into focus. Tissue roses and pleated paper bells, crisscrossed by miles of crepe paper, hung from the ceiling. The decorations rocked to and fro in the feeble breeze generated by the fans the club members had brought in.

The bridal table, festooned with carnations and roses, tall white candles, and yards of ribbon, stood at the far end of the room. A five-tiered wedding cake, decorated with sugar roses and topped with tiny porcelain bride and groom figures, had a table all to itself. A third table was piled high with packages.

The best man in a sport coat and the maid of honor in her

yellow cocktail dress stood near the entrance. He held a bottle of whiskey and poured a shot for Stephen. She held out her hands to retrieve the gift from Celina. Young, fresh-faced girls wearing their Sunday best carried each gift to the table in the corner.

Kimmie, radiant in her gauzy, lace-trimmed gown, and George, tense and tugging at the collar of his dark suit, greeted their guests. Celina hugged and kissed Kimmie. "I'm so happy for you."

"This is the best day of my life." Kimmie placed her cheek against Celina's. "I'm looking forward to an invitation to your wedding." She glanced up at Stephen's smiling face and whispered. "I'm so glad to see you happy."

With deep satisfaction, Celina sighed. It felt so good to belong to someone. She scanned the crowd and found Pattie waving wildly. Marty in his first-communion suit and Tommy in short pants ran to greet them. The boys clung to them as they crossed the room to where the Pasniewski and Harchak families sat together at a long table draped with a white cloth.

Pap and Baba sat with Judith Harchak's parents. Uncle Stanley and Aunt Vera filled out the circle. They spoke in Polish and laughed, their voices rising and falling in rhythmic cadence. The old ladies fanned themselves and tucked wisps of snowy hair back into place from time to time. The old men spoke rapidly, gestured with their hands and slapped a knee for emphasis, oblivious to the younger generation around them.

Tomas and Joe Harchak stood up and shook Stephen's hand, and Johnny slapped him on the back. "Let's get something to drink."

"What would you like?" Stephen asked Celina with a smile.

"Let's see. A rum and coke, but if they don't have rum, I'll take a highball."

"Cripes, Missy, you're getting fancy with your drinks."

"I want to try something different."

Pattie chimed in. "I'll have a rum and coke too."

"See what you started." Johnny winked, and the two young men strolled off, talking and laughing as though they had known each other since they were kids.

Pattie clasped her hands together. "Isn't this the most beautiful wedding you ever saw?"

Celina watched the wedding party take their places at the bridal table. On either side of the bride and groom, their parents beamed with pride. No sooner were they seated than the assembled guests picked up their forks and tapped their glasses, the sound of a thousand tiny glass bells in chorus. Blushing, the couple stood up and kissed. The crowd applauded and cheered.

The best man held his glass high and extolled the virtues of the bride and groom, then everyone toasted the newlyweds. "*Na Zdrowie!*" echoed through the hall.

Pap tapped Tomas on the arm and spoke in rapid Polish, accompanied by much hand waving and head shaking. He repeated the word *starosta* several times. Tomas turned to him, an apologetic tone in his voice, and answered in equally rapid Polish. When the short exchange ended, Celina leaned toward her father. "What were you talking about?"

"Pap's disappointed that the *starosta* didn't speak in Polish."

"Starosta?"

"The best man. And he said when you kids get married, he wants us to greet you with bread and salt like they do in the old country. He misses the old ways."

It was at times like this that Celina wished her parents had been willing to teach her Polish, but for some reason they seemed embarrassed to teach the old country's language to their children. There had been no room in their lives for anything other thanAmericanization and hard work.

After the bride's table had been served home-style with bowls and platters laden with festive food, the guests rose from their seats and filed past long tables weighed down with ham, chicken, kielbasa, halupki, rigatoni, potato salad—more food than anyone could eat.

Andy, like a male cardinal trying to entice his mate with small treats, encouraged Ellen to take a morsel of this or that, but she refused almost everything. At the table, she passed up a cup of coffee because the smell still made her nauseated. "I don't think this morning sickness will ever end," she whispered to Celina. Her face reddened as the women cheered after she had eaten a piece of nut roll he brought back from the dessert table.

The beer and hard liquor flowed.

Although the fans kept the sultry air moving in the cavernous hall, one by one, men removed their coats and ties and unbuttoned their collars. Women fanned themselves as best they could, and children playing tag ducked around the adults. The guests chattered and tapped their glasses with their forks. The newlyweds kissed.

Early in the evening, the Swing Kings arrived. While the band set up, ushers, unsteady on their feet, pushed chairs and tables against the wall and cleared a spot for dancing. Stephen and Celina strolled through the wide-open double doors to the grassy area outside. He struck a match and lit a cigarette, but didn't offer her one.

"The night we met we were standing right here, and you

offered me a cigarette."

Smoke drifted from his mouth. "I remember." The corners of his eyes crinkled. "I was pleased when you said you didn't smoke."

"Really? You don't like women to smoke?"

"No, I don't, but I don't like men to smoke either." He put the cigarette to his lips and inhaled. "Once you start, it becomes a weakness." He dropped the cigarette, rubbed it into the ground with his foot, then, placed his arm around her shoulder. "It's a rotten habit. Yellow stains cover your fingers and you burn holes in your clothes."

Everything about Stephen was thoughtful and Celina liked that.

Back inside the hall, couples turned and skipped in wide circles to the quick-paced music. Celina smiled. "They're playing an *oberek!* Let's dance." They joined the others and danced till they were out of breath.

During a brief intermission, her heart sunk when she noticed Tomas lurching toward them. She frowned. *He's plastered.*

Tomas threw one arm over Stephen's shoulder, and slurred words tripped over his thick tongue. "So, this is your *Magyar.*" He patted Stephen's chest and shared a conspiratorial look. "Them john-bulls don't call us Magyars and Poles, they call all of us hunkies, stupid bastards." He clutched at Stephen's sleeve. "And they go around telling them god-damned Polack jokes."

He continued patting Stephen's chest. "But I was sayin', you're the one my only daughter picked. She's a good girl. Damned good girl...she hain't afraid ta work...cooks, cleans, irons. Good at plantin' a garden."

Tomas wobbled, stepped closer, and spoke in a loud

whisper. "But damn it to hell, look at this beautiful little girl. Would you believe she has an ugly temper?" He leaned even closer. "Works hard, but don't want to listen." He snorted and leaned against Stephen's chest. "Have to watch that." With a knowing look, Tomas nodded. "Keep her in line."

Celina's face burned. She wanted to scream 'shut-up, shut-up.' But she stood there mute as a statue.

Before the music resumed, Stephen said, "Mr. Pasniewski—"

"No, no, call me Tomas. Tomas, that's my name."

"Tomas, how about if we go over to the bar there and get a beer."

"Sure. Sure. That's where I was goin' anyway."

Stephen led him to the bar, then back to the table. Celina stood nearby.

Tomas plopped into a chair with a grunt. "You know my wife here, Marian's her name. Sometimes I call her Mar but she doesn't like that." He leaned against Marian. She steadied the deadweight he'd become. "Hain't that right, Mar?"

His wife sighed a very small sigh. She glanced at Ellen then up at Celina. "That's right, Tomas. I like my given name."

He cocked his head in Stephen's direction. "See, what'd I tell ya?" He patted a nearby chair. "Here, sit down, I wanna know how you're goin' to take care of that little girl standin' right there. She's a good girl. But has an ugly temper, yeah an ugly temper. Don't want to listen."

Celina was mortified but didn't know how to stop his rambling lecture.

"Can't figure that out. No reason for it." He swayed onto Stephen's shoulder and squelched a belch. "No reason for it at all. Her mother don't have a temper. Sometimes the looks that girl gives ya could curdle milk, before it comes out of the cow that is." Tomas doubled over with laughter at his joke. He sat up and ran his arm across his eyes.

Marian reached over and touched his shoulder. "They're playing a polka, maybe the kids want to dance."

"You don wanna dance, do ya?"

"I'd like to take Celina out there for a few turns around the floor."

"Well, hell. Don let an important man-to-man talk get in the way of your dancin'."

Celina could stand no more and stepped forward, but a strong hand stopped her. "I'll take care of this," Andy said.

He approached Tomas. "Hey, Dad, it's awful hot in here. Let's go outside." Before Tomas could balk, Andy had his arm. "They just tapped another keg and a lot of the guys are trying it."

"Okay. Okay." He got up, patted Stephen's chest and raised an eyebrow. "Remember what I told ya." Andy led him to the door.

He mother and grandmother sent comforting looks to an enraged Celina, who scowled as her father and brother disappeared into the crowd.

Stephen stood up and held out his hand. "They're playing a slow dance."

Still frowning, Celina watched the dancers.

He grinned. "Is that the look that will curdle milk?"

Surprised, and even less sure of herself, she glanced at the group. Marian, Ellen, and Baba, trying to hide smiles and averted their faces. Celina stole a look at Stephen. He stood there holding his hand out to her.

She reached out to him and they stepped onto the dance floor. She stumbled over the words. "I'm so sorry…about…that. My dad doesn't get drunk too often, but when he does, he gets falling-down-stupid drunk."

"Don't let it bother you. If my dad were here, he'd be putting it away too." They glided around with the other dancers. "At least he let me know what I'm in for."

She playfully smacked his arm. "Oh, you." He drew her closer and they finished the dance.

At dusk, the bridesmaids gathered around the untouched wedding cake and the groomsmen announced that it was time for the *Oczepiny* Ceremony, the unveiling of the bride, and the bridal dance.

Chairs were scooted back as men and women reached for their wallets and purses, and children ran to their parents for a coin to throw into the apron.

The groom and the other men stood apart from the festivities. The band struck up a merry tune and all the single women and girls circled Kimmie. The maid of honor took her position behind the bride and carefully removed her flowing veil.

After the veil had been set aside, a new circle of both young and old, all matrons, gathered around the seated bride in her billowing white gown. Kimmie's mother, tears filling her eyes, stepped up to her daughter and replaced the veil with a petite lace cap to cover her hair, symbolizing her new status as a married woman. The women hugged and kissed the young wife, who had now become one of them.

Kimmie retrieved her bouquet. Celina and Pattie joined the other single women gathered into a tight bunch and waited for the bouquet to sail in their direction. With solemn dignity the bride closed her eyes, lifted the bouquet high, and tossed it over her shoulder. After a moment of silence, an arm held the flowers aloft. Pattie had caught the bouquet and amid giggling congratulations from other women, her face glowed.

"I caught it. I caught it." More loud applause spread through the hall. Pattie buried her face in the flowers and a red-faced Johnny took ribbing from the men round him.

The band paused. The best man stepped up to the microphone and announced the bridal dance. All the guests took their places in line and waited for an opportunity to dance with the bride and to throw money into the apron tied round the maid of honor's waist.

The best man and groomsmen kept the line moving, and each guest had only a few seconds to twirl the bride around the floor. Celina took a few turns with Kimmie. She kissed and congratulated the young wife and as she spun away, she tossed a folded bill into the apron. The groomsmen offered shots of whiskey to each adult. The shot was to be downed before receiving a piece of wedding cake from the trays held by the bridesmaids.

The whole family laughed when Celina swallowed the liquor. Her eyes watered, her throat burned, and her stomach felt as though it were on fire. She fanned herself and giggled. Stephen chuckled and hugged her.

At the end of the line, the bride's and groom's families took their turn whirling the bride around the dance floor. Finally, George came out of the shadows to dance with his wife. With a proud smile, he tossed his wallet into the apron, as dictated by tradition. His wife was now in charge of the household money. The hall resounded with cheers and applause. He spun Kimmie around, lifted her into his arms, and raced out the door into their waiting car. Soon after, the overindulged guests started to file out behind them.

Tomas, too drunk to drive, refused to allow anyone except

Andy behind the wheel of his car. Followed by Ellen and the boys, Andy drove his parents home.

Arms wrapped around each other, Stephen and Celina strolled through the maze of cars and pickup trucks to his car. He spoke softly. "I'd like to talk to your parents about us soon."

Celina murmured, "Yes, soon."

The moon was a sliver of itself, and millions of stars filled the black sky. At the door, they kissed long slow kisses. "I'll see you tomorrow," he said when they pulled apart.

"Um-hum." She smiled. "I wish you didn't have to leave."

"I don't want to."

She reached up and put her hands on his shoulders. "Sometimes, when I think about it, meeting you, falling in love…being together seems unreal…like a dream."

He pulled her close. "It's all real, and we're going to have a wonderful life together."

Wrapped in each other's arms, they stood motionless for a long time. Stephen broke the silence. "When I left Hungary, I had to concentrate on finding a way to the United States and making a living once I got here. Until I met you, I didn't realize how much I wanted someone to love and how much I missed family life."

His eyes were soft and thoughtful. "I can't thank Aunt Terez enough for taking the chance, for agreeing to be one of my sponsors, vouching for me to the immigration authorities. How else would I have met you?"

The porch light clicked on and Stephen chuckled. "I believe that's a signal from on high." They shared one last kiss then Celina watched him disappear into the darkness before she opened the back door.

She crept into the house and noticed the back of Marian's

housecoat disappearing up the stairs. Tomas, still in his blue suit and Sunday shoes, snored with abandon from the living room couch. Celina remembered her earlier embarrassment as she climbed the stairs.

CHAPTER 12

Daylight flooded Celina's room. She grabbed her housecoat and descended the stairs. Tomas' voice hung in the air as she approached the kitchen. In an instant, her anger at him rekindled.

His pallid face sported bloodshot eyes and razor stubble. He sat at the table looking like he wished he were dead. Celina managed to control her irritation as she poured a cup of coffee, all the while ignoring him. She spoke to her mother. "Are we going to church this morning?"

"I am. But I don't know about your father."

Tomas, an elbow on the table and his head in his hand, said nothing.

"Hey, Dad, you up to Father Schmidt's sermon this morning?" Johnny said with a glint in his eye.

"Don't get funny with me. I had too much wedding yesterday."

He shot Celina a look. "Get me some coffee."

She drummed her fingers on the side of the cup. Her stomach turned over. *After what he said yesterday, he expects me to wait on him this morning.* Her answer rang out like a glass bell.

"No."

Tomas winced and held his head. "What? You too busy to get your dad a cup of coffee?"

"I'm not getting it. That's all." Her fingers tightened around the cup.

His face contorted in anger. "You get that coffee."

"No." Her voice rose to a near squeak.

"You don't tell your father no."

She turned on him. "I'm not doing it. I might curdle the milk."

"God damn it, get the coffee." He slapped the tabletop with the flat of his hand.

Although her face was as immovable as a stone, her stomach knotted into a tight wad. She looked him in the eye. "I felt like a fool standing in the middle of that dance floor yesterday, and I'm not taking your orders today."

"Marian, you hear what your daughter's saying?" Tomas sputtered.

"Listen, Tomas, you were drunk and you shamed her in front of her new young man yet. You should say you're sorry."

"What? She can't take a little joke?"

"Has she ever in her life been the kind of girl who would take that kind of talk as a joke?" Marian's voice rang out with exasperation.

"It was the booze talking. Just because a man's a little drunk, don't mean a daughter should disobey her dad." He drew his hands across his grizzled face.

Celina refilled her cup and moved toward the back door.

"You get back here."

With her heart pounding and fear clutching at her stomach, she shook her head. "No."

Tomas stood up, and Johnny stepped in. "Leave her alone, Dad."

"What the hell's the matter with her?"

"You hurt her feelings, saying she has a bad temper and telling Stephen to keep her in line. She's a good kid."

"She's too damn touchy. Must be on the rag or something."

Marian swung round. "Tomas, you shut your mouth. It's Sunday morning and God

hears you talking." She grabbed a cup, filled it, deposited it in front of him, and pushed the cream and sugar across the table.

"There's your coffee. You happy?"

He mumbled under his breath.

Celina choked down a small sip of the sweet, cream laced-liquid. She ran her hand through her hair and wished that she could take stupid drunken talk as a joke, but she couldn't. She was shaking inside, but on the surface she appeared to be nothing more than stoic.

Before Mass the congregation sat subdued. Most of the men, slack-jawed and hung over, wiped their sweaty faces from time to time, and most of the women, tight-lipped and huffy, fanned their faces with unread bulletins. When a baby squalled, half a dozen men winced.

Marian poked Celina with an elbow. "Kimmie's dad looks a little green around the gills."

A small breeze drifted through the open windows and stirred the stink of hang over breath. Celina shivered at the smell. It conjured up images of Duxbury grabbing her wrist and dragging her around the desk.

Marian looked at her. "You all right?"

"Yes." She nodded. What else could she say? It was best that her parents be kept in the dark about the incident.

Tomas' unshaven face echoed the same greenish tint exhibited by many other men, only greener. She gloated. *I'm glad they're sick and hope their wives cook greasy fried pork chops for supper and the smell makes them sicker. Why do they have to get so drunk and make everybody around them embarrassed and miserable?*

Stephen and Aunt Terez slid into the pew behind them and Celina brightened. He leaned forward and whispered to her. "Looks like a lot of these people should be home in bed."

She nodded. "Too much of a good time, I guess."

Father Schmidt's car roared up the hill.

In less than a minute, followed by two altar boys, he raced from the sacristy to the altar. At the opening blessing his pace slowed. During the sermon, it was slower still. He droned on and on about practicing the virtue of moderation in all things. Kids squirmed. Adults craned their necks and examined their watches.

Unrepentant men stared at the ornate ceiling, at the plank floor, or out the stained-glass windows. Vindicated women looked at their fidgeting husbands, at other smug women, and at the frowning Father Schmidt. Their bulletins flew faster as they fanned themselves, and they nodded in tight-lipped approval. At last, the sermon ended.

After the final blessing, Terez and Marian stopped to chat. Heads together, they left the church. Anna Jankowiak joined them. The three ladies stood in the shade cast by the church and spent many minutes deep in conversation. Their shoulders shook in quiet laughter, and their hands fluttered through the air in excited gestures until all but four or five vehicles had driven away. They sent indulgent smiles toward Celina and Stephen, and sly smirks at Tomas and Charlie who stood near the car, shifting from foot to foot and consoling each other.

Tomas pleaded, "Marian, come on, let's go." The three women took their time saying their good-byes. At last, Charlie and Anna climbed in their pick up and waved as they rumbled by.

"Don't forget to stop for the paper," Marian reminded her husband.

"I don't wanna read the paper today."

"Well, maybe the rest of us do."

"Jesus Christ."

"Tomas, you just left church."

He said nothing but slowed to a stop in front of the Main Street Drug Store. Celina hopped out and picked up the *Pittsburgh Press*. Tomas drove with his left arm and head out the window. Marian sat with crossed arms staring through the windshield. Celina with the newspaper on her lap, delighted in her dad's misery.

Back home, she tossed the paper on the kitchen table. "Since nobody's coming for Sunday dinner, Stephen and I are going over to Aunt Terez's place and then for a ride, okay?"

"Yeah, your dad's sleeping on the couch already; I don't think he'll want much to eat till tonight."

Celina cleared her throat. "What were you and Terez talking about after church?"

"You and Stephen, of course. Terez said he's written his parents about you."

"He said he was going to." Celina couldn't conceal her pleasure that he had contacted his parents about her.

"From what she says, he thinks the world of you. And we both think you're good for each other."

"He makes me happy." An image of Stephen's face drifted through Celina's mind.

"You made a good choice. He's a good man and a hard worker."

"I'm glad you like him."

"He's the same as you with the books. Terez said he's read everything in the house. That's when he's not looking for work, or fixing her place up or spending time with you."

"He can do almost anything." Pride filled Celina's voice.

"Did you tell him about wanting to go out and be a newspaper reporter?"

"Yes. He said that journalism is getting more difficult to break into. It's becoming what they call a real profession, and a college education helps. Reporting is more sophisticated than it was ten or twelve years ago, during the war."

"Do you think he's talking that way because he thinks a woman should stay home?"

"No, he's not like that." She shook her head. "No."

Marian looked doubtful. "I hope you're right. But—"

"Look, Mom, his family thinks everyone should be educated and get ahead."

"Well, in a free country like the United States, women stay home. They don't go out in the world like a man, the way women do over in communist countries."

"For Pete's sake, Mother," Celina said with a huff. "Why is it that people think if a woman's smart and educated, and dreams her own dreams, she'll grow hair on her chest and develop five o'clock shadow?"

"There's nothing wrong with a woman working till she gets married," Marian answered. "You can't go wrong working in a nice place like Duxbury's. But a woman is supposed to be the helpmate and her husband, the bread winner."

Celina rolled her eyes. She was sick of hearing how nice Duxbury's was, especially since the attack. "If you had to work at that store, you might not think it's so nice." Quickly she added, "Stephen's mother works at Budapest University, and his father is a bookkeeper. And they do everything together. They're happy."

Tomas yelled from the living room. "What the hell are you two yapping about?"

"An article in the paper, that's all," Marian answered.

"Don't talk so loud."

They fell silent, filled their coffee cups and riffled through the paper while Celina waited for Stephen.

He arrived at two. Once in the car, he pulled Celina to him and they kissed. "How long has it been since I've seen you?"

She laughed. "Hmm, let's see, it feels like days, but mass ended only four hours ago."

On their way to his aunt's house, Stephen stopped near the abandoned tipple. "If you take the path away from the tipple, you'll come to a meadow filled with tall grass edged with mountain laurel and oak trees." He reached for Celina's hand. "Want to take a walk?"

Under the bright sun, they strolled down the path.

"I haven't been this way since I was a little girl. Johnny and I used to sneak away from the house to play in the woods. We pretended we were on the Lewis and Clark Expedition, exploring the wild western frontier."

A rabbit startled them when it jumped out of the grass and zigzagged out of sight. A few steps further, they noticed an indentation in the ground. Four baby bunnies, their eyes closed, slept in a nest of soft grass. They tiptoed past.

"Let's sit over there." Stephen pointed to a large boulder at the edge of the field.

Perched side by side, he reached for her hand. "I have something to tell you, but I don't know where to start."

"Is something wrong? Duxbury isn't causing trouble, is he?" Concern laced Celina's voice.

"No, no. But sometimes good news can sound like bad news at first."

"What is it?"

He put his arm around her. "The confirmation letter came. I'm an adjunct professor at Duquesne University."

"Stephen, that's wonderful."

He threaded his fingers through hers. "Faculty orientation is a couple of weeks away.

Once I'm there, I'll have to spend most of my time preparing for and teaching classes." He kissed her hand. "The university will provide living quarters while I look for an apartment."

Celina lowered her gaze. "It is wonderful news but...when will you be able to come home?" A familiar bleak emptiness enveloped her and made her feel hollow inside. *Martyn left and never came back. Bobby left and never came back. And now Stephen. Would he leave too? And...I won't think about it.*

His voice overrode her thoughts. "We'll have a week's break in mid-October."

"Almost two months." She blinked hard to hold back the tears. "That's a long time."

His arm tightened round her shoulder. "If I juggle everything carefully, I believe I can come home on at least a couple of week-ends."

She rested her head against his shoulder. "I'll miss you."

Tears threatened to fall and she blinked again. "Don't go."

He put his hand under her chin and lifted her face to his. "I want you to come with me."

"I wish I could," she said in a hoarse whisper.

He hugged her close. "I have something I want to show you." He reached into his pocket and retrieved an envelope.

The envelope was folded into a small square. He unfolded it and lifted the flap. His fingers reached inside and retrieved a piece of very thin paper folded into a smaller square. Celina was curious and craned her neck to see what was written there. He grinned like a kid as he unfolded the paper.

A sparkling ring lay right in the center of the tissue paper. It was the most beautiful thing Celina had ever seen. A diamond surrounded by smaller stones set in gold. It twinkled in the sunlight. Taking her hand in his, he whispered, "Will you marry me?"

Her eyes filled with tears. "Yes. Yes, I will."

He slipped the ring onto her finger. "We'll be together as soon as possible." He kissed her fingers and turned her hand over and kissed the palm. Soon their lips touched and they clung to each other. He slid her down and they lay together in the tall grass, hidden from the world. He slid his hands beneath the thin material of her blouse, caressed her breasts and rubbed his thumb across the taunt nipple. His hands were gentle and strong. Celina tugged at his shirt. His breath became hot against her as she unbuckled his belt. He slid over her and she felt the power and weight of his body. Her heart pounded, but a wave of guilt washed over her. "We can't do this."

He didn't move, only rested his cheek against hers. Their breathing slowed and he rolled onto the ground beside her. He stared at the sky and Celina watched him. "You angry?"

"No." With a wry look he added, "But I didn't want to stop. You?"

"No. And I'm still trying to compose myself."

"You'd have felt terrible and guilty if we hadn't stopped, wouldn't you?"

"Yes." Celina blushed.

"Okay. Then we'll have to wait…and see how long we can hold out the next time."

"Stephen!" She tried to sound indignant.

He tilted his head to one side to look at her. His arm slid under her shoulders, and he pulled her onto his chest. "We're probably the purest couple in the entire world, waiting until we are blessed by the church."

Her ear rested over his heart and she could hear its rapid beating. "We do have to wait, but…"

"Well then." His dark eyes scanned her face and he softly kissed her forehead. "We should get married as soon as we can. What do you think?"

Determined and a bit giddy, Celina agreed to do exactly that.

"We have to talk to the priest and get the license. That might take a while. But the mid-term break isn't that far off. Would that give you enough time to do whatever brides do to prepare for weddings?"

"I don't see why not." Her face glowed. "The most important thing is talking to Father Schmidt."

"Then mid-October is okay with you?"

She nodded. "Um-hum. That's eight weeks away, but it's not too long." In eight weeks she would be with Stephen forever, and she couldn't be happier. It seemed like a dream.

He scanned the clouds hovering above them. "My one big concern was that you'd want to wait longer."

She had already spent too many years of her life waiting and alone. "No, I don't want to wait."

They sat up and he slid her onto his lap. "Well then, no more waiting. We'll talk to Father Schmidt about an October date."

"I'll call him and make an appointment."

He leaned back against the rock. His eyes scanned her face. "I'm looking forward to spending the rest of my life with you."

He reached for her hand and examined the ring. "This was my mother's engagement ring. A few days before I left, she brought it out from a hidden place and told me to give it to the woman I would one day marry...give it with her blessing."

The ring sparkled in the sun. "I'll always treasure it." She rested against him and contentment filled her.

"It's been passed down in my father's family for three generations." He ran a finger over the clear stones. "I hope that maybe in a few years we'll be able to go to Budapest and you can meet them." He smiled. "I know they'll love you as much as I do."

"I'd love to," Celina whispered. "I want to get to know your whole family." The ring that joined her to the man she loved, connected her to a family who lived thousands of miles away. "Does Aunt Terez know about the ring?"

"I told her I'd ask you to marry me today." They walked arm in arm and stepped out of the tall grass near the car. Stephen grasped her around the waist with both hands and lifted her high into the air. "Now we can tell her you said yes."

#

Later, that afternoon they entered the house through the kitchen and the screen door slammed behind them. "We've talked to Aunt Terez, and now it's time to talk to my parents," Celina said.

He held her close. "I wouldn't be surprised if they know."

Celina scrunched her face. "Aunt Terez?"

He lifted an eyebrow. "I wouldn't be surprised at all."

Marian stepped into the kitchen from the living room, a broad smile on her face. She called out, "Tomas, the kids are here."

"Tell 'em to come in and sit down."

They entered the living room. Tomas looked much better than he did that morning. He sat in his usual spot on the couch. *The Ed Sullivan Show* played on the television and he got up, padded across the room, and turned off the flickering black-and-white image. Marian stood in the doorway, her hands clasped. The evening sun glinted through the windows and a small breeze ruffled the curtains.

"Sit down. Sit down." Thomas waved an arm.

The joy-filled day had pushed their earlier argument out of Celina's mind and she sat with a smile.

"You two have something to say?"

Celina looked toward Stephen. "I've asked Celina to marry me, and she said yes. And we would like your approval."

Tomas slid to the edge of the couch. "I approve, and we celebrate."

He nodded to his wife. "Marian, get the bottle, the good stuff."

Marian left and he turned to Celina. "Your mother and Terez have been on the phone clucking like two old biddies." He ran his gnarled hand over his forehead. "Tried to, but didn't get much sleep with them blabbing for the last hour."

"I knew my aunt wouldn't be able to keep it to herself." A grin spread across Stephen's face.

Celina's father grinned. "One of the Kolariks picked up the phone while your mother was talking about you two living with us or Terez till you find a place of your own. With that party line, I'll wager that whole damn county knows by now." Enjoying himself, Tomas sat back. "Pattie's mom's probably on the phone this very minute." He chuckled. "Them women are burning up the wires."

Marian returned from the kitchen carrying a small, doily-covered tray laden with four shot glasses and a bottle of Jack Daniels. Tomas filled each glass to the brim. The liquor ran down their fingers when they clinked glasses together for a toast. "*Na Zdrowie!*"

Celina and Marian demurred when Tomas refilled the glasses, but the men tossed down a second shot.

"Now Celina, let's see your ring," Marian said, reaching out with excitement.

She held out her hand. Tomas nodded with satisfaction.

Marian took the hand and turned it to and fro. "It's beautiful." She looked up at them.

"I'm happy for both of you." She sighed with the satisfaction of a mother who had, at last, seen her aging daughter marry well. "Our daughter is getting married."

A small commotion arose outside. Frankie barked and Johnny yelled, "Down, dog!" and the screen door slammed.

Pattie, flushed with excitement, led the way. "Where are they?"

Tomas shot a conspiratorial glance at Stephen. "Told ya."

Pattie rushed in, stopped, and grinned wide. "We came as soon as we heard."

Under his breath Tomas grumbled. "You musta flew."

"Let me see. Let me see." Pattie squeezed Celina's hand. "It's beautiful." She looked up at Stephen, and a long rapturous breath escaped her.

Johnny congratulated Stephen with a handshake and his sister with a kiss on the cheek. "Have a wedding date set?"

Celina answered. "We're going to talk to Father Schmidt soon."

#

Monday at noon, Celina and Pattie sat on the park bench under the oak tree nearest the dairy bar. "I'm going over to the *Weekly Messenger* again. I wish Harry Cherriten would give me an answer about that job. Since the position is temporary, I need something like that."

She hurried through the park and crossed the street. Stopping in front of the newspaper office, Celina saw Marge Duxbury's green Buick speed by, almost clipping a sedan parked in front of Taylor's Hardware. The woman had taken to spending more and more time at the store, criticizing everything from Earl's method of giving orders to Harold's frayed cap.

Celina peered through the *Weekly Messenger's* open door. The odor of carbon ink on newsprint drifted out to her but the clattering machines were quiet. She stepped inside. The deluge of notes and clippings she noticed weeks earlier still flooded the bulletin board and appeared broader and longer than it had back then. She stepped up to the unattended counter and called, "Hello."

Sarah Monahan sat at one of the cluttered desks writing a letter. She looked up and came round the partition to greet

Celina. "I heard the news about your engagement. I'm so happy for you. Your young man has been in to send telegrams a couple of times." She smiled and asked to see Celina's ring. "It's beautiful! I imagine that you'll be marrying soon."

Sarah pressed for a wedding date, but Celina replied that she had not yet decided. After all, they hadn't yet talked to the priest. "I'm still interested in the job here. I hope to work here until I'm married and eventually at another paper when this job is finished."

Sarah sniffed. "A lot of young women do that at first. If my Jerry had lived, I would have quit after a year or so to stay home."

Celina steered the conversation to her quest for employment and the discussion she had with Mr. Cherriten about the job opening.

"I gave Harry my resignation letter on Friday." Sarah said and her eyebrows came together. "He's known about this for a couple of months, so he's had plenty of time to hire someone."

"Then he hasn't mentioned anything about who will take your place?"

"No, it drives Edgar crazy, but that's the way Harry does things. He'll procrastinate and procrastinate till the last minute." She patted Celina's shoulder. "Don't worry. I don't know anyone else who wants to work here."

"I guess I'll come back in a day or so."

"My final day is coming up and I'll be getting my first Social Security check next month."

"It must be a relief to know you'll have an income."

"It is, and I have a picture of the man who made it possible. Franklin D. Roosevelt is hanging on the wall in my parlor right next to pictures of my husband and my parents. If it hadn't been for him and his New Deal, I'd have to work till I dropped dead."

Sarah looked around the cluttered office. "I better get back to work before Edgar comes in from his lunch."

"Do you think I'll hear from Mr. Cherriten soon?" Celina shifted from foot to foot.

Sarah shook her head. "I can't say. You might hear something this week or maybe next week. Like I said, more often than not, he waits till the whole place is in an uproar and Edgar's having a fit before he makes a decision. That's the way it works around here."

Celina left the office and hurried back to Pattie in the park. She rushed through her lunch and they walked back to the store. "I'd hoped Mr. Cherriten would've given me an answer by now, but Sarah said he puts decisions off till the last possible minute."

"Well, look at it this way. At least Duxbury isn't around that much."

"Yeah, but I want out of that store. I can't stand going in there and seeing him and having to pretend everything is fine and dandy. And I want to work at the newspaper, so I can get some experience."

"But when you and Stephen get married, will you keep working here?"

"I'll have to quit here since he'll be working in Pittsburgh. Sarah said the job was temporary anyway, but some experience should make it easier to get another job in the city. And I can take night classes at the university."

"I guess you and Stephen talked about all this."

"Yes, of course. We want to get married when he has time off during the mid-term break, but when I told my mom she said that we should wait till next June. It caught me off guard, since she has been harping at me to get married since I graduated from high school."

"What about your dad?"

"I think he's just happy I'm getting married and that he won't have an old-maid daughter on his hands."

"What are you going to do?"

"I don't know. Stephen and I don't want to put it off. But you know my mom. She might dig in her heels and try and force us to wait till next spring. I've got to think of a way to convince her that October is a good month to get married."

"If you have to wait a year, you might not see him at all during the winter, especially if there's a lot of snow."

"I know, and I'm going to tell her that. Even with chains on the tires Dad and the boys get stuck on these roads."

"Why does your mom want you to wait so long?" Pattie took a sip of her root beer.

"Oh, I don't know. You know how bossy she can be." Celina shook her head. "I feel like I'm bickering with her or my dad all the time anymore, and I don't want to argue with them about this. Somehow I've got to win her over."

"Don't you think you'll be scared to leave home?"

"No, I'll be with Stephen. He came all the way from Hungary and he managed. Someday we'll go back to see his family. We even talked about going to France and Italy, too."

#

A steady stream of school shoppers paraded in and out of the store that afternoon. Celina helped Shirley Wilson fit two of her granddaughters with dresses and bobby socks. She stifled a laugh when the youngest held up a pair of pink underpants and yelled, "I want guchies for every day of the week."

Shirley shushed her quickly. "Bart gets a charge out of it when the kids do this sort of thing. He encourages them. Him and the boys carry on something awful when they go to the hardware store."

"How is the family?" Celina asked with a smile.

"You know Bart. He acts like a kid himself half the time. Him and his practical jokes."

Carrying their purchases, Shirley and the girls left the store while another shopper, her children in tow, came marching down the aisle. Mrs. Pinkerton kept watch from House wares. Her unflinching glare assured that no unwatched or unruly boy misbehaved. It would take her no more than a few seconds to charge out of Housewares, pass through Linens, and stand staring at him.

At closing time, Harold pushed his broom down the main aisle and Mrs. Pinkerton ran to lock the doors and flip the *Closed* sign. Once the sign was flipped, no latecomers were tolerated.

Celina and Pattie lost no time grabbing their purses, trekking down the basement stairs, and through the back door.

"Do you think Johnny will be getting me a ring soon?" Pattie asked, clutching Celina's arm when they reached the parking lot.

"He hasn't said anything to me, but I could ask him."

"Oh, would you, Celina?" Pattie squeezed tighter. "But I don't want you to be too obvious. I wouldn't want him to think I'm trying to find out or anything."

Celina smiled. "I'll think of something."

"I want to start planning our wedding, too. Just make sure

you bring it up in a real casual way, so he won't be suspicious."

"Okay. What do you want me to ask?"

Pattie pursed her lips and then grinned. "When is he going to get me a ring, already?"

"That's real subtle." They giggled. "You know Johnny; he'll be suspicious."

Pattie hopped into her car. "You'll think of something."

CHAPTER 13

Summer signaled its coming end. The trees along the road had begun to take on harvest shades. Purple plumes of ironweed stood tall in abandoned fields. A curled and mottled leaf wedged itself into the corner of the Hudson's windshield and clung there while Celina drove home. When she stopped beneath the old maples, it wobbled in a breeze and sailed silently to the ground.

She never tired of watching the old, unyielding hills create the magic of autumn. Nighttime chills and shortening days heralded the approach of September. It was beautiful but there was no time to waste. Her father would be home in a few minutes demanding his supper. She threw open the car door and rushed to her room. She savored the coolness of the empty house, unbuttoned her blouse, yanked up her skirt, and hopped from one foot to the other while pulling off her stockings and garter belt. Free, she tossed everything onto an oak chair in the corner to be replaced by jeans and a blouse then dashed down to the kitchen.

The surface of the beige porcelain cook stove was warm since a few hot coals had kept the fire alive all day. She shook the grate and the stove belched smoke. "Damn it." She coughed, waving it away before opening the bottom draft and damper. The smoke cleared, she threw a few twigs and egg sized lumps of coal into the firebox. In seconds the fire sprung to life.

Dinner was half cooked when Marian came up the basement stairs. "The sky's getting pretty dark. I hope Ozzie gets here with the coal before it starts to pour. The coal bin's cleaned out and ready for this year's load."

Every fall, for as long as Celina could remember, her mother ordered house coal to be delivered before the nights got too frosty. Sweaty and dirty, her father and brothers would open the creaking cast iron door of the chute built into the foundation, and shovel tons of fuel into the bin in the basement. Later, Marian would eye the pile with a satisfied nod.

Celina slid the cast-iron pan over the firebox. "So, Ozzie's delivering today?"

"Yeah, said he'd be here right after work. Ten tons will do us till spring, unless it's a really bad winter."

Frankie, who lay sprawled on the back porch perked up his ears and jumped to his feet. Puffing his muzzle with air, he growled and hurled himself across the yard and down the lane.

Marian reached up and loosened the knot in her yellow plaid babushka. She slid the head covering back over her hair and retied it at the nape of her neck. "That must be him. I'd better show him where to dump it."

"You'd think he'd know by now."

"You know Ozzie. He could dump that load anywhere. Remember the time it ended up right against the coal chute door and Dad had to shovel for half an hour to get the chute

215

open?"

"Oh yeah, how could I forget that." Tired and hungry at the end of a long day, Tomas had cussed aloud with every shovelful he lifted before the door was freed.

Marian stepped off the porch as the truck approached. Celina went to the screen door and watched Ozzie's battered dull-red, dump truck lumber up the lane. The safety chains fastened to the tailgate clattered against the truck's dented side panels. His mammoth, rusted vehicle rumbled past the maple trees and up to the corner of the house. Panting, Frankie raced behind.

The truck stopped and Ozzie poked his long, narrow head through the open window.

A battered, too-small brown fedora perched at a jaunty angle above his receding hairline. He spat tobacco juice into an empty bean can he kept on the seat beside him and called out, "Where'd ya want this dumped?"

The racket from the rumbling truck drowned out Marian's voice so she gestured, waved, and pointed. Ozzie acknowledged her directions and tipped a grimy finger to the brim of his hat. Gears ground, the motor roared, and the truck lurched forward. Marian, with Frankie at her side followed the smoke-spewing, swaying hulk around the house.

Celina didn't hear her father's jalopy approach, but from the corner of her eye, she noticed his truck bounce its way up the lane. He parked, jumped out, and slammed the door. Like a baggy shaped goblin, he slapped at his dirty work clothes. Puffs of dark powdery residue rose round him. His hair was plastered to his head and a band of dirt-free flesh glowed where the cap had protected it from the clinging bug dust of the mine.

"Ozzie here already?" he asked.

Celina stepped onto the porch. "Yeah, he went round back. Mom's showing him where to unload."

Tomas strolled round the side of the house. A few minutes later he returned, followed by rattling and clanking. The red truck rumbled to a stop under the maples and Ozzie, in grimy flannel shirt and rumpled brown work pants, jumped out. "Sure could use a beer."

"Hey Celina, bring Ozzie and me a beer."

Celina grabbed two beers from the refrigerator and took them outside. Ozzie spit a stream of tobacco juice against a tire and maneuvered the wad of chew out of his mouth. With a forefinger as grimy as the coal he had delivered, he removed the last remnants of tobacco before taking a swig. He threw his head back and closed his eyes as his Adam's apple bobbed. When he removed the almost-empty bottle from his parched lips and held it aloft. A blissful expression lingered on his face as he wiped his mouth with the back of his hand.

"Nobody appreciates a cold beer like you, Ozz," Tomas said with admiration in his voice.

Ozzie pulled a wrinkled red bandana from his back pocket, lifted his hat, and swiped the bandana across his forehead. "Damn right. Workin' out in that infernal heat, loadin' coal, shovelin' coal, walkin' on piles of coal, deliverin' coal, dumpin' coal, breathin' coal…makes a man thirst for something cold to wash down the bug dust."

Tomas slapped Ozzie's back. "Celina, get a couple more," he called into the kitchen.

Frankie lifted his ears and scrambled to his feet. Johnny, encased in drying, blackened mud, his cap tipped at a jaunty angle, rounded the corner. He tossed his dinner bucket on the porch and grinned. "You fellas having a coal miner's convention or something?"

"Naw, just havin' a beer before Ozzie heads out. Celina, get your brother a beer."

When she returned, the three carbon-black apparitions were sitting in the shade. "Damn it Johnny," her father said with a grunt. "You're muddy as hell again. Make sure you get those boots good and dry or the skin's gonna rot off your feet."

"I always set my boots out in the sun as soon as I get home." He bent over and untied the knots. "Had a close call today."

"Oh, yeah?"

Johnny pulled his waterlogged boots and socks off exposing wrinkled white feet then rested his arms on his knees. "Yeah, Mike, Charlie, Bart and me were up near the end of the tunnel setting some new timbers the foreman sent in. We were hoisting one into place, and shale started slipping down. We stopped to listen and more shale and loose rock pelted us."

Tomas reached for the sodden, smelly boots and tossed them onto the sunny porch then he and Ozzie set their beer aside and turned their full attention to Johnny.

"Honest to God, it happened so fast, a couple of stones hit me. Charlie shoved me aside and Bart yelled, 'Run.' I fell on my knees right against the rib of the tunnel. Not a second later a boulder broke loose. I swear to God, it didn't miss any of us by more than an inch."

He finished his beer. "Scared the hell out of me. When I looked up, Mike's eyes were about bugged out of his head. Bart swore he'd never let any of his grandkids work in the mines and Charlie said he's getting too old for this kind of shit."

"Where was Mezovsky?"

"He didn't come in again today. Probably hung over."

Ozzie clucked and wagged his head. "That mine hain't safe. Hain't safe, I tell ya. Men's telling me there's close calls almost every day."

Tomas turned to Johnny. "Your section's the one where Carl got nailed last winter when a rock the size of a football hit his shoulder. Damn near ripped it off. That shoulder's never gonna come back to what it was." The corners of his mouth turned down. "Carl says he's okay, but anybody can see he favors that arm."

"Hain't he the one who lost two fingers a few years back?" Ozzie asked.

"Yeah, two fingers on his right hand."

"Holy cripes."

Johnny sighed. "And what about old Harry Simko? Poor bastard's about ready to retire and buggered up his arm a couple of weeks ago. He won't be coming back."

"What happened?" Ozzie leaned toward Johnny.

"As far as I can tell, he was working on a coupling between two mine cars and they moved before he could react. He screamed at the top of his lungs till somebody came to free him. He was holding the arm to his chest and blood was running down his shirt and pants when they took him out."

Tomas pointed to his foot. "I've been lucky. After thirty some years, all I got was a busted foot and one missin' toe."

The men shook their heads and Ozzie waved his empty bottle. Celina, shaken by everything she heard, brought three more.

"Thanks," he said and took a long swallow. "I'm sure as hell glad I'm haulin' house coal for Glacier Heating." He pointed to the dump truck. "Nothin's going ta fall on me in that bucket-a-bolts."

"Well, if Charlie hadn't been so quick today, they'd have hauled at least one of us out of there on a stretcher. Cripes, that was close."

"I told ya over and over that Charlie's the guy to trust down there, didn't I?" Tomas asked.

Johnny nodded.

Marian called from the kitchen. "Supper's getting cold." She poked her head out the door. "Ozzie, you staying for supper?"

"Naw. The old woman'll be wonderin' what the hell happened to me. I better get home." His baggy pants flapped around his skinny legs as he struggled to his feet. He stretched. "Old body hain't what it used to be." He counted the money Marian handed him, climbed into the truck's cab, and set off down the lane.

Marian clucked and fussed about Johnny's close call. Tomas advised him to always pay attention to Charlie. "He knows what every creak and whisper coming out of those tunnels mean. If you had to trust your life to anyone, Charlie would be the guy."

The day drew to a close and fog settled between the hills and over the houses. Thunder rolled far in the distance. Soon it rolled loud and long overhead.

At first, the rain fell in dainty droplets then the clouds released a downpour. Like an angry fist, the rain pounded the roof and windows. The house grew hotter and stuffier while they waited for the storm to pass. Lightning knocked out the power, making it too dark to read. Celina thought about the story her father told her when she was a little girl, the one about the angels rolling beer barrels across heaven. In an odd way it still comforted her.

At a few minutes past nine the power came back on and her father, quietly reciting his prayers in Polish, padded through the house and climbed the stairs to bed. Johnny had fallen asleep on the couch, his raspy snoring flooding the living room. The book he had intended to read slipped unopened from his chest to the floor.

The phone rang and Marian, reciting the prayers of her rosary at the kitchen table, motioned for Celina to answer it. It was Stephen. She tiptoed past Johnny and dragged the phone by its long cord into the hallway. They recounted the day's events as the storm faded away.

She told him about Johnny's close call. "One of these days somebody is going to end up in the hospital or worse."

"What about Andy? Was he there too?"

"No, he's not working in that section right now. Thank God."

Stephen tried to quiet her concerns. "All those men are experienced miners, and like you said, they look out for each other."

Celina told him about her visit to the newspaper office. "Getting this job is taking a lot longer than I thought. But Sarah said not to worry, so I won't."

"I've got some news too. I received another letter and a contract from the university. I've signed it. Even if I wanted to, there's no backing out now," he said with a smile in his voice.

"You'll be teaching at a university. It's really exciting."

"Well, it's a definite improvement over the time I was a waiter in a Hungarian restaurant."

They both laughed. "Finally, I'm beginning a real career in this country." He added, "Did you talk to you parents about the October date?"

"Yes, but my mother insists that we have a summer wedding."

"What's wrong with October?"

"She thinks the separation is good for us."

"But what we think of the separation is more important, isn't it?" There was a sharp edge in his voice.

"Yes, it is. I know."

"Will I see you tomorrow night?"

"Of course."

"We'll make a decision then, okay?"

"All right, we'll work something out. I love you. See you tomorrow."

The electric lights flickered as Celina returned to the kitchen. Marian sat at the table sipping cold coffee. "Was that Stephen?"

"Yeah, we're going out tomorrow night for a while."

Celina pulled a chair out and sat down. She wanted to make her mother understand that she dreaded the separation. She'd had one separation from somebody she loved and she never saw him again. An uneasy fear lurked in her heart and she couldn't stand the thought of going through that again. She was determined to explain that both she and Stephen wanted an October wedding. "Mom, about the wedding, neither Stephen nor I want to wait till next summer."

"What's your rush? You'll have the rest of your lives together."

Celina lowered her eyes. "I don't want another long separation from someone I love. It's too hard to be left behind waiting and worrying."

Marian said nothing.

"Mom, he'll be almost a hundred and fifty miles away, it'll take hours of driving to get back here, and if we have a bad winter, we might not see each other for months."

"It's not that many months. It's not like he's going to war or anything."

"Why are you being like this? You wanted me to get married and I'm ready to marry someone I love, but now you're making it so hard. Why?"

"If you wait, he'll miss you enough to want to settle down here. Then you won't have to leave at all."

Celina was taken aback. *She expects us to live in Kenville. How can she put that kind of restriction on us?* "How can you say that? He signed a contract, and he doesn't want to settle here right now."

Marian set her cup down with a thump. "Don't you love your family and want us to be together? Can't he teach school here?"

"Why would you even ask if I love our family? You know I do. I can still love everyone here and be with the man I marry. Besides, the high schools here don't teach Russian. Half of them don't even teach Latin and French anymore. And he wants to be at a college. That's where he belongs. "

"He might want to stay here if he thinks about it."

"I don't want to stay here either. I want to become a newspaper reporter and I want to be with Stephen. And we're going to see the world together." Celina swung her arm out in an expansive gesture. "There's a lot going on out there, and I want to be part of it."

"You're being selfish," Marion snapped. "I'm glad you're getting married, but what about the rest of us? Don't we matter at all?"

It was as though a punch had landed in Celina's stomach. She was shaken. "I've always done what you and Dad ask. But now I want to live my own life. Stephen and I both want a close family. We'll be back for all the holidays and during the semester breaks."

Marian shook her head. "Families stick together."

"We won't be that far away. You know I was thinking of working at a city newspaper somewhere before I even met him."

"That was just girlish talk." Marian sat back and crossed her arms.

"No, it wasn't. I need more than what's here in Kenville."

"You're going to have children someday. They'll need grandparents." Marian was determined to cling to her argument.

"They'll have grandparents."

"Stephen's parents are over there in Hungary. Your kids won't get to know them. And we'd be more than a hundred miles away."

"Mom, you're being unreasonable."

Marian waved away her argument. "You listen to me. When Pap got aboard that steamship in Germany, he left everybody he knew in Europe. It was the same for Baba. They had no family here, not until us kids were born. When I was growing up I had no grandparents, no aunts, no uncles. I remember looking at the English kids, the ones whose families had been here for generations. They had grandmas and grandpas, and I was jealous. They had everything."

Marian folded her hands and spoke softer. "Before Pap and Baba left Poland our family lived in the same place in Galicia forever. They were close-knit farmers. They celebrated weddings, and christenings, and cried at family funerals. The same as us, they worked hard for every little thing they got."

Celina's shoulders slumped. How could she disagree when

she knew how hard it had been for her parents and grandparents?

"When Pap and his younger brother Jozef reached Ellis Island in 1900, Jozef stayed on the ship and sailed to Brazil. Pap never saw or heard from him again. Nobody knows what happened to him. For years, Pap talked about him and the great dreams he had but Jozef might as well have died the minute that ship sailed out of the harbor. Pap had no way of contacting him."

"I didn't know that."

"That's what happened. He was my uncle and I never knew him," she said bitterly.

Celina thought about Bobby and Marty and how they went away to war and never came back. Pap walked away from his family when he left Poland and never went back, and when his brother sailed out of New York they never saw each other again. It was becoming more and more difficult to dispute her mother's argument.

"Your kids should have grandparents and aunts and uncles. Blood relatives they can depend on. You can't turn to strangers in cities if you need help."

"I understand what you're saying Mom, and that's what I want. But we're not emigrating or going to war. We'll be close enough. And Johnny and Andy are here."

Marian stood up. The lines in her face seemed etched deeper than ever. "If you leave, you might be like Uncle Jozef. And I don't want that. I want my family." She turned toward the stairs. "Goodnight."

"Mom, why won't you see that it's not the same?"

"I don't want to talk about it anymore. Goodnight, Marcelina."

Her stomach churning, Celina rested her elbows on the

table and her face in her hands. *What am I supposed to do? If I stay here, I'll have my family but I'll probably lose Stephen and be alone again.*

Johnny came in, went to the refrigerator and opened the freezer. "Want some ice cream?"

"No."

He filled a cereal bowl to the brim and drizzled chocolate syrup over the mound. "You sure you don't want any?"

"I'm sure."

He sat down across from her. "I heard you and Mom talking. Are you going to ask Stephen to stay and live here?"

"How can I? There are no jobs for him here. Besides it's our life. Why does Mom always think she can tell me what to do?"

"She's used to it. She's been telling you what to do all your life."

Celina pushed her fingers back into her hair. Johnny was right. Their parents had always had the final word in everything they did.

"Say, I didn't know we had a great-uncle in Brazil," Johnny said.

"Me either."

"Do you think he's still alive?"

"I don't know." She was irritated and upset. "And right now I don't care."

"Listen, Missy, you can't let Mom and Dad run your life forever."

Celina didn't answer.

"Remember when you wanted to go to college after high school and Dad put his foot down because of the expense?"

She nodded.

"It would have been hard, but you could have worked

your way through, and Andy and I could have helped. That wasn't right, Missy. You and Marty were the only ones who wanted to go beyond high school."

"Yeah, I know. I guess I wanted to do it for him as well as for myself."

"You'd have been happier if you had had the chance."

"But—"

"But you can have your chance now. Stephen will help you do whatever you want. I know he'd be one hundred percent behind you if you want to go to college, because he told me."

Tears filled Celina's eyes. "Mom is making this so hard."

"You've got to make up your mind and do it." He patted her arm.

She said nothing.

His old impish grin appeared. "Maybe we could distract Mom and Dad with another wedding."

She lifted her eyes to his smiling face. "What are you talking about?"

Johnny pulled his chair closer to hers. "Pattie's birthday is next week, and I'm going to take her to the Harbor Inn for dinner on Saturday and…" He stood up. "Wait here."

He bounded up the stairs and returned with a small velvet box. "I'm going to give her this." He opened the box.

Celina stared at the princess-cut diamond set in a gold band. "It's beautiful. She is going to be so happy."

"It took four months of slaving at the mine to get this thing. And by spring, we'll be home free with the rest of the money we need."

"You and Mike still planning to go into the auto business?"

"No. we've been thinking about what Dad said…that most men fix their own cars. So, we decided to open an auto parts store instead. Sell everything from jumper cables to Simonize."

"That's a swell plan. When are you going to open up?"

"We're working on that. The experience I'm getting at Kasper's is helping more than I thought. Wilcox's son, the one we were trying to buy the garage from, has been stalling…trying to get more money out of us. I don't like the way he talks to us, like we're dumb or something. We're not playing along anymore. So, we're looking into buying Taylor's Hardware. Old man Taylor has been talking about retiring for years."

"Have you told Pattie?"

"That's why we're going to have a nice, quiet dinner for her birthday. She's going to be a part of this venture, too. I want her involved in the business. A man and his wife should be partners, don't you think?"

"Oh yeah, I do."

Celina stood up and squeezed his shoulder. "I'm really happy for you. And make sure you're careful in that mine.

CHAPTER 14

How do I tell Pattie about the engagement ring without giving too much away? I have to be careful, because I don't want to spoil Johnny's surprise. As she thought about their engagement, a little glimmer of hope sprung up in the back of her mind. *Just maybe Mom and Dad will change their minds when they find out about a second wedding coming up.* The blue morning sky brightened up just a little.

Duxbury's black Cadillac sat in its place behind the store when she got to work. Her stomach turned over. Oh *Boga*, he can't be back from the latest trip already. Her eyes darted around the outside of the building then into the office window where she had seen him standing on the day he had attacked her. The window was empty. *Should I wait for Pattie or go in alone?*

Fed up with being afraid of him and everything else, she grabbed her purse and her lunch and stepped out of the car. *Damn it, that bastard can't scare me forever.* Before she had time to stop herself, she marched across the parking lot. Sweat collected on her back and dampened her hair. *Why didn't I keep Dad's knife with me? Why? Why? Why?*

Her throat tightened. *When I get inside the basement, what if he's between me and the stairs? What'll I do? What if he grabs me? Oh God, I should have held onto that knife.*

Celina reached the door. She berated herself. Stephen took care of him. Stephen wouldn't let him bother me again. He'll stay away.

She clenched her teeth and stepped inside. One bare light bulb dangled from the ceiling. It reflected the light from the whitewashed walls. The water pipes overhead clattered. Tapping came from somewhere out of sight. Duxbury himself stood near a lopsided stack of pallets. He held several brass fittings in one hand. He stared at her but said nothing. Then he nodded in her direction.

She bit the inside of her lip, glared directly into his small, bloodshot eyes, and strode past him up the stairs. At the top of the steps she took a furtive glance over her shoulder to be sure he wasn't following her. He was still down there leaning on the pallets and rolling the brass fittings around in his hand. Her heart thumped in her chest.

A few seconds later Pattie darted up the stairs. Her eyes fluttered and her red head bobbed. She was breathless. "I was getting out of my car when I saw you go in. You okay? I'm so sorry I wasn't here. Why didn't you wait for me?"

Celina filled her lungs with air. "I had to come in here on my own, and I did it." She had faced the fear that had stalked her for weeks, and she was glad.

"But you didn't have to."

"I suppose, but I needed to. I'm glad I did it."

"You sure you're okay?"

"Yeah. It's time to go out to the floor."

The clanking and banging coming from below increased. Harold, dragging his broom, came in from sweeping the sidewalk. "Mornin' ladies."

Earl, carrying his ever-present clipboard, strolled out of the office. "The boss is back. He's giving Sam orders about the water pipes." He tapped the clipboard with the tip of his fountain pen. A blot of ink spread across the page. "I told him those pipes were leaking like a sieve."

"Will they take long to fix?" Celina asked.

"It wouldn't have if the boss had listened to me three months ago. Who knows how long it'll take now." He turned toward the basement stairs. "You might have to go across the street to," he cleared his throat, "use the ladies' room today." With Earl's strict Calvinist upbringing, he still had difficulty mentioning bodily functions in mixed company. He marched down the stairs and joined his employer.

"Did you ask Johnny about the ring?" Pattie whispered.

Celina returned the whisper. "I didn't have to."

"What?"

"He mentioned it on his own."

Pattie squeaked with pleasure. "Did he say anything about the setting or anything like that?"

"No. He didn't say a word about the setting." Celina didn't have to lie.

"What about when he's getting it?"

"I don't know that exactly, but I can say that I am glad you're coming into our family." Celina reached out and hugged her.

Pattie glowed. She wiggled the fingers on her left hand. "I'm so excited I can hardly stand it. I hope I don't have to wait too long."

#

That evening when Stephen arrived, he lingered outside speaking to Johnny, who was lounging on the porch. As the two young men stepped into the kitchen, Celina heard him congratulate Johnny on the upcoming engagement.

Inside Tomas and Marian greeted them from the living room. "Come on in here."

The evening news was on the television and Tomas pointed at the screen. "Looks like Hungary's president, what's his name…. Nagy, is pushing back at the Russians. Hey, Steve, you think he'll get some breathing room?"

Stephen grimaced and his brow furrowed. "I've been keeping up with this, and I'm afraid the government's moving too fast. The Soviets are going to clamp down."

"We saw newsreels during the war; the bombing and the concentration camps. You'd think everybody in Europe would have had a bellyful of killing and want to stay home," Johnny said.

"Everybody in Europe wants the Soviets to stay home." Stephen's eyes were fixed on the flickering screen.

"I feel sorry for those poor people over there, with all the death and destruction. Only God knows if the family Pap and Baba left behind are still alive," Marian said.

Stephen frowned and shook his head. "Television doesn't do the carnage justice. It'll take fifty years to rebuild some of those cities."

Johnny got up and adjusted the sound on the television. "Ike said that during the war, Warsaw was bombed worse than any other city in Europe, even Berlin. Is that right?"

"Yeah, what the Nazis didn't destroy, the Soviets went in and smashed into rubble. Then they took it." Stephen shook his head. "And they wouldn't hesitate to go in with their guns and tanks and do exactly the same thing to Budapest."

"Nothing against your country, but I hope the United States stays out of it." In her usual abrupt way, Marian said, "Enough of our boys have been killed."

Tomas pointed at the flickering screen. "The other day on the television, John Cameron Swayze said Ike's sending military advisors over to Indochina. It looks like the commies are picking another fight over there."

"We don't need another war," Celina spoke up. "Ike should leave well enough alone.

Indochina can fight its own wars."

"They're sayin' the Commies will run right over us in our own country if we don't stop them over there," Tomas argued.

"Dad, how do we know that? Don't you think those people are as sick of killing as we are?"

"Hey, Missy, the government knows better than we do," her father said.

"Maybe the government should be run by women who wouldn't rush out and start shooting and bombing every time somebody gets a hair up their butt," Celina snapped.

"War hain't about getting a hair up somebody's butt; war is serious."

Johnny intervened. "When you think about it, how many more American boys can the government send around the world to get shot up or killed? Especially if it's for people we don't know anything about, and who don't know us?"

Stephen cleared his throat. "Did the newscast say anything about the United Nations getting involved?"

"Didn't hear anything about the U.N. Seems to me they talk too much and don't do enough." Tomas shifted in his seat.

"Somebody has to keep the peace. I'd like to see the U.N.

have enough influence to protect Hungary."

Tomas shook his head. "I can't see how all those different countries could sit down together and agree on anything. Look at the president and congress…they're at each other's throats all the time, and they're all Americans."

"The U.N. is just getting started; it might end up doing some good." Stephen added with a hopeful nod.

"By the looks of it, it'll be a long time before they settle anything," Johnny said.

"Well, we should do something ourselves," Celina said. "Stand up and refuse to go to war unless our country is being invaded. That way there won't be any more Koreas and nobody will go to Indochina."

Johnny's eyes narrowed. "It sounds good, but it won't ever happen, because there's always somebody in some government stirring things up."

Celina stood up. "I say our boys shouldn't be hauled off to get killed in some war they don't even understand."

"Nobody's arguing with you about that," Johnny agreed.

Her voice shaking, Marian said, "Why should women have to worry about their sons or brothers getting blown to bits?"

"That's right, Mom. We women have to speak up."

"Women's place is to back their men, especially when it comes to war," Tomas roared.

"But Dad, if wives and mothers spoke up, leaders might think twice before they send somebody else's sons get shot at. The rich boys stay home, and it's people like us that end up getting killed."

Tomas' face glowed red and his cheeks puffed out. "War is men's business. Women stay out of it."

Stephen stepped in. "We're not going to solve the world's problems tonight."

He reached for Celina's hand. "Are you ready?"

"Yes."

He turned to Marian and Tomas. "I won't keep her out late."

Tomas got up, went to the television, and fiddled with a couple of knobs. "Joe Friday's on tonight. Don't want to miss *Dragnet*."

When they stepped out onto the back porch, Celina pushed back her hair with a huff. "Why won't people take a stand? If they don't, I'm afraid that someday Marty and Tommy will in end up in Indochina or some other godforsaken place."

"I don't know honey, but there's no use arguing with your dad about it."

"I know."

Stephen slipped his arm around her waist and they strolled to his car. "Where do you want to go tonight?"

"The drive-in."

"We don't know what's playing."

Her eyes twinkled. "We probably won't see much of it anyway."

Once in the car, Celina relaxed. "Saturday will be your last full day here. What time do you have to leave on Sunday?"

"Around one o'clock. After church."

She slid closer and rested her head on his shoulder. "I know you have to leave. I just don't want you to."

After pulling into a slot at the drive-in, Stephen adjusted the speaker. They waved to Mike and Stella, who drove by. "Let's go over to the concession stand and get something to drink."

Hand in hand they strolled to the painted cement-block building and ordered two cokes. On the way back to the car

Johnny and Pattie pulled up next to them. "Where are you parked?"

Stephen pointed to his car. "Right over there."

Johnny pulled in beside them.

"I wonder what those two are up to tonight." Celina said and sipped her soda.

At the car, Stephen leaned out the window toward Johnny and smiled. "We won't need any popcorn tonight." Johnny chuckled and led his girl to the concessions.

Darkness fell, the movie started and Celina cuddled into Stephen's arms. They gazed into each other's eyes. He reached up and ran his hand over her hair. His lips brushed her forehead, her eyes, then finally her mouth and they shared a lingering kiss.

As they pulled apart, he murmured, "Let's elope."

Excitement and anxiety shot through her. "I wish we could."

"It would solve a lot of problems. We're engaged and we want to be together. It seems logical to me."

"Me too. But I have to deal with my mom. She thinks if we wait till next summer you'll decide to stay here permanently."

He drew back and looked hard at Celina. "What did you tell her?"

"That you're committed to the university and you have a right to follow your dreams. But she didn't want to hear it."

"I'll go and talk to both of them, your mom and dad."

"Not yet. She's not listening to anything I say. She probably wouldn't listen to anyone.

He rested his head against the back of the seat. "How did this get so complicated?" Their eyes met. "If I talk to them, I can tell your mother that as soon as we're married your family will be my family. I want us all to be as united as possible. She's got to understand that."

Celina reached for his hand and ran her fingers over the scar on his arm. She brushed her lips across the scar. "When Mom was a kid she was lonely for grandparents and other relatives. It must have really bothered her because now, she wants all of us as close as possible. Having lost Martyn in the war seems to have made her more possessive."

"If she doesn't change her mind, will you'll change yours?"

"No, never."

Stephen closed his eyes. "Your mother is making problems where there should be no problems."

"Well, Johnny is giving Pattie an engagement ring this weekend. Maybe their wedding plans will be enough for her to come around."

"You don't believe that do you?"

She grimaced. "Not really. Mom is clinging to all of us. When Marty was killed, she went to pieces. Thank God Andy and Ellen have settled under her wing or there would be real trouble there."

"Pittsburgh isn't that far away. We will be able to come back here every few weeks."

#

After Sunday Mass, Father Schmidt greeted the parishioners at the open doors of St. Stanislaus. Vestments fluttering in the light breeze, he stopped Stephen and Celina. "Congratulations young man, on your good fortune."

"Thank you, Father. I'm a lucky man."

"Yes indeed. Not only have you won the heart of this beautiful young woman, you will be teaching at my alma mater. There isn't a better Catholic university than Duquesne. I have many good memories from my years spent there." A broad smile spread across the priest's face. "Wonderful school, wonderful school."

"Thank you Father. I'm looking forward to settling into the department's routine."

The priest turned to Celina. "And you, young lady, we will have to discuss a wedding date."

"Yes, Father." She looked up at Stephen. "We've been talking about that."

Tomas, Marian, and Terez joined them. Terez's flower-covered straw hat bobbed. "I'm proud of this nephew of mine." She patted his arm with a gloved hand then squeezed his arm.

People strolled toward the cars but before they went their separate ways, Stephen pulled Celina aside. "I'll stop by before I leave."

Marian piped up. "Too bad you can't stay for Sunday dinner."

Celina shot a quick look at Stephen. He appeared not to have noticed the sarcasm she picked up in her mother's voice.

At one o'clock, Stephen drove up the dusty lane and parked under the maple trees. Celina went out to meet him. "Let's go inside. Mom and Dad want to say good-bye. Johnny and Pattie are here too."

Stephen whispered. "Did Johnny give Pattie the ring?"

"Oh yes. He's smiling like the Cheshire cat and she's been floating on a cloud all day."

They stepped into the kitchen where the family waited. Pattie rushed up to them. She wiggled her fingers and held out her left hand for Stephen to admire. "We're engaged too. Isn't it wonderful?"

He hugged her and said, "I know you two will be happy."

Tomas strode through the living room doorway. "Marian, get the bottle and some glasses. We gotta drink to the engaged couple." He poured a shot for everyone, held up his glass, and made a toast. "To my son and future daughter-in-law. *Na Zdrowie!*"

Glasses clinked. *"Na Zdrowie."* Shots were downed.

Pattie gasped and fanned her face. "Wooo, that stuff's hot." Johnny went to the sink to get his fiancé a glass of water.

Tomas reached for the bottle, about to pour a second round to toast Stephen's new job, but Stephen spoke up. "Thanks, but I'll have to pass on this one. I have to drive, and it's time for me to go." The family hugged him and wished him well.

Celina walked out with him. The day was bright and sunny with a whiff of falling leaves in the air. Locusts hummed in the trees and dozens of birds gathered on the power lines. They stopped beside the car and he kissed her mouth. "I miss you already," he said. They stood, silent, holding onto each other for a long moment. Their foreheads touched. "We'll write each other, and I'll call at least every other day."

"We'll write. And I'll wait for your calls." Her chin quivered, and she blinked back tears.

He held her close and spoke softly against her lips. "I love you."

Celina murmured, "I love you."

They shared one last kiss, and he cleared his throat. "It's time for me to go."

He got behind the wheel, slammed the door, and waved. Celina watched the car disappear down the lane. She lingered for a long while, there in the shade of the maple trees. *I waited for such a long time, then we found each other, and now he is gone. How can this be happening again? How?* She stared down the empty lane and asked herself the same question over and over again. She had no answer.

I wonder if God does single out one person or one family for more punishment than they deserve. She would not allow herself to dwell on the question. She remembered how the whole family had stood here and waved good-bye when Martyn left for the war, and his death in Germany. She looked down. *This is the same spot where I stood when I watched Bobby drive away before he was sent to Korea.* She blinked hard and with leaden steps, returned to the house.

Johnny and Pattie stood near the table. "Don't be sad, Missy, he'll be back before long. Stephen said he expects to make it home on at least a couple of week-ends."

"The time will go fast, you'll see." Pattie chimed in.

With a half-hearted smile, Celina nodded. "Yeah, I know, but it was so hard to watch him go."

"Now you'll have time to start saving money for your wedding," Marian said from the doorway.

"And we can look for wedding gowns together and pick out the colors of our bridesmaids' dresses," Pattie added. "My bridesmaids have to wear lavender. That's why I'm letting my hair grow out its natural color, so I won't clash."

"My God, you mean the woman I'm going to marry isn't a natural redhead!" Johnny gasped, held Pattie at arm's length, and repeated his favorite phrase from *Casablanca*. "I'm shocked, shocked."

Everyone, even Tomas, laughed.

"It's time to get supper started," Marian announced and the men wandered outside.

Celina wanted to go outside too. She wanted to take a long

walk, past the barn and the pond, through the meadow where the tall grass grew, to the secluded place where Stephen had asked her to marry him. Instead, she did what she was expected to do and joined her mother and Pattie in the kitchen. She set the table and nodded and smiled while Pattie babbled about her wedding plans. Celina stirred the sour cream and onions into the cucumber salad. Marian tended to the cook stove and fried thick slices of ham.

"The tomatoes are getting ripe. Looks like we'll have to lug the canning stuff out of the cellar again," Marian observed.

Celina's heart ached. *I really don't want to hear about lavender dresses, regardless of how beautiful they are. I want to think about Stephen, not dragging canning supplies from the cellar.*

"Celina did you hear me?" Marian asked.

She looked up. "No, what?"

"I said that Baba and I will do most of the canning, and you'll only have to bring a couple dozen jars up from the cellar and sterilize them."

"If I help, it'll go faster. I need to learn all these things now," Pattie said and wiggled the fingers of her left hand.

"I'll do it. It won't take long." Celina turned back to what she was doing.

The afternoon passed. Johnny drove Pattie home, and Celina held her breath when the phone rang. Marian called, "Celina, it's Stephen."

They talked and for a few minutes she was happy. When he hung up, she listened to the dial tone before replacing the receiver in its cradle. A cold emptiness burrowed its way through her heart. She trudged up the stairs, threw herself across her bed and cried, then finally chastised herself for being childish. She got up and glanced at her puffy face in the mirror. *I can't go around feeling sorry for myself. That won't do Stephen or me any good. I have to get out there and do something.*

CHAPTER 15

Celina stood and stared at the front door of the *Weekly Messenger's* office. *How long will I have to keep pestering them before I find out whether I have a job?* She stepped inside the cluttered room and asked to speak to Mr. Harry Cherriten. Edgar, wearing a purple plaid shirt and white trousers, came round the partition. "This is Sarah's last week. Did you know that?"

"Yes." She nodded.

Edgar drummed his stubby fingertips on the desktop. "I'm going to tell you like it is.

My brother and I wanted to hire our nephew, who nobody expected to get into college. But somehow the kid made it, so we need somebody until he drops out. He'll be home before Thanksgiving. Can you start on Monday?"

Surprised, Celina nodded. "Yes, yes of course."

"When the kid comes back, the job's still his. Understand?"

"Yes."

"Okay." Edgar jabbed his stubby thumb over his shoulder toward the desk Sarah would soon vacate. "When you get here, I'll show you the ropes. Sarah's our proofreader and fact-checker. She has other duties too, but we'll get to that when you start."

"Okay. What time do I come in?"

"Be here at eight o'clock. If I'm on time, everybody had better be on time."

"Okay, Monday at eight."

Elated, Celina skipped across the street on her way back to Duxbury's. She couldn't wait to tell Stephen that she had gotten a job with a newspaper, even if it was temporary. But she decided to avoid, for as long as possible, telling her parents about the temporary part. It was more important that she have real experience to put on an application to work for a bigger paper. A huge weight had been lifted from her shoulders; she'd never have to be in the same building with Grover C. Duxbury III again.

It had been so hard to walk back into that store after *it* happened. Now she'd never have to set foot in there. She'd never have to pretend that everything was fine and dandy when she despised the place and despised Duxbury. She'd never have to wash storefront windows, or clean the janitors' closet, or wipe sticky fingerprints from the glass counters, or polish the store's woodwork. Knowing all that made leaving even better.

When she got back, Earl stood waiting at the front entrance, hands on hips and elbows jutting out at his sides like a skinny kite. As she approached, he held up his clipboard and tapped it with his closed fountain pen. "Ahem. Celina you were off the premises," he checked his wristwatch, "for nine minutes. What do you have to say for yourself?"

She couldn't help but smile broadly. "Yes, I was off the premises. I was at the *Weekly Messenger* office, where I will begin a new position next Monday. And Earl, I'll shorten my lunch break by ten minutes today so I won't deprive Duxbury's of the nine minutes worth of work I missed this morning."

Earl sputtered and a few flecks of saliva landed on the clipboard. "But you can't leave. You've been here for three years. Your departments are well-organized, and who will help me with the orders?"

Celina grinned wider. "Remember last year when I asked about the promotion to office manager? You said the job was more suitable for a man. Well, there must be plenty of men who'd love to work here. I'm moving on. And I am giving a week's notice as of right now."

Mrs. Pinkerton and Harold had stopped what they were doing to listen to the exchange. The older woman crossed her arms over her ample breast. Harold nodded several times, rearranged his cap, and continued pushing his broom toward the basement door.

When Celina stopped at her station behind the counter in Women's Apparel, Pattie stood, waiting. "I didn't hear all of it. What happened?"

"His mouth dropped open, and he looked like a big, homely baby pigeon chirping at me," Celina said, after repeating her conversation with Earl and Pattie giggled. "I loved telling him I was quitting. And I loved that he didn't get the chance to try and make me squirm over a lousy nine minutes." She leaned close and whispered. "And I'll never have to see Duxbury again."

"I've got to get another job now, too. It won't be the same here without you."

"I hope you get one at the bank."

"Yeah, that…"

Earl strode by, tapped his clipboard, and the two saved the

rest of their conversation for later.

Sitting on the park bench at lunchtime, Celina unrolled the top of the brown paper bag and pulled out an apple turnover. She broke it in half and shared it with Pattie.

"This is good. Do you think your mom will show me how to make it?"

"Sure. In fact, when the weather gets a little cooler, maybe we can get her to make nut rolls on a Saturday when we can help."

"And I can surprise Johnny with something I baked."

"He loves this stuff. He can eat a whole nut roll in one sitting."

While they finished their lunch a few leaves drifted down and landed at their feet. Bushy-tailed squirrels busied themselves darting through the grass and stashing acorns under the sod.

Pattie leaned back on the bench. "A lot's happened this summer, hasn't it? Both of us are engaged and you got the job at the paper. I'm happy."

"Me too."

"You don't sound like it."

"I'm worried about Stephen. I want to be near him to make sure he's all right."

"Oh, he'll be all right. He made it all the way from Hungary, didn't he? You don't think he'd let anything happen now, do you?"

"No. But I still feel lost without him."

Celina threw a few crumbs toward the sparrows pecking nearby. "He called last night. Said he got there around dinner time and settled in to his," she grinned, "cell, as he calls it. It's a tiny room with only a bed, dresser, and study table. He plans to start looking for a place this week." She turned to

Pattie. "Have you and Johnny talked about the business he and Mike plan to open up?"

"Yeah. It'll be a lot of work and worry at first, but Johnny says that after a couple of years, the money will be coming in."

"If you get hired at the bank, it'll be good experience for the future."

"That's another reason why I have to get out of Duxbury's. Stacking blue jeans, flannel shirts, and jockey shorts isn't helping me prepare for anything."

Silence fell between them.

"Are you really going to let your hair grow out its natural color?" Celina asked.

Pattie lowered her head and used her fingers to part a segment of her hair. "Look, you can see the roots already. I don't want to look like Piper Laurie anymore."

"Why not?"

"There are more important things than trying to look like a movie star."

"A lot more important things."

"Before I go back to the store," Pattie said as they stood, "I'm going to the bank and check on my application." She rushed down the street to the three-story, limestone building with Corinthian columns, and stepped up to the massive glass door. Absently, Celina watched her stride in and wondered what Stephen was doing. *I hope he's not too busy to miss me.*

The day dragged on but finally it was over.

"Is your mom still canning tomatoes this week?" Pattie asked as they strolled through the parking area.

"Yeah."

I'll come over and help."

"I don't know why she wants to start so early. Most of

them won't be ready till the middle of September." She frowned. "And tomatoes make such a mess. You have to scald them, peel them, cut them up, and squish them into quart jars."

"I'm glad she's doing it now since I need to learn all these wifey things. Will your baba help?"

"Oh yeah, but she's worried about Pap and doesn't want to leave him for too long. He's been sick lately. The doctor says old age is catching up with him. His heart isn't as strong as it used to be. He's been keeping Kwiaty near the barn because he gets out of breath when he goes out in the field after her. You know how he loves that horse."

"Yeah, my pap is slowing down too. But my baba keeps chasing him out of the house to go fishing, or to the hardware store. She says he can't just sit on the couch and wait to die."

Celina nodded. "It's sad."

"Yeah. I can't imagine what it's like to get old."

"Me either. We're lucky to be young today. Now that Korea's over, there are no more wars to fight."

"Thank God we don't have to worry about that."

Celina sighed. "Yeah. You want to come over for supper?"

"Sure, I'll stop at home and change, and tell my mom where I'm going."

They got into their cars. Celina turned right on Main Street and Pattie turned left.

That evening, Stephen called. "I'm coming home right after classes tomorrow. I'm not waiting till Labor Day."

More cheerful than she'd been for days, Celina called her best friend. "Stephen's coming home for the weekend. I can't wait."

"We'll make plans to do something fun."

\#

On Friday afternoon, Celina stood under the maple trees staring down the lane; her anxiety lifted when she saw his car coming. He jumped out, grabbed her, and swung her high into the air before planting a big noisy, kiss on her cheek. She slipped her arms around his neck and they indulged in a long and lingering kiss.

He slid his arm around her waist and they walked toward the house. "Tell me more about the job at the newspaper."

"They had planned to hire a nephew but he is in college for now. I'll be proofreading and fact-checking. I hope I'll be able to write for the editorial page, maybe something about mine safety since there are so many coal mines around here. I'm not sure what else is involved, but Edgar, that's Mr. Cherriten's brother and partner, said he needs someone to take over Sarah's job. Today was her last day."

"Didn't they want to have you start while Sarah was still there so she could train you?"

"I guess not. In fact, if I hadn't gone to the office, I don't know when they would have called me."

"They don't sound too well organized."

"But they get the paper out every Thursday so they must be doing something right. And I'm so glad to be getting out of Duxbury's that I won't mind dealing with their disorganization. I just hope I'll be able to cover some general news like school board meetings and maybe some of the high school events. I know I'll do a good job."

Johnny's car roared past them and he beeped the horn, waved, then pulled up to the house. His bright eyes peered out of a smudged, dusky face. "Hey Stephen, good to see you. That sister of mine has been moping every day since you left."

"Johnny! I haven't been moping."

Stephen laughed. "So you missed me, huh?"

"Well, yeah." She flushed bright pink from her collarbone to the roots of her hair.

Johnny plopped down on the back porch and set his dinner bucket and cap on the top step. He kicked off his boots and looked up, a broad grin splitting his grimy face. "Okay, okay, then if you weren't moping, you must have been contemplating the major philosophical problems of existentialism."

"Oh, what do you know about existentialism?"

"I know it's a popular word the eggheads use when they have long faces about the state of the world."

Stephen, amused at their bickering, changed the subject. "Say, what's going on this week end?"

"There's a dance at the Polish Hall. I'm not sure which band is playing, but I hope it's the Swing Kings. Pattie said there's a good movie at the drive-in. And there's always the Pizza Place afterwards."

Stephen turned to Celina.

"I'd like to go to the dance tomorrow. How about going to the movie tonight?" she said.

"I'll call Pattie as soon as I get cleaned up and that's what we'll do." Johnny chuckled and walked inside.

#

Celina rushed through her Saturday chores, dusted the living room, cleaned the kitchen, and began scrubbing the back porch. She swished the broom until the porch floor was a froth of suds. Then she tossed several buckets of water across the slick wooden planks. Ripples fanned out and sent streams of suds over the edge and she laughed when Frankie snapped at the popping bubbles.

Sweeping the excess water onto the grass, she noticed her mother and father return from shopping in town. He carried an armload of parcels wrapped in brown paper tied with string. "Open the kitchen door, will ya," he said.

"Dad, you're going to leave tracks across the floor."

"I gotta take this stuff in. Open the door before I drop something." She opened the screen door, and he took three long strides into the middle of the kitchen. He dumped the packages in an untidy pile on the table, took a few more steps then disappeared into the living room.

Celina looked skyward, drew her wet hands down over her face, and swore under her breath. Tomas heard her through the open door. "What are you gripin' about?"

"You messed up my clean floor, that's what."

"A few footsteps hain't gonna hurt it. Now quit complainin'."

This family will never change. Celina lugged the pails and broom to the pantry and yanked the door shut. She pulled the pink cotton babushka off her head. "Damn it anyway."

Marian stepped into the kitchen. "Now what?"

"In case nobody noticed, I just finished scrubbing the floor and the porch is still wet. Couldn't anybody wait five minutes till I put the carpets down so the place doesn't get all tracked up?"

The multicolored rag rugs lay in a small pile on one of the chairs. Celina marched to where they lay. She grabbed them and tossed one in front of the sink, one in front of the stove, and one in front of the door.

"Okay, the carpets are down," Marian said. "Now I have groceries to put away."

"Fine," Celina snapped.

Tomas called from the living room. "Cook some of that kielbasa we got, and boil some eggs. I'm hungry."

For a long moment, mother and daughter eyed one another. Celina refused to flinch and Marian said, "Go and get ready for your date. I'll do it."

Celina ran up the stairs. *This family is so inconsiderate. They don't care that I spent the whole day cleaning. They just tramp through the house without even asking if it's okay.* She threw herself across the bed and stared at the ceiling for a moment, but she didn't have time to wallow in her frustration. She gathered her things and trotted down to the bathroom to get ready for the dance.

She was just finishing when Stephen arrived early. They took a long drive before meeting Pattie and Johnny at the Polish Hall.

CHAPTER 16

After Sunday Mass, Stephen took hold of Celina's hand. "Let's stop in at the rectory and talk to Father Schmidt about a wedding date." He checked his watch. "We'll have time before I leave."

They knocked on the rectory door, heard shuffling inside, and a wave of anticipation rushed over her. *In a minute we'll be talking to the priest about our wedding ceremony.* She looked up at Stephen and his eyes, full of tenderness, were fixed on her. *This is really happening.*

Father Schmidt flung the door open and led them down a narrow uncarpeted hall to his study; a room Celina liked at first sight. A large desk piled high with papers and books dominated the space. Stacks of *Time* magazine filled an arm chair. An ancient typewriter sat on a rickety stand, and books lined the shelves on the walls. A crucifix hung on an uncluttered panel between two windows. The priest, who Celina had known all of her life, waved an arm. "Sit down. Sit down." He took his place behind the desk and patted his ample stomach. Pleased, he looked from one to the other and assured them that Holy Mother Church would sanction and bless their marriage. "Have you set a date?"

For a long moment, Stephen and Celina looked at each other. Father Schmidt fidgeted in his chair and cleared his throat.

"We'd like to get married soon, in October, but my parents aren't happy about it," Celina said.

Father Schmidt sat up straighter and cleared his throat again. Embarrassed concern settled on his broad features. "Sometimes there's an issue of," he patted his portly middle once again and sheepishly eyed them both, "a little one on the way with some couples." He hurried on. "If that's the case we can have you married in no time."

Celina's cheeks burned. She looked down at her engagement ring and remembered the impassioned moments after Stephen had given it to her.

Stephen leaned forward in his chair and explained. "Father, it's not like that. Celina is not pregnant. We love each other and want a life together. Her parents aren't happy about it because they want us to wait a year, and neither of us wants that."

Still ill at ease, Celina tried to avoid looking directly at the priest.

Father Schmidt's round face settled into an uncomfortable grimace. "I'm sorry I misunderstood, but there are," he coughed, "times when couples want to move the date up for the reason I mentioned."

He redirected his question to Celina. "So, tell me why your parents are not happy about the wedding date."

She proceeded to explain their predicament, about Marian's desire for all her children to settle near home and that her mother wanted Stephen to stay in Kenville to teach at the local high school, once they were married.

The priest ran his fingers over his shiny scalp. "You have a problem all right. Does your mother...your family...understand that opportunities to teach in a good Catholic university don't come along every day?"

"I don't think she sees it that way, Father," Celina answered.

For a long moment, he stared at the ceiling. "Unless you know someone on the school board, there is no chance of getting on here in the local district. And being Catholic won't help." He shifted in his chair. "They'll be very polite and tell you there are no positions available, and that will be the end of it."

He waited for Stephen and Celina to absorb what he'd said. The priest tipped his chair back, tapped the ends of his fingers together, and stared into space. In his own good time, he continued. "Why don't you apply for your marriage license, get the blood tests out of the way, and check with me when everything is in order? Maybe something will change by then."

Stephen ran his hand across his chin. "If we move forward on this, maybe something will change."

The discussion ended and the priest ushered them back down the narrow hallway. At the door he reminded them that with the Lord's help, all would be well.

The couple left the rectory. Celina had more hope than she'd had since Marian surprised her with the story about Pap losing touch with his brother after Ellis Island.

Not entirely convinced that Father Schmidt could help them, Celina asked Stephen's opinion.

"Well, your mom and dad are more likely to listen to him than to us."

"Yes, you're right. The priest's opinion is definitely more

important than ours. He has always been so kind, but do you think he'd really do that for us?"

"Honey, I don't know. We'll get the blood tests and license and see what happens."

"We'll have to do it during the week," she said. "Public offices are closed on Saturdays."

"The Labor Day holiday is next week, and since my classes are on Monday, Wednesday, and Friday, I can stay till Tuesday afternoon. We can have the tests done and get the license on Tuesday, before I leave."

#

Promptly at eight the next morning Celina entered the *Weekly Messenger* office. There was no sign that Sarah had ever been there. Edgar sat at one of the desks pounding the typewriter keys and slamming the carriage to its return position.

She stepped round the partition and smiled. "Good morning."

Without raising his head, Edgar held his hand up. "Hold it right there. Have to finish this."

While she waited, Celina looked around. The place was more chaotic than during her interview with Harry Cherriten. The wastepaper baskets overflowed with sandwich wrappers and rumpled old newspapers. Pencils with broken points littered the shelf next to the pencil sharpener, and unfilled ink bottles served as paperweights holding down stacks of unkempt documents and letters.

Edgar tore the last page from the machine. He examined it and without looking at her asked, "You ready to start?"

"Yes."

"Okay, let's give you a little tour around the place. After that I'll put you to work." He raised his right arm and shot the hand into a forward-march position. "This way."

They stepped through a doorway at the back of the room and walked down a long corridor. The heavy odor of paper, ink, and machine oil hung in the air. "We're a small operation here. Harry and I, along with two full-time and one part-time employee, take care of everything. For now you'll be one of the full-time people."

The plank floor creaked under Edgar's heavy footfalls. They walked to the back of the building and he flung open a door that had once been white, but was now a dull gray. The area around the doorknob carried the imprints of a thousand ink-covered fingers.

They entered a room filled with huge machinery.

"Does your family buy our paper?"

Celina nodded. "Yes, it comes in the mail on Saturdays."

"Good, then you know what it looks like. How it's laid out."

"Yes."

"Since we're a weekly," Edgar said, "we cover only local news like weddings, family reunions, obituaries, and legal notices. Things like that."

They stopped in front of a machine, and even Edgar's bulk was dwarfed by its size. He continued talking. "Plus, school announcements, sports, homecoming, and the spring prom. The way I see it…if people want national news, they can watch the television or get the *Pittsburgh Press* delivered."

He shot a question in Celina's direction. "What do you think?"

She said what she knew he wanted to hear. "Local news is what we look for in the weekly paper."

"Right."

"Now this is where we do our printing. We have sturdy equipment. This Linotype machine has a few years on it, but it's reliable and does what we want it to do. Harry keeps it in tip-top condition."

Celina stared at the monstrosity with its pulleys, gears, and buttons.

Harry Cherriten sat hunched over the Linotype machine's three-part keyboard. He held several slips of wrinkled paper in one hand. A stack of notes sat in a basket at his feet. A clothesline had been strung around the room, and dozens of notes and typed sheets, attached with wooden clothespins, were spaced out along its length.

Harry did not look up until Edgar yelled for his attention. "Hey, Harry. I'm showing the new employee around."

The beanpole of a man glanced in their direction, unfolded his body, and jumped to his feet. "Hello, hello. Welcome aboard." He whirled around and patted the Linotype machine. "How do you like our fire-breathing dragon here?"

"I didn't know printing equipment was so big," Celina responded.

A wide grin split his thin face. He leaned against the machine and threw one foot over the other in a long-legged nonchalant pose then sucked air between his teeth. "Some of it isn't, but this…. this magnificent piece of machinery is trained to do everything I command." He nodded toward the machine. "She's a little temperamental from time to time, but considering her age, she's doing okay."

At that moment, Edgar's eyebrows flew up. He puckered his brow, and shook his head from side to side with quick short jerks. "Harrrrry."

At a loss to understand Edgar's twitching, Celina stepped away from the gesturing man. "How old is it?"

"This Linotype machine is sixty-five years old." Harry paused for effect. "Old enough to collect Social Security!" His sandy moustache twitched and he burst into laughter. "Get it—old enough for Social Security."

She laughed and Edgar frowned. "I tried to warn you about Harry's dumb jokes," he said. "But no, you didn't pay attention and fell for it. You had to ask."

He stood there, his mouth in a thin line, while Harry cackled, pulled a hankie from his hip pocket, and wiped his eyes.

"Oh, come on Ed. That's a funny one."

"It is not."

"Is too."

Celina wanted to laugh just because Harry was having such a good time, but Edgar's behavior caused her to have second thoughts and she pulled her face into sober lines. "If it's that old, how do you keep it running?"

Before Harry could say a word, Edgar interrupted. "Just tell her, Harry. Okay?"

A chuckle bubbled from Harry's mouth. "Aw, come on Ed."

Edgar's chubby cheeks flattened, his eyes narrowed, and Celina thought his face looked like a bashed-up old pie pan. He eyed his brother.

"Okay, okay." Harry stood back and admired the machine. "I stocked up on parts from as many old machines as I could find, and I got some good stuff from a newspaper in Philadelphia that was converting to offset printing."

Still chuckling, he went to a dusty window and pointed. "See that building across the alley? That's where I store my extra Linotype parts."

He turned to Edgar. "You want to take her over and have a look?"

"No. She has to get started in the office."

"Cripes, Ed. You're such a spoilsport." Silently, Celina agreed with Harry.

"We have a paper to get out."

Harry raised his arm in an expansive gesture that encompassed the entire room. "I know. I get it out every week."

Celina followed Edgar back to the cluttered front office. They stopped at the desk Sarah had used. "In spite of Harry, we do get this paper out on time every week." He took a deep breath and tapped the side of his head with his forefinger. "It takes a lot of thinking and planning. I'm the thinker and planner. I will write the stories, and you will proofread and double-check facts."

"I'd like to have a chance to do some reporting…get some experience as a journalist." Celina said.

Edgar eyed her for a few seconds as though he were trying to size her up. "That's not what you were hired for. Harry and I do the real reporting. Vera Clark does the society and women's page. You know our freelance reporter, Vera Clark, don't you?"

"Yes, I've met her," Celina answered. The weight of her status at the new employee got heavier.

Edgar picked up a handful of typed sheets and rearranged them. "Once we get this material edited, it's ready to go to Harry for placement on the pages. Got that?"

"Yes."

"Everybody reads high school sports and family news first. So, we can't have a single mistake on ballgame scores, engagements, weddings, anniversaries, or birth announcements. And never, *ever*, make a mistake on an obituary. Or one of us will be pushing up daisies next to the dearly departed when the family gets through with us."

Celina smiled and Edgar frowned.

He shoved a sheet of paper toward her. "Here, double-check the information on these boys. They're new army recruits. After that, do the hospital discharges."

Edgar bent over his desk and rummaged through the stack of papers. He pulled a couple of sheets free. After you're done with that, proofread this guest editorial by our state legislator. Make sure his grammar and spelling are perfect. We can't have our politicians sounding like uneducated clodhoppers."

In spite of Edgar's negativity, Celina still hoped to at least be considered for a small assignment. "Err, um, who covers things like township meetings, the chamber of commerce, and who writes editorials?"

"I told you, Harry and I cover all the real news, and the traffic accidents, and police beat. Vera covers ladies' meetings and all church related functions like weddings, baptisms, and funerals. And I am the only one who writes the editorials. That's it. Nothing else. Understand?"

Celina nodded. "Yes." She focused on the drab green desk and the unkempt piles of papers lying there. "Is there anything else I should know today?"

Edgar removed his glasses and squinted. "This place is a pigpen. Sarah didn't empty the wastepaper baskets, water the plants, or run the vacuum cleaner the way she was supposed to, the whole last week or so before she retired. That'll be your job now. She always did it on Thursday or Friday, but you might as well get things cleaned up today and do it again on Friday."

Celina drummed her fingers against the side of her thigh and scrutinized the office and sighed. It looked like there was no escape from charwoman's work in the world of business.

Edgar continued. "I make the coffee in the mornings, so you'll have to empty the coffeepot and clean up around there before quitting time. Don't want bugs crawling around on the cups."

Celina sat down at Sarah's old desk. She checked and double-checked facts and proofread the articles Edgar pulled out of the typewriter. By two o'clock, she had a headache from listening to the typewriter carriage slam back to its original position at the end of every single line Edgar typed. And she was disappointed that she wouldn't have an opportunity to try her hand at reporting or editorial writing, at least not yet. She eyed her boss. *I'll keep asking and sooner or later he'll give me an assignment.* She rubbed her neck and blinked a few times before going back to proofreading.

An hour before quitting time, she carried trash to the rusted barrel behind the building, found the vacuum cleaner in the closet, and swept up several weeks worth of crumbs, pencil shavings, and dust bunnies. Her head throbbed harder from the sweeper's roar.

She'd just pushed the machine into the broom closet when Edgar called out. "Don't forget to water the geraniums. Our mother brought them in, and she wouldn't like it if they died."

After work Celina met Pattie. "You won't believe the day I had. Harry tells jokes that aren't funny, and Edgar gets miffed and yells at him. Actually, Edgar yells instead of talks."

"Is he as bad as Earl?" Pattie asked.

"I haven't decided yet." Celina rubbed her temples. "Vera

came in with a piece on old Mr. Grischam's funeral. She interviewed some out-of-town relatives from Philadelphia and New York so it's a long piece. Edgar liked it and said that the family will buy extra papers and send clippings to everyone. That was the only time he smiled all day."

Celina pulled her hands down over her face. "Harry, and his helper Robbie, started using the Linotype machine this afternoon. It's as big as St. Stanislaus' church organ and makes a racket as loud as Pap's old tractor. Harry called me back to show me how they use the hand-fed flatbed printing press. They feed it one sheet of paper at a time."

"Can I come in and see everything?"

"I'd have to ask Harry. No, I had better check with Edgar first."

"Sure doesn't sound anything like the store. Do you like it?"

"I think I will after I get used to Edgar and all the commotion. The newspaper is so different from Duxbury's. Harry and Edgar bicker about deadlines all the time, and there are scraps of paper hanging from a clothesline."

She put her hand to her forehead. "Right now I have a sickening headache."

"Duxbury didn't come in today," Pattie said, "and Earl's enough to give me a migraine. He told me I'd probably have to wash the windows myself on Friday." Pattie looked up at the sky and tapped a polished finger at her chin. "I wonder if I'll have to do windows if I get on at the bank."

"I wouldn't be surprised."

"It was kind of strange without you at the store today. Earl said Duxbury might not hire anyone till it gets closer to Christmas. So Mrs. Pinkerton and I have to take turns in Ladies. Everybody said to tell you hello, and to come over on your lunch break."

"I will. But you'll have to let me know when Duxbury isn't around."

"When are you going to start being a reporter?"

"It doesn't look like I'll be doing that for a while. Harry and Edgar do most of it, and Vera does the women's news." She laughed in spite of her disappointment. "You won't believe this...I have to empty the wastepaper baskets, sweep the floor and water the plants. I guess women get stuck doing that kind of stuff everywhere they go."

Pattie's eyebrows shot up. "Aren't you disappointed?"

"Yeah, but at least I'm out of Duxbury's."

It was getting late so they hugged and went their separate ways. When she arrived home, Celina headed straight to the bathroom and found some aspirin. She took two. After running upstairs and changing her clothes, she trudged down to the kitchen, and went through the motions of preparing the dinner.

Marian peeled potatoes at the table. "You aren't saying much about your new job."

"I have a headache."

"You never get headaches. What's the matter?"

Celina raised her hand and touched her forehead. "It was hectic and noisy in there today."

"So, what's it like?"

She told Marian about proofreading and fact-checking, and Edgar slamming the typewriter carriage.

"Well, you wanted to know about the newspaper business," Marian said as she placed the silverware on the table. "I guess it's not as glamorous as it is in the movies with Katharine Hepburn." She gave Celina a sideward glance.

"Mom, I didn't think it'd be like in the movies." I wish

you could be a little kinder, a little more encouraging once in a while.

"Maybe you should have stayed at Duxbury's. It's a nice store."

"No."

"I don't see what's wrong with Duxbury's. Pattie seems to like it."

"I left that store, and I'm glad. I don't plan on ever going back." *And you will never know what happened to me there because I'm protecting you from knowing.*

The cellar door opened and Tomas lumbered in. He sat down and pulled socks onto his knobby feet. "How soon's supper ready?"

Celina filled his plate and carried it to the table. "Right now."

He slid his coffee cup toward her. "Coffee ready?" Weary from a long day, she vaguely wondered if women would be expected to wait on men forever.

He added cream and gulped down a mouthful. "How's the new job?"

She sat down and told him about her day. He leaned back in his chair and grinned. "That Harry and Edgar sound like Laurel and Hardy from the movies, don't they Marian?"

"They're a couple of strange birds, if you ask me," she remarked.

Marian had just poised the butcher knife over the spice cake she baked that afternoon when they heard Frankie scramble out from under the porch and tear around the side of the house.

"Johnny's home. Celina, get your brother's plate ready."

"And get me another cup of coffee."

"Can't anybody do anything for themselves around here?"

Celina said, looking directly at her father. "I have a splitting headache and I don't feel like waiting on people right now."

"For Christ's sake. I'll get it myself." Tomas' chair scraped the floor as he pushed it back and loped to the stove. He turned around. "You'd better get off that high horse, Missy. I don't like the way you're actin' lately."

"I'm tired, that's all." She didn't want to be rude to her father, but unless she became quarrelsome and confrontational no one paid any attention to her concerns.

That evening Stephen called. He asked about her first day at the paper and sympathized when she told him about the brother's antics—Edgar's dictatorial attitude and abrasive tactics which irritated her, and Harry's exuberance which made her want to leap to his defense.

"I like Harry, but with Edgar, it's not possible." She paused. "Oh, I just thought of something. I have to ask him for a couple of hours off next Tuesday so we can apply for the marriage license."

"How do you think he'll react?"

She drew a breath. "From what I've seen so far, he won't like it at all. I'll offer to stay over after work to make up the hours, that's all. If Harry were the one I had to ask, I'm sure he'd wave me off and say, 'take your time.'"

"Do you want to postpone getting the license for a couple of weeks?"

"No. I'll stay late and get all the work done, so he shouldn't be too upset. Surely he'll understand how important this is."

They discussed their day and after a few minutes, Stephen said, "I went to a jazz club called the Hurricane Lounge with a couple of other professors. We had a few beers and spent a couple of hours talking and listening to great music. When you come to Pittsburgh, we'll go there. And you can forget about that curmudgeon, Edgar."

"I'd love to, but I don't know anything about jazz."

"Neither do I. All you have to do is sit and listen. I like living in this city."

They said their goodbyes. "I love you and will be home Friday in the late afternoon," Stephen said.

"I love you too. See you Friday." She hung up the phone and wondered what else he did in the evenings with his new friends, but Celina couldn't allow herself to be jealous.

#

Upon entering the office the next morning, she saw Edgar swiveling in his chair and reading newspaper clippings. A cup of black coffee sat next to a half-eaten portion of berry pie. He looked up. "Coffee's fresh, and the pie's in the top drawer of the empty desk."

Celina put her things on her desk and poured herself some coffee. She tried the pie. "This is really good. Did your wife bake it?"

"Heck no. My mother lives with us…she's the one who picked the berries and made the pie." He looked at Celina over the rim of his cup. "My wife isn't much of a cook."

A minute later he tossed his plate onto an empty desk. "Wash this stuff before you get started this morning. Check the coffee pot too. I had two cups and so did Harry and Robbie. Make another pot."

Put out at the way men automatically assumed women were the dishwashers, Celina gathered the dirty dishes into an out-basket, and took them to the janitor's sink. *They never ask, just tell. "You there, the one wearing the skirt, you make the coffee, you wash the dishes. And me, the one wearing the pants, I sit back and watch you."*

Celina cleared her throat. "Edgar, I need to ask you something."

"What?"

"Next Tuesday morning I have to take an hour or two off." She added quickly, "but I won't take a lunch break and I'll stay over after work to make up the time."

Edgar stopped what he was doing and turned slowly in his chair. "You want to take a couple of hours off...a week after you start here?"

"I really have to."

"What is so important?"

Celina didn't want to tell him about the blood tests and marriage license, so she stated that she had to go to Clearfield for an appointment when Stephen had a day at home.

"He's the guy who sent the telegrams from here a couple of times. I remember him."

"That's him. I do need to take a couple of hours off. I'll be back as quickly as possible."

Edgar breathed deep and sighed noisily. "I suppose. But you had better plan on staying until you get your full eight hours in. I don't like employees taking off anytime they please."

She swallowed hard. "Thanks Edgar."

"Yeah. Yeah." Edgar turned to the pile of work on his desk. He grabbed a handful of notes and flung them in Celina's direction. "The stuff on the Duxburys' thirty-fifth wedding anniversary is in there. Marge wants a big spread with pictures. When you read that one, make sure you pretty it up as much as you can. Then I want to see it."

Celina picked up the papers and began to read.

He interrupted. "I thought I told you to make more coffee. And get that mess cleaned up in the desk drawer. I don't know why Harry puts food in the empty desk."

"Anything else you would like right now, Mr. Cherriten?" Celina said in her best professional voice. But her stomach tied itself into knots and her fingers tightened around the notes she held.

"Come to think of it, you can go down to Smith's Grocery and pick up a couple of pounds of coffee." He looked at his watch. "You can do that while you're on lunch break. The petty cash is in this drawer."

He turned his attention to his desk. "Now, I have work to do."

Every time Edgar opened his mouth, she liked him less. She examined the notes on the Duxbury anniversary and shuffled through them. Her skin crawled when she thought about the man. She picked up the typed sheets and read about Grover C. Duxbury's graduation from college and his engagement to Margery Smithfield of Newark, New Jersey. She read about their Niagara Falls honeymoon, the birth of their three sons, and the expansion of the family business from a small store to a sizeable establishment. The piece even included news of their recent vacation to New York City.

Celina corrected Marge's misspelled words and added punctuation where needed. She broke long paragraphs into short ones then gave the piece back to Edgar.

"Did you like working over at Duxbury's?" he asked.

"It was okay."

"Everybody knows G. C. drinks too much. Do you know anything about his drinking?"

"I can't say that I do."

Edgar threw his head back. "You don't know much, do

269

you?"

She wasn't about to tell Edgar Cherriten anything she didn't want to tell him. "Look, Mr. Cherriten, I worked in Ladies Wear. I was an employee. I didn't have any reason to know the Duxburys."

"Know anything about Earl Hartisty then?"

"He loves the store and takes over when Mr. Duxbury goes out of town."

"Hmm. Anything else?"

"No."

Edgar turned back to his desk, slipped a sheet into the typewriter, and began to type. Within the hour, Celina's head throbbed. She eyed the clock and wished for quitting time.

When she met Pattie after work, they watched Duxbury's black Cadillac move away from the store. It was followed by Marge's Buick. "She was in and out of the store all day. They had the office door closed but I could hear them arguing."

"Did Earl say anything?"

"No. He just yelled at everybody to get back to work, even when we were working."

"I am so glad I'm out of there." She disliked Edgar Cherriten, but at least she didn't have to step into Duxbury's realm and be in his presence five days a week. At the store she had to be polite, respectful, businesslike, and pretend nothing untoward had happened. His role was that of upright citizen, and she had to play the loyal employee. He had attacked her and gotten away with it.

CHAPTER 17

At suppertime, Johnny announced that he and Mike planned on quitting the mines by November. They had signed a lease and planned to open their store before the weather got really cold.

"I guess you're gonna do it," Tomas said. "But be sure you get yourself some land. Every man has gotta have his own land so he don't starve to death if there's no work."

"What does Pattie think?" Marian asked.

"She wants to quit Duxbury's and help out."

Between bites Tomas said, "Shirley Creek's still paying good. And you're throwing your hard-earned money into a business that's pretty iffy." He shook his head and continued eating.

"Listen, Dad, I'm not like you and Andy. I hate working underground in the pitch dark, the coal dust in my eyes, my nose, my throat; I'm sick of it. I want to work in the daylight and fresh air." He nodded slowly. "And I want the ground below my feet instead of above my head."

"Well, damn it, I don't want you failin' like I did when I went out west during the Depression to find work on

Boulder Dam. It makes a man feel damned little when he can't support his family and has to come crawling back home with nothing in his pockets. At the mines you can make enough to buy a piece of land and hold onto it. Plus, if you didn't make it work, them John Bulls will go around saying you're a dumb Polack who can't run a business. Look how they go around telling those damned Polish jokes. You never hear them telling English jokes."

"The English are so boring that nobody wants to waste a joke on them." Johnny teased.

"That hain't funny, Johnny."

Johnny became serious. "Dad, those people don't know us. They try to fool themselves and pretend they're better than other people, so they make up dumb jokes."

"Well, I don't want them getting a chance to try and look down on you. Look how they showed Poles in that movie…. the one, what was it…*A Streetcar Named Desire,* with that Stanley Kowalski character. It insulted Poles, and all those big-shot movie people said it was a great story. I'd like to talk face to face with the bastard who wrote that story."

"It was only a movie."

"People believe it, though. They like thinking we're dumb, or mean, and giving us less than our due."

"Well, people are going to see that I'm no dumb Polack. I'm one of the smart ones. I've already outsmarted Wilcox's son when he tried to bilk us on the garage we wanted to buy. I plan to have more than one store in the next few years. And there are plenty of people who will buy auto parts from me."

"I hope you're right, son. But I still think you should stick with your own, and don't trust any of those big shots out there." He pushed his coffee cup toward Celina, appeared to think better of it, and asked Marian for a refill.

After supper, Celina waited for Stephen to call. But no call came.

The next evening she hung around the living room, hovering near the phone.

Marian noticed. "Why don't you go out to the garden and pick some green peppers and I'll take them over to Baba. She's helping Aunt Mary make chowchow tomorrow."

"I might miss Stephen's call."

"It won't hurt him to call back."

"Mom, I want to talk to him. Okay?"

Marion crossed her arms and scrutinized her daughter in silence.

The phone rang and Celina scurried to answer it. She carried it around the corner to the hallway. Stephen's voice sounded tinny and far away. "Did you get a couple of hours off on Tuesday?"

"Yes, Edgar was crabby about it, but he gave in. Now tell me what you've been doing."

"I've been busy meeting my colleagues and finding my way around campus. The English Department is across the hall from us, and some of those professors love the beat artists, especially the poet Allen Ginsberg. The beatniks have been around since the 1940s, and their main concentration seems to be off-beat literature. There are a few oddballs in the department, but you find them everywhere, I suppose."

Celina thought she'd like to interview the bohemian characters who seem to enjoy breaking all the social norms. As she prepared for bed, she mused about the type of questions she would ask if she ever had the opportunity.

#

On the Friday before Labor Day, Celina composed obituaries, edited engagement announcements, and proofread a few pieces Harry had set aside for the next week's edition. She glanced at the clock every few minutes, and Edgar's voice clanged in her ears.

At noon he got to his feet. "I'm going to the chamber of commerce lunch. I'll be back later."

Glad to see him go, Celina poured over the stack of notes on her desk. She looked up when she heard the screen door open then close.

The top half of Harriet Grayhill's face was visible above the partition. "Hello, Harriet. It's been a while since I've seen you."

"I spent a few weeks with my sister in Erie."

"How's she doing?"

"Getting old and cranky, but her health is good."

"What brings you here today?"

"I have a Women's Society announcement. Summer's almost over and our meetings will start up again at the end of September."

Celina examined the neatly typed sheet of paper and using a pencil as a pointer, went over the wording with the older woman.

When Harriet left, she moved back to her desk. A couple of minutes later, the older woman returned. She cleared her throat and Celina looked up. "Do you want to add something to the announcement?"

"No, but, well...I hope you won't think I'm prying, but I do talk to Terez almost every day. So I know a lot of things."

She grimaced and scanned the wall above Celina's head.

"Is something wrong?"

"No, no. It's just that...well, I feel I should tell you

something."

"Come around here and sit down."

Harriet sat next to Celina's desk. In slow, measured tones she began to speak. "A long time ago, when I was away at college, fate brought a young man into my life. His name was Brandon."

Harriet sighed and glanced around the room. "Oh, I did love him."

Celina didn't speak. She listened.

"But not enough, I guess. He wanted to marry me, but my parents wouldn't hear of it, because I would have to leave home and follow him to Washington, D. C. They told me to come home, and I came home to teach. He went into government service. We wrote to each other for almost a year, I pleaded with him to come here and I refused to join him there. After a while, he stopped writing."

Celina reached out and patted Harriet's blue-veined hand. "I'm sorry."

The older lady blinked tears away. "I know how difficult it is to leave one's family, but I hope you won't make the same mistake I made all those years ago." She leaned forward. "Each of us has the right to live our own life." Her pale eyes large and intent, she continued. "Savor your life while you're young, because it loses that savor when you're old." The light glinted off her white hair and she repeated her words in a small voice. "It loses its savor when you're old."

Celina sat there mute. Finally she stammered, "Thank you for telling me about Brandon. And, and for the advice."

Harriet smiled. "I saw his picture in the newspaper several years ago. He's an official in the Eisenhower administration, you know. He's successful just like he said he'd be."

Celina patted Harriet's shoulder.

The older woman pulled a cotton hankie from her pocket, wiped her eyes. "I really have to go. I have so many things to do."

Tears burned Celina's eyes as she watched the plump, little woman progress down the street. Confident and reserved, Harriet had been carrying the burden of regret for over forty years.

Heavy-hearted, Celina returned to her desk, picked up a handful of notes, and plopped down in her chair. She blinked several times. Edgar returned. Her head throbbed.

An hour before quitting time she left her desk to tidy the office. She collected the wastepaper, watered the plants, and emptied the coffee pot. Tugging on the vacuum cleaner, she dragged it out of the closet. In the midst of the battle with the machine, she looked up. Stephen stood smiling at her over the partition. She dropped the sweeper and was around the partition in seconds. "I am so glad you're here."

He gave her a quick peck on the cheek and looked in the direction she had come from.

"Oh, Stephen. This is Mr. Cherriten. He's the person who keeps the paper running smoothly." She didn't like her boss, but she was determined to be pleasant, even if she choked on the words.

Edgar came forward, and thrust out his hand. "Nice to meet you, Maszaros."

Stephen took his hand. "Mr. Cherriten."

Edgar eyed Stephen. "You want to have a seat and wait?"

"Thank you, no. I have to be on my way. My Aunt Terez is expecting me."

"Well, it was nice to meet you." Edgar turned back to his desk.

Stephen spoke quietly to Celina. "I'll be over right after

dinner."

"Yes, see you then."

When the door closed behind him, Edgar spun around in his chair. "I wonder what his story is."

Celina shot him a questioning look.

He screwed up his face and stared at the door. "Since he's from Europe and well educated, I would think he'd be interested in sophisticated women. Wouldn't you?" He opened his desk drawer and retrieved a silver-colored fountain pen, removed the top, and began to write.

On the defensive, Celina questioned him. "Why did you say that?"

He didn't look up. "I was just wondering."

"Were you implying something?" She stared at his back till he looked over his shoulder.

"No, nothing. Don't forget to water the plants." She decided that Edgar was a hateful little troll as well as a snoop. In spite of herself, she fought the urge to second-guess her relationship with Stephen.

The hours Celina and Stephen had together flew by like a happy dream. They spent Friday night laughing at the comedy of Dean Martin and Jerry Lewis at the movies, and Saturday at the Polish Hall dancing to the music of the Swing Kings. When the band played the last dance, Stephen held her close and they swayed to the music.

"I'm a lucky guy," he whispered.

She looked up into his dark eyes. "We're both lucky."

The dance ended and the couples drifted off the floor. Johnny and Pattie slipped through the chattering throng. "Hey, you two want to go to the truck stop for coffee and pie or something?"

Celina nodded, and Stephen turned to her with a twinkle

in his eye. "Sure, but don't forget we've got to get up for Mass in the morning. We have to stay on Father Schmidt's good side and let him know we're serious about our spiritual obligations."

Pattie's eyebrows hovered near her bangs. "Jeez, my parents wouldn't let me miss church even if I was dying. If I tried to get out of it, my mom would have a heart attack or something."

Celina smiled. "Okay, let's go to the truck stop and go to Mass in the morning."

On the drive home, she studied Stephen's profile in the darkness. "Remember when we were dancing the last dance?"

"Um hum."

"You said you were lucky."

"I remember."

Deep lines cut across her forehead. Edgar's words echoed in her mind, and she worried that she wasn't refined enough for someone like Stephen. "There are a lot of sophisticated women out there. Why did you find yourself attracted to someone like me?"

"Why would you ask that question?"

"I was just wondering."

"Because you're genuine, you don't waste time putting on silly airs, and you're honest. We think alike. We're the same religion. And you're beautiful." His voice was light. "We belong together."

He steered the car into the tall grass at the side of the road and switched the engine off. "You know I'm not a loner. I need someone in my life, someone to love." He took her hand and kissed her fingers. "I love you. I don't know what else to say." Pulling her closer, he rested his forehead against hers. "And you argue politics with your dad."

The dark cloud Edgar had placed in her mind evaporated. "And Dad's not easy to argue with."

He wrapped his arms around her.

A thrill excited her and she hugged him tight. "I love you so much."

"I love you, and I need you," he said in a husky whisper.

He kissed her and slid his hand along her neck and down the front of her blouse, Waves of excitement rushed through Celina's body; the wave of guilt took much longer to catch up.

The porch light was on when he kissed her good night.

On Labor Day, Stephen brought Aunt Terez to the house for a picnic.

Marian was in her element, wielding pots and pans and giving orders to everyone within earshot.

When she ducked into the pantry for a scoop of flour, Tomas tiptoed into the kitchen. He placed a finger over his lips and closed the screen door in silence. Celina couldn't help but smile. Even though her dad was gruff and old-fashioned, he was a good and likeable man.

Andy, Ellen and the kids arrived and the boys raced to the house. Andy yelled at them to slow down, and Ellen carried the domed cake carrier holding her coconut-frosted marble cake.

The place bustled with activity. Mike and Stella pulled in a few minutes later. Mike went round to the back of his car, popped the trunk, and brought out a case of Yuengling beer.

"Hey, where do I put this?" he yelled.

Tomas pointed to a galvanized wash tub so Mike and

Johnny buried the brown bottles deep in the melting ice.

Pattie wandered outside and followed Johnny to the shallow fire pit he had dug and circled with fieldstone. He stood back and admired his handiwork and slipped his arm around her shoulder. They stood close and spoke quietly.

Celina called through the screen door. "Hey. Mom needs help."

Dressed in shorts and blouses and wrapped in aprons, Celina and Pattie set to work filling the blanched cabbage leaves for the halupki. Pattie twisted her mouth in concentration as she worked. Frowning, she wiped her hands on her apron. "Look at this. The cabbage rolls are still lopsided and fall apart before I get them in the roaster. I'll never learn how to do this."

When all the stuffed treats were ready for the oven, Marian scattered a few loose cabbage leaves over the halupki and placed the lid on top.

"Making those things is a lot more work than I thought," Pattie announced as she washed her hands.

Outside, Tomas opened a bottle of beer, found a comfortable place under a tree, and ordered the young men to build the bonfire with the dry wood piled nearby. Johnny positioned several wads of newspaper in the fire pit under the dry kindling, struck a match, and the blaze crackled and spit and roared to life.

Marian yelled through the open window, "Make sure you take turns watching that fire. I don't want it spreading into the grass."

Two hours later, Tomas led the boys to the corn patch and they scurried between the rows reaching for plump ears, twisting them and pulling them from the stalks. Johnny and Stephen, with their T-shirt sleeves rolled up, moseyed to the tool shed and found the digging fork. Stephen flung it across his shoulder as they headed to the garden to dig potatoes.

Andy and Mike sat under a tree sipping beer until the boys ran back from the garden. They asked their dad to cut elderberry branches into sticks for roasting the frankfurters. Tomas laughed as Andy and Mike followed the boys to the edge of the yard. "You didn't think you'd get away with doin' nothing, did ya?" He took his spot in the shade.

Stephen placed the scrubbed potatoes next to the ears of corn stacked like cordwood beside the inferno. "The embers look about right." They tossed the spuds onto the glowing coals and used forked sticks to roll them onto hot spots.

The boys rushed toward the fire, but Andy yelled and grabbed them by the backs of their shirts before they got too close. "You two stay behind Uncle Johnny, you hear. Nothing will be ready to eat for another hour."

Later, the hungry boys stood near their father to watch Stephen brush the coals into a smooth layer with a long stick. Mike tossed the corn onto the hot ashes. "Corn'll be ready in a couple of minutes."

The boys ran to the house. "Baba, we need frankfurters to roast."

"I'm starving." Johnnie snatched a piece of chicken from the big yellow glass bowl on the picnic table.

Tomas pronounced the roasted vegetables ready to eat and they used the elderberry sticks to forage through the dying embers and retrieve the potatoes and corn, burned black by the intense heat of the fire. The women giggled when Mike yelped and blew on his fingers after holding onto a charred cob of corn a second too long.

Marian sat down on the edge of the porch, leaned against the railing, and sipped the beer Tomas brought her. She watched her family enjoying the day and smiled with contentment.

Soon enough, lightning bugs blinked their way up out of the grass, and Johnny raked what was left of the fire into a small mound. Marian turned on the porch light and Celina helped the boys push marshmallows onto the ends of long sticks. "I want to cook my marshmallow by myself," Marty announced.

Celina choked back laughter when, dismayed, he held up a charred, black lump of sweet air that had been a puffy white marshmallow only a minute earlier.

The sun sank below the horizon. The dying embers descended into ashes, and a barn owl called. Andy and his family headed down the lane toward home. Mike and Stella soon followed.

"I'm gonna call it a night," Tomas said. He approached the screen door and stood silhouetted against the yellow light of the kitchen. "Nice Labor Day picnic. A lotta men complain about him, but I say, God bless John L. Lewis and the United Mine Workers, or we'd a been digging coal on this Labor Day, not celebrating it." He stepped through the door and disappeared.

Stephen kissed Celina good night and called to his aunt who was inside chatting with Marian. "Aunt Terez, are you ready?"

It was a perfect day and Celina slept well, feeling her own contentment.

#

Tuesday morning, Stephen stopped in front of the newspaper office and waited until Celina jumped into the car.

"Edgar's in a rotten mood this morning. He doesn't like that I'll be out of the office."

He gave her a peck on the cheek. "Edgar knows you'll be back before noon, doesn't he?"

"Yes, but he's still annoyed."

He maneuvered the car away from the curb and Celina clasped her hands together. "I've got butterflies."

"Me too. Did you tell your parents where you were going?"

"No. I didn't want my mom questioning me. She'd start that business about waiting a year and us setting up housekeeping here. She won't listen to reason, and I don't want to talk about it anymore."

"I hope Father Schmidt can do something to help us."

"He'd be the only person she'd listen to."

A week later, a manila envelope addressed to Celina Pasniewski arrived at the newspaper office. Edgar held it up to the light and turned it over in his hands. "What's this?"

"Oh, that's the paperwork I needed." Celina stepped up but he continued to grasp the envelope. She reached for it and pried it from his fingers.

After work, in Duxbury's parking lot, Pattie jumped up and down with delight. "You'll never believe what happened today. I got the job at the bank. I start next week."

"Oh Pattie, that's swell." Celina hugged her.

"Yep." Pattie threw her shoulders back. "I got it. I can't wait to tell Johnny, and my parents, and your parents, and everybody. You have to tell Stephen when he calls."

"I will."

"You'll never believe what else happened."

"What?"

Pattie's eyebrows shot up high to meet her half-red and half-brown bangs. "Marge Duxbury came in, and she looked like she was ready to kill everybody in the store. She stomped into the office and started screaming even before the door was shut. I heard her yelling about the books being a mess and money being pissed down the drain."

Celina interrupted. "Did she say that?"

"That's what she said."

Pattie took a deep breath. "Then that darned Earl rushed over to the office and things quieted down. From then on, all we could hear was mumbling. After a while, Marge marched out and stopped dead…right in the middle of the store. She turned around and marched back to the office, forgot her pocketbook and had to run back for it. Everybody was staring. She stopped in front of Harold and Sam and told them to stop looking at her like a couple of dopes and get back to work."

"Jeez." The Duxbury's resembled the characters in one of those weird movies about rich and miserable people. "How can things be that bad over there? I mean, even though we had some slow times, there are a lot of customers, and the store's been around since Duxbury's grandfather's day," Celina marveled.

"We always have people moving through, but maybe his, you know…" Pattie lifted her hand to her mouth and tipped her head back, "has been causing problems."

"Could be. He never paid much attention to how things worked around there. If it wasn't for Earl, the place would fall apart."

"That's the big news from Duxbury's." Pattie reached into

her car and pulled out a magazine filled with pictures of wedding dresses and wedding cakes. "Do you want to go shopping for wedding gowns on Saturday? If we can't find anything in Clearfield, we can go to Altoona in a week or two."

"Okay. I'll start really early so I can get the housecleaning done before Mom and Dad go grocery shopping."

That evening after supper, Celina switched on her nightstand lamp and wrote Stephen a letter, telling him that the wedding license was safe in the bottom of her sweater drawer. She also told him Harriet's story about Brandon, then she plumped her pillows and sat back on her bed to reread several of his letters.

She held them to her heart and stared out the window at the early autumn sunset. The moon was rising when she turned back to the letters. In a recent one, Stephen told her that he and a couple of friends from the department had gone to the Hurricane Lounge again.

We left the school and walked up to what they call the Lower Hill. It's part of a busy neighborhood called the Hill District which is a large Negro community here in the city. The club's interior was long, narrow, and smoky. The place was noisy with people, both black and white, laughing and talking about everything from baseball to Eisenhower's presidency. We ordered beer and listened to the musicians playing cool jazz. A guy named Ramsey Lewis played the piano. There were a lot of couples there, and I'm looking forward to bringing you. Even if you don't know anything about jazz, you'll like the atmosphere, the people, and the music.

Celina folded the letter, returned it to its envelope, and slipped it into the packet she had tied with a narrow pink ribbon. She stared at the ceiling and wondered what he was doing at that very moment. She wanted so much to be with him that her heart hurt, and she wished that she didn't have to live through another minute of separation. She could only imagine what it would be like to be married to him, live in a city, and go to jazz clubs. She had great expectations for the future. At her bedroom window, she stood for a long while, gazing at the star-sprinkled sky.

#

In a short time, work at the newspaper, proofreading, editing, and soliciting advertisers became routine, and the racket rising from Edgar's typewriter faded unnoticed into the background. Occasionally, Harry, his thin hair standing on end, rushed into the office and asked Celina to help flip and fold the papers as they came off the press.

When the Linotype machine ran smoothly and the press inked properly, he strutted around the clattering, hissing contraptions like skinny rooster about to flap his wings and crow with delight. But on days the machine malfunctioned, his hair stuck to his forehead, his moustache sagged, and he lugged his ink-and-oil stained canvas bag of tools from the storage building across the street. Robbie scurried back and forth carrying machine parts of all shapes and sizes, while Harry hovered over his equipment like a surgeon, focused on the ailing patient he vowed to keep alive.

The time she spent inhaling the odors of paper, ink, and machine lubricants while watching Harry and Robbie perform their tasks in synchronized motion, made having to spend the rest of the week with Edgar almost bearable. She longed for Friday afternoons when Stephen would stop by and she'd have the weekend as a reprieve from barked orders, complaints about missing notes, and demands for a more tidy office.

Celina berated herself for being the only person in Kenville who hadn't known what Edgar Cherriten was like to work for. She came to the conclusion that Edgar was the reason why no one else applied for the position, and she was glad when she heard that his nephew was ready to quit college and demand her job.

One Friday afternoon, Edgar spun around in his chair and wondered aloud if there were any Elizabeth Taylor types at the university where Stephen worked, or if the coeds swooned over him.

Celina had resolved not to let him bait her. But she did want to grab the fountain pen Edgar held, pull the little silver lever that controlled the ink flow, and spray ink all over his face. Instead she smiled. "I'll have to ask him."

On the first weekend of October, the maple trees were bright red and gold, and a chilly wind carrying a hard frost was in the air. Marian had already retrieved all the winter coats and gloves from the steamer trunk in the closet under the stairs.

Celina ran to the door when Stephen stepped onto the back porch and hugged him hard. "I've missed you so much."

"I've missed you too," he said then kissed her.

They clung to each other until they heard Tomas call out. "You two going to stand out there all night? You're letting the cold air in."

"Are you hungry, Stephen?" Marian stepped into the

kitchen. "There's leftover pierogi and I can fry up some of the brook trout Pap and Uncle Stanley brought over this afternoon."

"Thanks, but Aunt Terez had a big dinner ready when I got home."

"How about some coffee then?"

Before he could answer, Tomas joined them. "The coffee is on and the cream's fresh."

"Sure. That sounds good."

Tomas sat at the kitchen table and motioned for Stephen to take a chair. Marian poured the coffee, and Celina sliced the nut roll.

Frankie, ever on the alert, scrambled from his place on the porch and ran to greet Johnny and Pattie as they strolled toward the house. They entered the kitchen and he spotted the nut roll. "We're just in time."

CHAPTER 18

Celina rushed home from work. Edgar had had a bad day, and he shared every miserable minute of it with her. She stepped on the gas and ignored the potholes and ruts in the road.

His voice rang in her ears. "Don't sharpen five pencils at once. You'll wear out the pencil sharpener. Why do you need such sharp points anyhow?" He badgered and droned. "When you talk to those merchants be forceful and push them. Make them buy advertising space."

"I picked up a new account from Wetzel's Greenhouse and got Miller's Grocery Store to take out a half-page ad," she retorted. "Even the Kenville Feed Store agreed to take out a half page."

"That's not good enough. I've got advertising space to fill."

Celina snapped, "There's not a single business in this whole county that I haven't tried to wring a nickel out of."

"Try Duxbury's and Nadar's Shoe Store again. They can afford full-page ads. Hound them till you get something, and that's final." Edgar huffed.

Celina dialed Nadar's and was politely told that the store's business was brisk and unless things slowed down they would not change their advertising schedule. She called Duxbury's and spoke to Earl, who told her they were doing business as usual and would continue advertising for holidays and special sales only. "Don't you have anything better to do than pester every business in town?" Red-faced, Celina slammed down the receiver.

Her racing mind had her so occupied she failed to notice sights she usually noted along the way. The dusty trucks and cars that filled the gravel lot at Shirley creek, some of them relics from the 1930s with headlights like giant, metal-backed glass eyes perched above their fenders usually caught her eye. But Edgar's carping was all she thought about. She was home before she knew it, parked under the trees, and stomped into the house. She ran upstairs, changed clothes, and pushed Edgar's puffed-up and angry face out of her mind.

In the kitchen, the homemade noodles Marian had drying on the table were ready to cook. When Celina stirred the kettle of simmering soup, large chunks of beef rose and dove among the vegetables. She fanned the steam rising from the broth, inhaled its fragrance, and remembered she hadn't eaten a thing since breakfast. The long-handled dipper rested nearby and she filled a small bowl. She had finished the last spoonful when Marian came up from the cellar.

"I counted forty-eight quarts of tomatoes, thirty quarts of green beans, thirty of applesauce, and as many pickles, beets, jelly, and chowchow. That's not bad. And we still have the potatoes to dig and sauerkraut to make."

Marian washed her hands and tested the noodles for dryness. "Is the water boiling?"

"It will be in a minute. I tried the soup. It's good."

"Well, get the table set. Dad should be home any minute and Johnny won't be far behind."

"There's enough here for an army. We'll be eating it for a month."

"You know Ellen still isn't feeling too good with this baby. She hates cooking right now, so I'm going to take some over to them, and there'll be plenty for Baba and Pap too."

"Good."

Celina knew all too well that Tomas liked his supper on time each and every evening. He never dawdled on his way home from work, but tonight his supper waited. He was fifteen minutes late. The soup simmered and the noodles cooled.

A growing sense of unease settled over the two women. Marian stepped out onto the back porch and looked down the lane. "He's still not home. Johnny might be here before Dad, tonight." Marian tried to conceal the frightened expression that crossed her features. "I hope nothing happened at the mine." She caught herself and said, "It must have been that old truck. It broke down."

Celina stared at the large-faced clock on the kitchen wall. If it was the truck, Dad will be as mad as a hornet when he gets here. But Boga, please don't let it be trouble at the mine.

She watched her mother through the open door. "Maybe Dad and Charlie got to talking and he forgot the time." She decided to change the subject. "Edgar spent the whole day griping and complaining, and I couldn't wait to leave the office." The comment didn't even register an *I told you so* from her mother. Marian's attention was elsewhere. Small talk vanished.

The clock's hands crept around its face to half-past the hour. "Mom, something must have happened at the mine."

"I'd better call around to find out." Marian jumped up and went to the telephone. "The line's free. I'm calling Anna."

A minute later she returned to the kitchen. "Charlie's not home either. Something's wrong."

"I didn't notice anything when I drove past the mine on the way home." Then she remembered how distracted she'd been by Edgar's behavior.

A few more minutes passed. "This isn't good. Anna said she'd call Sally Wilson and see if she knows anything," Marian said, wringing her hands.

The phone rang and they both jumped. Marian rushed to pick it up. She nodded and spoke in an undertone. Her face pale, she replaced the receiver and turned to Celina. "There has been an accident at the mine. Let's go."

Celina pulled the car into the dust-and-gravel covered mine lot where other families had begun to gather. She followed her mother to the mine office, a low-slung gray building not far from the portal. The boss stood in the open doorway. Before anyone asked a question, he scanned the crowd, raised his hands, palms facing out and shouted. "Everybody keep calm now. There's been an accident, and right now I don't know any more than you do. But I can tell ya that a rescue team's already on its way into the mine."

From the back of the group, Stu Kazmark called out. "How many down there? Who's on the rescue team?"

"I'm tellin' ya all I know. When I find out something," he pointed, "I'll come out of that office behind me and let ya know."

Word spread, and relatives and friends gathered. Celina saw Charlie's pick up park. Anna jumped out, ran across the gravel lot, and joined them.

A minute later, ashen and shaking, Ellen rushed through

the gate and edged her way through the crowd. Her belly strained the buttons on the printed maternity dress she wore.

"Ellie, you didn't drive here by yourself did you?" Marian asked.

"No. My dad brought me…Mom's watching the boys.

"*Dobry. Dobry.* That's good."

Rumors flew through the gathering people and many speculated that it could have been an explosion.

An old timer's scratchy voice shouted above the crowd. "No, that hain't it. If it had a been an explosion, we'd a heard or felt it. Had to be black damp, no oxygen in the air down there. Maybe methane. Could a been methane gas." He pulled his sweat-stained cap off, revealing thin white hair. He bowed his head. "If it was gas, they're all done for."

A stout woman wailed. "Shut up, you. You don't know. Nobody's dead. You hear me?"

Sally Wilson stood a few feet away and spoke up. "Shirley Creek has a bad roof. Maybe there was a roof fall."

The old man agreed. "Yeah. Yeah. Most likely a roof fall."

The wailing woman's face crumpled. "Not the whole roof."

"God damn it woman, the roof in one of the sections then." He replaced his cap and spat tobacco juice into the dust.

Marian and Celina paced back and forth between the mine office and the car. Minutes later, Pattie and her mother ran up to them. "Have you heard anything?" Pattie' voice trembled and fear gripped her face.

Several people shuffled closer to hear Marian answer. "All we know is that a rescue team's been sent in. They're not saying any more than that. People are talking, but nobody knows any more than we do."

"Who's on the rescue team?" Anna asked. "If we knew who they are, we'd know who isn't down there."

"They aren't saying," Marian replied.

Celina walked from small group to small group. She approached a mechanic who worked above ground and spoke to him for a short while. It was dark when she returned. "Did you find out anything?" her mother asked.

Celina ran her hands through her hair. "The mechanic said he wasn't sure, but he thinks Dad's on the rescue team, so it wouldn't have been his section. He mentioned a couple of other guys who are on the rescue team."

"Did he say who is down there?"

"No. He wouldn't even speculate about that."

Low-riding ambulances, their sirens blasting and lights flashing, rolled through the front lot. The drivers maneuvered their vehicles through the crowd and parked as close to the mine entrance as possible. They jumped out, pushed through the men, women, and children, and went straight to the mine office. A woman tried to stop them. She grabbed at their shirts and tried to question them but the crew avoided her, and one man grumbled that they knew nothing.

Someone turned on the lights. The ambulances stood out stark and white against the encroaching night, and murmuring knots of shadow people shifted from one foot to the other. A paneled station wagon squeezed into the lot. It was the Presbyterian Church Ladies; they offered hot coffee. Most people couldn't take a swallow; others gulped it down gladly, appreciating the kindness.

Marian and Anna stood stoic, their lips moving in silent prayer.

Father Schmidt came by. His round head and black clerical garb were covered in the grey dust that more than a hundred feet had disturbed as they shuffled through the parking area. He stopped, spoke quietly, and prayed with the women. He bowed his head and prayed that Our Lady intercede with her Son for the protection of the trapped miners and the rescue team. He prayed that everyone be brought safely to the surface, and said amen.

Pattie prayed. She bit her lip and her chin quivered. Tears spilled out, and she clung first to her mother and then to Celina. She repeated again and again: "They'll be okay. They'll be okay." Her mascara slid down her face, mingled with the rouge on her cheeks, and settled at the corners of her mouth.

Ellen's eyes filled with tears, she swiped at them, and leaned against the car. Celina opened the sedan's back door so that Ellen could sit inside. Then she found a blanket in the trunk and draped it around Marian's shoulders. The women were silent, yet alert to every movement and noise coming from the mine entrance.

It was past midnight when a wave of sound spread through the crowd and the steamy breath of dozens of people rose in the chilly autumn night air. The boss stood up and announced that it had been a roof fall. The trapped men were in the first left section about a mile back from the entrance.

"That's Andy's section," Ellen blurted out.

"Johnny and Charlie are in there, too." Marian covered her mouth with her hand.

Sally Wilson blanched white. "Bart's in there."

Someone in the crowd cleared his throat and called out. "Is that all you have to say? You got to know more than that."

The crowd buzzed like a hive of disturbed bees. The boss raised his hands for quiet. "The team reported that rock and shale are blocking the tunnel. There's some water but not much…and they said they heard the sound of tapping coming from the rails. They used a three-pound sledge and tapped back so the trapped miners know they are coming."

Celina heard a man rasp, "Must have been rotted timbers that gave out. First left had a weak roof, all right, and the damned place is nothing but dripping water and mud."

Johnny and her dad often grumbled that ground water had weakened the mine's roof. They were infuriated with the superintendent for dragging his feet on getting supplemental roof supports in place. Mike had threatened to call the union. Even one of the bosses, a company man, had complained about conditions. Celina prayed. *Oh, please, Jesus, help us. Bring them out all in one piece. Please, please take care of Johnny, Andy, and Dad. And Charlie, Bart, and Mike too.*

She craned her neck to see the wall clock in the mine office. It was a minute past three a.m. She glanced around and saw some miners' families sitting on the ground. Men, women, and children slouched against car tires and huddled together like frightened cattle trying to keep warm. Others dozed inside their vehicles. Some had stretched themselves out in the back of pickup trucks. All remained alert and tuned into the comings and goings around the portal.

Celina watched the clock's minute hand crawl toward four a.m. She ran her hands across her face, and her chin quivered. She needed and wanted to support the others, but felt alone and needy herself. She blinked back tears and realized she had a splitting headache.

She wished Stephen were there to lean on. Startled, she realized that he had no idea what had happened here tonight. He was far away. *Unless a dozen men die, this mine accident wouldn't even be in the newspapers. Miners get killed by ones, twos, and threes every day, and nobody outside notices or cares.* A ragged breath escaped her. *That's the way it's always been, the way it will always be.*

She dozed off, and when she woke up the sun had tinged the horizon. Golden white rays shot up and over the low hills. Marian had already crept out of the car and stood with her hands on the small of her back staring at the mine entrance. The others woke up and stretched. Pattie's neat red hair with its brown roots was flattened in back, and her bangs stuck to her forehead. Her tears had washed the mascara away, and her perfect nails had been bitten into ragged tatters. Her eyes met Celina's. "What time is it?"

Celina stretched to see the clock. "Almost seven o'clock."

A paneled truck carrying the Presbyterian Church Ladies bounced across the parking lot. Wrapped in heavy sweaters and wearing sturdy shoes, the women set up steaming coffeepots and food. Their offerings included pieces of bread wrapped in wax paper, donuts, and cake. Celina accepted the coffee gratefully and urged Ellen to eat a bite or two of buttered bread and drink a swallow or two of coffee.

A ripple passed through the crowd. Someone had spotted movement at the portal. The ambulance drivers jumped into their vehicles and the motors roared to life and as one, the crowd moved to the entrance. The mass of cold, stiff, achy people buzzed and inched forward. "What the hell is goin on?" a man called out.

A voice called back, "Looks like they might be bringin' a body out."

Celina blinked hard so she wouldn't cry and tried to squeeze ahead, but the police pushed the worried family members back. An officer swinging a billy club bellowed. "This here's a rescue effort. You people stay outta the way."

Half an hour passed. Three quarters of an hour passed. The sun hung above the multicolored, frost-singed hills.

Marian paced and pulled at her thin hair. "*Boga*, what's going on down there?"

Once again, the mine office door opened and the boss stepped out onto the porch. A small group of men stood behind him. Police officers stood on either side of him. He raised his hands and yelled. "Okay everybody, quiet down now."

The buzzing and grumbling stopped. Pattie wiped her nose. Marian and Anna clung to each other. Ellen's big belly got in the way as she lurched out of the car. Celina stared at the bosses' face.

"Like I told ya earlier, the miners were in the first left section, about a mile back from the entrance. Nine miners were in that section and the connecting tunnel. The rescue team has moved rock and other debris, and some busted timbers, to get at 'em. Everybody on the rescue team is safe."

Celina sucked in a big gulp of air. Thank God that Dad's safe, but what about Andy and Johnny?

He paused for a second. "Of the nine miners, three were unhurt. Four were injured. They're being brought out," he pointed to the queue of white vehicles, "and the ambulances you see over there will be taking them to Philipsburg Hospital."

The boss shifted from one foot to the other. "I'm sorry to say that two of miners who were down there didn't make it."

Men removed their caps, women stood at attention, children were quiet. The crowd held its collective breath, waiting for him to continue.

The boss sucked in some air. "The two miners who died in the mine were Bill Mezovsky and Bart Wilson." Bart's wife, Sally clenched her hands into white-knuckled fists. Her knees buckled, and a long wailing sound rose from somewhere inside her. Her oldest son helped her stay on her feet. On the other side of the mine lot, Libby Mezovsky stood silent and pale as a ghost. She pulled her crying children close, whispered to them, and turned to her brother who hovered nearby.

Tears rolled down and dripped off Celina's chin. *Two more women are widows and more kids are fatherless. Oh, Boga.*

The boss cleared his throat and continued. "The Company offers its deepest sympathy to the Mezovsky and Wilson families. You know the Kettlemore Company is always concerned for the miners' safety. This was one of those tragic accidents that couldn't have been avoided. We couldn't have known something like this would happen."

A low grumble rolled through the crowd. The families of the two dead miners said nothing. What could they say? Their men were dead and nothing would change that. The company would offer condolences and then hire new men to take their places. With bowed heads, they walked heavy-footed toward the mine gate.

An old man croaked. "Couldn't have known? Like hell they couldn't have known."

The policemen, with their shiny badges, stood with their legs spread. They held their billy clubs in their right hands and tapped them against their left palms. They were on the ready in case the crowd should dispute the company's official statement.

In spite of her grief for the others, Celina felt great relief that her brothers and father were alive. She saw her feelings mirrored in Pattie's face as together they released a quiet sigh.

The boss continued. "The four injured miners are: Peter Oliver, Stu Girgurich, John Kublak, and Johnny Pasniewski." Pattie shrieked and fell into Celina's arms. Marian shed silent tears, and Celina's face hurt as she strained to see which stretcher Johnny was on. She didn't know if she could be strong enough to support Pattie and her mother, and she wished more than ever that Stephen were there to lean on.

"These men are being readied to be taken to the hospital at this very minute. The families can follow the ambulances out." The boss straightened up. "The three uninjured miners are Charlie Jankowiak, Andy Pasniewski, and Mike Tyska." Anna clung to Marian and heaved sobs of relief. Ellen plopped back down onto the car seat. Her belly bounced, she tittered, she cried, she wiped her eyes, and blew her nose. She looked up at the sun above the trees and whispered. "Oh, *Boga, Boga.* Thank you, Jesus. Thank you, Jesus. Thank you, Jesus."

#

Many hours later, in the hospital waiting room, Celina was told she could see her brother for a few minutes. She climbed the stairs in the echoing stairwell and found Johnny's room. She tried to pat down her unruly hair and smooth the wrinkles from the clothes she had been wearing since yesterday. She peeped around the corner of door 223.

Arms at his sides, Johnny lay under white sheets pulled up to his armpits. One leg, encased in heavy white plaster, protruded from beneath the sterile sheet. Narrow gauze strips covered one side of his face from forehead to chin. His closed eyes were black and purple and swollen. His curly brown hair poked through the bandages and stood out in all directions. Celina crept closer to the bed. She leaned over and kissed him through the bandage. He was asleep. She crept away.

CHAPTER 19

Shaken by the accident, Johnny's hospitalization, and Marian's emotional reaction, Celina failed to react when Edgar's grunted, "Get back here as soon you can." She explained that she needed to stop at the hospital and check on her brother during visiting hours. Edgar's verbal barbs and callous tone were no longer able to shock her. Without a word, she left the office.

Everyone thinks problems don't bother me, and that I'm strong, but I'm not. I'm scared for Johnny. And I'm worn out with the responsibility of being strong for Pattie and my mom. I don't know if I can cope. But I have to.

The afternoon sun flooded room 223 with bright light. Johnny had his head turned away from the glare when he noticed her standing in the doorway. He spoke through purple, swollen lips that weren't able to curl into his usual smile. "Come in. I'm not as bad as I look."

She stepped up to the bed and tried not to stare at his mangled body.

"I'm glad you came."

"I stopped in last night, but you were asleep."

"They knocked me out with that morphine."

She scanned his swollen face, bandaged shoulder, and leg protruding from under the sheet. He was pitifully helpless. Determined to keep up a good front, she tried to be cheerful but tears filled her eyes. She offered a shaky smile. "You look like Pap's horse kicked you across a pasture."

"I feel like a meaner horse than Kwaity kicked me halfway to Philadelphia."

She wiped her eyes and asked how he was doing.

"I'd laugh, but my face hurts too much," he said quietly. "That damned mine tried to kill me, but I wouldn't let it. I'm still alive." A raspy breath escaped his discolored lips. "I prayed, really prayed down in that hell hole that we'd get out alive."

He tried to shake his head and flinched. "After the roof fall, Charlie checked everybody. Bart and Billy were dead. Bart's head and upper body were crushed like he was no more than a piss ant. In the light from Charlie's lamp, I could see his hand with the wedding ring on it sticking out from under pile of shale and rock."

Tears stuck to Johnny's eyelashes. "And Billy, the poor bastard, all that was left of him was his legs and boots sprawled out in a puddle of muck and blood."

Celina wanted to say something but she was speechless, standing mute at the side of his bed.

He stared into her face. "That's no way to die. They should have lived to be old and gray and died in their sleep." A tear slipped from the corner of one swollen eye.

"You don't have to talk about it if you don't want to."

"Missy, I gotta talk to somebody. I can't tell Pattie or say anything to Mom and Dad."

"If you're okay talking about it, I'll listen." She pulled a chair closer to the bed, sat down and reached for his hand.

"There's no way to explain how god damned dark it is down there. A night with no moon or stars is bright compared to that darkness. I guess I should be grateful that we could hear the rats scurrying around. They hadn't disappeared into a safer area. When Mike relit the carbide lamps, I could turn my head enough to see what happened to Bart and Billy." His face twisted. She knew he was having a difficult time composing himself. "Charlie told the rest of us to stay calm…that the rescue team'd get us out."

"Those three men clawed at the rock and cleared some space between us and the tunnel. Mike puked and started to shake when he lifted some of the rubble from around Bart's body and saw what was left of him." Celina's stomach churned and she held his hand tighter.

"The bodies, the puke, and the stench that filled the place. I don't know how Charlie and Andy kept from puking, too. But I know they were mad as hell. With every rock or splintered piece of timber they moved, they prayed for God to curse that bastard, Kettlemore."

Celina patted his hand.

"The space was so cramped it was hard for them to move around in there."

"I'm so sorry you had to go through all that. I'm sorry that any of you did." She blinked hard and drew a long breath. "We're all so glad you made it. Dad was on the rescue team. Did you know that?"

"Yeah. I heard swearing when they broke through, and I could tell that some of it was coming from him. I saw the light from their lamps and was never so glad to hear his voice in my whole life. When he called our names, it sounded like music to me."

"You've been through a lot." Tears rolled down her face. "I don't know what we'd have done if…"

"Well, god-damn it, I made it." His voice softened. "I just wish Bart and Billy had."

She hugged him and he winced. Tears continued to flow down her face no matter how hard she tried to stop them.

"Quit crying, will ya?"

"I'm trying, Johnny."

"Pattie bawled her eyes out the whole time she was here. And Mom couldn't stop bawling when her and Dad came in." He pointed to the foot of the bed. "And even though Dad tried to stand there like the stone-faced Polack he thinks he is, I saw his old chin quiver a couple of times."

She wiped her tears and blew her nose. "You didn't tell him you noticed, did you?"

"*Boga*, no. It would have broke his heart if he thought we could see he cared about any of us."

She smiled. "Well, thank God."

He tried to move his body, grimaced, and swore under his breath.

Celina jumped up and called the nurse, who came and shooed her out of the room.

After he had received a shot, she was allowed back in. "It doesn't look like any of your teeth got knocked out."

"No, and I don't remember how I scraped the hide off my face. Maybe it happened when I hit the ground. I remember the noise of the rock and coal breaking loose and then the dust about choked me. I blacked out till I heard Charlie calling my name. It was funny." Johnny tried to smile. "When I opened my eyes his nose was right up against mine, and I said, 'You're yelling in my face.' He patted my cheek and said I must be okay."

"I'm glad Charlie was with you."

"Me too. He's a tough old bird like Dad—said he'd been through worse."

"I wonder if he'll retire now."

"I wouldn't be surprised. He said he wants to live and see his grandkids grow up." Heavy sadness filled his voice. "Bart won't see his grandkids grow up…and he loved those kids. And Billy, even though he was hung over half the time, he won't get to see his little girl go to First Communion, and the other kids go to Confirmation, or graduate from high school, or anything."

After a long moment she asked, "What did the doctors say about your shoulder and leg? How bad does it hurt?"

"Right now, I'm not feeling much of anything since the nurse gave me that shot. But when it starts to wear off the leg and foot hurt like hell. Did they tell you I lost part of my foot, and a couple of toes are gone?"

She frowned. "Yeah. The doctors talked to all of us last night."

He coughed and laughed. "Now Dad won't be the only one in the family with bragging rights. All he lost was one measly toe."

He took a deep breath and continued. "The doc says that once I'm better and get used to the injury, walking won't bother me. My leg is mashed up pretty good. It'll take a while to heal. The shoulder doesn't hurt too much though."

He blinked hard and looked out the window. "I'm just grateful I have a shoulder and an arm. My fingers are still there and they work." He wiggled his fingers. "See."

Her chin quivered. "I see. Did the doc say when you can come home?"

"In a couple of days."

"Are you going back to the mine?"

"No. I can remember when we were kids, I'd see Dad coming home filthy and exhausted and taking a bath in that galvanized tub Mom kept behind the kitchen stove." His words were slurred from the morphine. "I told myself back then that I wasn't going into the mines. But I did anyway, because I figured Dad was a miner and I should be one, too. But I've hated every day of it…going down there with the dripping water and rats, breaking my back squatting all day, digging four-foot coal."

She squeezed his hand.

"No more mining for me."

"I'm glad."

Celina sat quietly and waited for him to continue.

"Mike's not going back either. When we were down there, and he was tapping on the rails hoping somebody would hear us, we swore that if we got out alive, we'd never spend another minute in a coal mine.

"We still have our plans to open the auto parts store." He lifted a finger to point at the cast on his leg. "When this thing comes off, that's what we're gonna do. We're gonna open J&M Auto Care." His purple lips formed a crooked smile.

"Do you think Dad and Andy will go back?"

"Yeah. I don't understand it, but mining's in their blood."

Celina glanced around the barren, gray-green walls of the hospital room and wished she could think of something to say.

"Hey, when's Stephen coming to see me?"

"He'll be here this evening. He had to stay and finish today's classes and arrange for someone to take over while he's gone." She longed to put her arms around Stephen and lay her head against his chest.

#

Two weeks later, Celina arrived home from work, tossed her jacket and purse on the chair in the hallway, and poked her head into the living room. Johnny dozed, propped up in the bed Tomas and Stephen had brought down to the living room. Most of the furniture hugged the walls, and the small fire in the belly of the heating stove kept the room warm. Marian hovered near the door.

Johnny hadn't been home an hour when Frankie began to whine and cry at the back door until Marian could stand no more. When she finally allowed him inside, he lay curled up and docile at the foot of the sickbed. Frankie's tail thumped the floor. Johnny's eyes were closed, but he spoke quietly. "I'm awake. Stick around."

"How are you doing?"

"Good enough."

"Pattie will be over pretty soon."

"I know. And she's getting to be a good little nurse. Checks my pills, helps me get up and move around, changes the bandages on my foot, and doesn't complain when I swear."

"She's come a long way in a short time," Celina said with a smile.

"Yeah. She's helping me get through this resting and healing stuff." A tender look crossed his face, and he nodded. "It means a lot."

"Good." Celina was filled with affection for her older brother.

"Remember, I told you that Mike and I have been negotiating a down payment on Taylor's Hardware Store."

"Yeah, I remember."

"Well, the deal's done. Mike brought the papers over this morning and I signed them."

"Oh, Johnny." She clapped her hands, pleased for him and the future he wanted.

"First thing we'll do is sell off the stock that's on the shelves and then we'll switch over to auto parts."

"You guys finally did it."

"Yep. That's one of the things that kept me from going nuts while we waited to be rescued. That and," he grinned, "I couldn't let Pattie down. It would have broke her heart."

"She was beside herself with worry while you were down there."

"I know. I told her I wasn't going back to the mines, but she wanted to be sure and asked me to swear on her rosary that I'd never step foot in a mine again. I swore. She's satisfied."

"I'm glad you did that for her. She won't worry now."

"Yeah. Hey, you know what her dad said?"

"What?"

"He'll loan me and Mike the money to pay off Taylor's free and clear. It's not that much so we can have him paid back in a year or two."

"Oh Johnny, that's swell."

"Now I have to tell Dad and Mom about it. You know how they feel about borrowing money."

"Yeah, but this'll be family."

He coughed and she gave him a sip of water.

Celina sighed. She was happy for her brother and she loved her family, but she needed someone too. That someone was Stephen, and he was miles and miles away.

"Thinking about Stephen?"

She nodded. "I wish he could have stayed longer. I'm so

tired of this separation. He's not here when I need him most."

"I've talked to him, and I know he wants to be here for you. Look how he's running back and forth from Pittsburgh almost every weekend. He's got to be sick of it too."

"We both are."

"I couldn't do what you're doing. I need to know Pattie is nearby and I can see her every day if I want to."

Celina looked down at her hands and touched her ring. "This long-distance relationship is more than I can stand. I don't know how couples managed during the war."

"Me either. What are you going to do?"

She stared across the sickbed and through the window to the autumn-hued day outside. "We wanted to get married during the semester break, and the break is about to start." She frowned. "Dad's talking about a big wedding, and Mom is still pressuring me about living here." She was silent for a moment. *I don't want to deal with any of this anymore.* "I don't know what to do."

"What's Stephen saying?"

"That he won't make the decision for me and that even if we wait till June, he knows

Mom won't change her mind."

"He's right, you know."

She frowned. "I know Mom and Dad want the family to stick together like we always have. They think if Stephen and I leave that we'll forget who we are, where we came from. But we won't. Everybody we love is here."

"What are you going to do?" he asked again.

"We've talked about eloping. I carry our rings with me on a chain around my neck all the time."

The yellow-green bruises around his eyes became round

circles and his brows rose. "Yeah. You're both over twenty-one. You could do it."

Concerned that Marian might be listening, she glanced over her shoulder. Celina didn't want another argument. Her mother would remind her how, just like in the old country, the whole family was swayed by Pap and Baba's opinions. She'd say that Celina and her brothers should show the same respect to their own parents and accept their authority when important decisions were made. "I wish Mom were more understanding."

"But you got to do what makes you happy," Johnny said.

"That's what Harriet told me."

"When were you talking to Harriet about this?"

Celina lowered her voice. "She told me that she met a young man named Brandon at college. They wanted to marry, but her father insisted that she return to Kenville and settle down. Brandon had other plans for them. In the end, she lost the man she loved."

"Harriet wouldn't have told you something that personal if she didn't think it was important." Johnny pressed his lips into a fine line. "What would you have done if you hadn't met Stephen? Marry just for the sake of getting married? End up like Harriet?"

"End up like Harriet, I guess." Celina sighed. "I suppose Mom and Dad would come around before long if we eloped."

"Sure they would. But I want to be there for the fireworks when you tell them." He smiled his old quirky grin.

"Wait, wait. I haven't decided yet." She squirmed in her chair. "Mom is still all frazzled and jittery over the accident. She's trying to hold onto all of us for dear life and I really don't want to upset her more."

He held out his hand. "Andy and I are still here. Pattie will be coming into the family soon. And when they see I can succeed out there in the business world and still be a good son, they'll understand that you can live your own life too, and there's nothing to be so worried about."

Celina brightened. "And Aunt Terez is here. She'd be part of the family, too."

He took a sip of water. "You know, Stephen's right. You have to be the one to make this decision."

"I know."

"Like Harriet told you, none of us want to spend our lives regretting what we didn't do when we had the chance," he added.

"You're right. When we first met, Stephen told me that everybody loves where they grew up, but he had to leave Budapest."

Johnny shifted his weight and swore under his breath. "Look at me. I'm all busted up on the outside. But before you met Stephen you were broken to pieces on the inside."

She knew there was more truth in that than she wanted to admit.

"Stephen isn't like Mom and Dad who hate to drive as far as Altoona. He won't mind driving back and forth from the city or you driving yourself back and forth. Besides, Eisenhower is having the interstate highway system built, and the drive will get easier every year."

She smiled. "You're covering all the angles."

"I'm just trying to help."

#

It was dark on Friday evening when Stephen pulled up to

311

the house. The full moon lit the way and fallen leaves swirled around his ankles as he approached the back door.

Celina ran out and he gave her a bear hug and quick kiss. Marian and Tomas sat at the kitchen table, and her father called to them. "Celina, get your man some coffee."

A voice came from the living room. "Hey, I'm in this house too."

Celina filled the cups and placed them on a tray. "We'll be there in a minute."

Stephen and Tomas moved into the living room. There was a knock on the door and Marian grinned. "Come on in. It's open."

Pattie popped into the bright kitchen.

They trooped into the makeshift bedroom and Pattie fluttered and fussed and helped prop Johnny up on many pillows.

"I wish Andy and the family were here. We'd all be under the same roof again," Marian said.

Celina and Johnny exchanged wry glances.

#

Stephen sat next to Celina at Sunday Mass. He linked his little finger though hers during most of the service. The low hanging autumn sun set the stained glass windows alight, tinting the parishioners with a rainbow of multicolored splotches. The congregation followed the ancient ritual of standing, kneeling, and sitting and Celina tried hard, but failed to concentrate on Father Schmidt's homily.

After the service and Sunday morning chatter in the parking lot, Aunt Terez rode home with Tomas and Marian, and Stephen and Celina drove around the corner to the rectory.

It was chilly, and she could see her breath while they waited for the priest to answer the door. "Hello, hello. Come in out of the cold. I trust you're here to talk about the wedding."

A smiling, white-haired, couple stood in the living room. "You remember Mr. and Mrs. Schimansky don't you?" Father Schmidt asked with a twinkle in his eyes.

Celina and Stephen greeted the older couple.

"My parishioners are good to me. The Schimanskys brought dinner and one of Mary's lemon meringue pies for dessert."

He excused himself from his guests and motioned Celina and Stephen toward the study. The coal furnace clattered and banged in the basement as they followed the priest down the hall. Papers and books still littered every flat surface in the room.

The priest smiled. "How is Johnny doing?"

"Really well," Celina answered. "He's using the crutches and getting around the house without catching them on the chair or table legs. Pattie has taken him out for a ride, and he wants to come to church next Sunday."

"I'm glad to hear that. Sit down, sit down." He folded his hands and rested them on the edge of his desk. "What's the latest news on the wedding?"

Stephen cleared his throat. "There isn't much to tell."

"What about the date?" Father Schmidt asked.

"Nothing's changed there, Father," Stephen said. "Maybe Celina should fill you in on what's been happening."

"You know how my mother feels."

The priest nodded. "She and I have spoken."

"Yes, well, she has been so worried about my brother and

now she never stops talking about the family staying together. She doesn't want to see her children scattered around the country."

Father Schmidt's brow furrowed and shook his head. "If you two marry soon and follow your own plans, how do you think your family will react?"

The corners of Celina's mouth turned down. "My dad would be mad that I didn't have a big Polish wedding, and I'm afraid my mom and Baba would feel betrayed. But Pattie and Ellen would be happy for us."

"I've talked to both Johnny and Andy. They understand," Stephen added.

"You two have a serious decision to make. And I want you to know I'll be praying for you." Father Schmidt had compassion in his voice.

"Thanks, Father." Stephen glanced at his watch. "We have to get back to the house. Have a nice afternoon."

On the drive home, Celina fiddled with her engagement ring. "Last summer we talked about getting married during the semester break. The time has gone by and the break's almost over, and—"

"You've been through a lot during the past few weeks. I'm not going to put any pressure on you right now. But we can't go on like this forever."

"What should we do?"

"You know what I want."

She sat back, crossed her arms, and looked out the window. Leafless trees, dry grass along the road, and the gray sky flew past. Time was slipping past too. She wanted to avoid making the decision, but it was hers to make. She knew her mother would not budge. Her parents still expected to be the final arbiters in her life.

Stephen drove in silence. There appeared to be no way out. *Mom refuses to understand that we can't stay isolated from the rest of the world forever. Why can't we continue being a close family and go out into the world, too? Don't people who have been here for generations do that?* Celina didn't like the answers she knew her mother would give.

When they passed the abandoned tipple, she remembered the day she sat on a railroad tie, alone and thinking. The anxiety she felt then, gripped her again. She considered what her life was like before meeting Stephen. The emptiness. The loneliness. The unhappiness. The silence in her heart.

Celina turned to his profile and spoke, the decision made and finally solid in her mind. "Stephen, let's go back."

"Now?"

"Yes."

"Are you sure?"

"Yes."

Stephen grinned wide and made a quick U-turn.

A huge weight had fallen from her shoulders but the rapid beat of her heart made her draw in a deep breath. "I'm getting nervous." His loving hand settled over hers as they retraced their way to the rectory.

When the priest opened the door he beamed with pleasure. "I knew you'd be back."

Twenty minutes later they stood on the sidewalk with the Schimanskys, and the priest waved them off. Celina was almost giddy. "Now I'm really nervous. We have to tell my parents."

Stephen kissed her forehead. "I'll take care of that."

Celina looked up into his dark eyes.

"I love you, Mrs. Meszaros."

She held out her hand and admired the wedding ring.

Holding his hand she could feel the ring on his third finger. They shared a kiss and then stood for a long moment, her ear against his chest listening to his this strong heart, and his chin on top of her head. Tranquility finally filled Celina.

Father Schmidt opened the door. Grinning he said, "Shoo, go home and tell your family. And don't worry about your mother. Tell her I'm stopping in later."

Arms entwined, they strolled through fallen leaves to the car.

"I love you, Mr. Meszaros," Celina whispered.

Walking arm in arm, and approaching the post-war built four-story apartment building near campus. Happiness washed over Celina. Things had gone more smoothly than she thought they would. Stephen convinced her parents to accept their marriage, Father Schmidt confirmed everything the young couple said, and peace reigned in the family. "Even though it was a spur of the moment idea, staying at the Harbor Inn for three days gave us a real honeymoon," she said.

"We may not have had the two weeks we wanted, but it all worked out."

The key grated in the lock and Stephen looked over his shoulder. "It's small, but cozy. I hope you like it."

They entered the apartment and stood in the pleasant main room. It was bright, the walls were painted a soft sea-green, and the hardwood floors were polished and spotless. A narrow archway led to the jonquil-yellow kitchen. A 1946 model electric range stood near a massive refrigerator. The checked yellow-and-black pattern in the linoleum busied the empty space. Celina spun on her toes and visualized the lacy curtains she would hang on the sparkling window above the sink.

Stephen put his arm around her and turned her playful spin into a slow waltz. "Well honey, this is it. What do you think?"

Her gaze moved round the room. "It's perfect." She pressed her face against his shoulder and his jacket held the scent of crisp cold breezes.

They shared a lingering kiss. He held her close for a moment then stepped back. "Let's go outside. I'll show you my office and the building where you'll be taking classes."

After locking the door, he placed the brass keys in her hand and her heart thumped. *My home. My husband. My kitchen. My life!*

The frosty ground crunched underfoot as they made their way across campus. A gust of cold wind swirled snow flurries around them as they darted into the warm building. Looking around, wide eyed and excited, Celina realized that her life had finally begun and that she could have the life she wanted.

I'm so happy that I'm me.

THE END

ABOUT THE AUTHOR

Carol Moessinger grew up in rural, central Pennsylvania, worked for the Navy Department in Washington, D.C., and married and raised her family. Her ethnic heritage, coal mining family, and educational choices support her desire to create a unique perspective and express deeper insights into human behavior as it is expressed in her writing. Ms. Moessinger's diverse interests have provided her opportunities to lead seminars and teach workshops on subjects such as Jungian spirituality, the New Testament, Celtic symbols, substance abuse, and coping with mid-life issues. She welcomes the term Renaissance woman. She devotes her free time to gardening, nutrition, and cooking.

Please visit Carol Moessinger online

http://www.carolmoessinger-historicromance.com
http://pcmoes.wordpress.com
https://www.facebook.com/carol.moessinger
http://twitter.com/CMoessinger

Made in the USA
Charleston, SC
25 April 2014